Book Two of The Siren Series

By Alisa K. Michaels

ꜟ A YA Novel ꜞ

Sale of this book without a front cover may be unauthorized. If this book is coverless, it may have been reported to the publisher as "unsold or destroyed," and neither the author nor the publisher may have received payment for it.

Copyright © 2020, 2025 by **Alisa K. Michaels**

All rights reserved. No portion of this book may be reproduced in any form without permission from the publisher, except as permitted by U.S. copyright law.

For permissions contact **Belen Books, LLC.**

This is a work of fiction. Names, characters, businesses, places, events, locales, and incidents are either the products of the author's imagination or used in a fictitious manner. Any resemblance to actual persons, living or dead, or actual events or places, oceanic demigods, or sassy Sirens is purely coincidental.

ISBN: 978-1-959715-12-2

Library of Congress Control Number: **2023931752**

Published by Belen Books, LLC
7901 4th St. N, Ste 300, St. Petersburg, FL. 33702 USA
Belenbookspublishing.com

Edited by Beverly R. Waalewyn & Paul L. Hight
Cover by Belen Media Group

2 3 4 5 6 7 8 9 10

Printed in the United States of America

For My Husband

"You can't cross the sea merely by standing and staring at the water."

–Rabindranath Tagore

Aria

Book Two of The Siren Series

PREFACE

The ocean holds a bounty of secrets, secrets hidden beneath undulating waves that tease of what is concealed below. Oftentimes, my overly zealous imagination journeys to ancient shipwrecks containing stolen treasures and violent misdeeds laid to rest in Davy Jones' Locker, with only whispers to speak of their existence. The thought makes my mind race as it wonders if something malevolent watches from fathoms below as unsuspecting sailboats glide along the surface, enjoying the spray of salty winds and the sound of the sails as they fill.

Shamelessly, I daydream of centuries ago when pirates ruled the seas upon galleons heavy-laden with gold doubloons, rare artifacts, paintings and jewels obtained through unscrupulous means. Stolen cedar chests heaving with their spoils are skulked away in the shadows of the ship, all the while their eyes sparkle with mischief as they laugh at what they have done... who they have killed.

Then perhaps, late one night as the pregnant moon hangs low in the heavens, they hear it.

"Don't be afraid," a voice sings.

"We're not afraid," they reply.

"Follow me... into the sea... in the ocean's waves we'll play."

Recklessly, they dive into the water unaware of their fate.

This time there are no passing flocks of seabirds to wake them from their trance; no clear mind advising them to swim back to the safety of the ship. Foolish hearts have already taken control, urging them forward, but the frigidness of the water engulfs them, and they realize all too late that they are merely men; a crew of murderous marauders swimming out toward the purple horizon in some sort of suicidal stupor.

Sadly, before any man can change his mind, the undertow grips their legs and begins to pull them out to open ocean. Unable to fight against its wishes, they close their eyes allowing their bodies to sink below the surface. A watery embrace devours them as their lungs fill with seawater, and they understand what is to come.

There will be no peace...

There will be no St. Peter...

There will be no forgiveness...

Rapidly, the liquid world begins to die away as they drift into the void, but in the distance, swimming toward them, are three shapes. As the shapes get closer, the men realize that it is three women; the first with long, curly locks; locks as crimson as the sun's unremorseful first light. The second, crowned with a golden-blonde cascade that resembles the sun's early morning rays. The third, adorned with jet black curls spilling downward like tentacles.

The last things they see of this world are their striking aquamarine eyes …

CHAPTER ONE

Bright-white, billowy clouds are coming in from the west, dotting the sky like cotton balls glued onto a cerulean poster board. The Mediterranean horizon once painted a dusty overcast-gray is now alive with shades of summer: amethyst, maize, emerald and an array of blue hues. Seagulls diving for breakfast a few yards offshore have now flown back toward the shoreline to consume their catch. I, on the other hand, along with my now six-year-old brother, Ando, find it almost impossible to move.

"Lena!" he bellows, tugging at the white, linen sarong covering my black one-piece swimsuit; pointing to the horizon. "What's that?"

Following in the direction that his finger is pointing, I squint to make out the bluish-black shape that seems to be shifting and squirming between the sky and the sea. The only way to describe it is sort of like when the satellite signal on a television gets distorted when it rains, but this signal seems to be sentient.

"I'm not sure what that is," I admit sheepishly, feeling that foreboding deep in my gut.

"Is it a whale?" Ando questions, looking over the railing.

Again, I strain to see what the large object is.

"I can't make it out," I huff feeling like a failure.

"I'm gonna get Mom and Dad," he informs as he races back into the villa, we have attained for our entire three month stay.

Standing alone, I survey our property, and I have to admit, the island of Capri is gorgeous. The four-mile-squared landmass is located in the Tyrrhenian Sea near the Sorrentine Peninsula. Capri, nestled on the southern side of the Gulf of Naples in the Campania region of Italy, is considered one of the jewels of the Mediterranean. According to my mom, it has been a travel destination since the time of the Roman Republic when she was born.

Our summer home is situated in the *Belvedere of Tragara*, which is a lofty panoramic promenade lined with villas overlooking the picturesque harbor. The house, constructed around a breathtaking quarter-of-an-acre garden, is a short ten-minute walk from the *Piazzetta*. Upon entering the property, guests are welcomed by an ornate gate, built in the early nineteenth-century by a local ironsmith. The single-level structure is comprised of handmade tiles, whitewashed walls and barrel-vaulted ceilings enhanced by cypress beams. A polished marble foyer accesses the great room, which is centered around a magnificent marble fireplace. As the caretaker informed us several times, the entire home is decorated with classic Italian furnishings including a collection of original artworks, a large, fully-equipped modern kitchen, three bathrooms and five bedrooms.

There is also a small laundry room for convenience.

The villa's landscaped garden features an impressive variety of native trees, meticulously kept flowerbeds, manicured lawns, and a rectangular reflection pond surrounded by patio furniture perfect for relaxing with a good book. The property's tree-lined terrace faces the garden and catches the warm breezes from the sea. According to the custodian, because of the location and the building materials used, the home is naturally cool and, in fact, has no need for central air conditioning.

How can we afford all of this?

No, we did not win the lottery. Mom has not fully explained, but when her human father passed away, she inherited all of his monetary assets as well as several acres of prime seaside property. Over the centuries, she has managed the estate and according to my stepfather, my mother is quite a wealthy woman. I remember vaguely the local banker shaking my mother's hand excitedly, rambling in Italian something about being at her and her family's 'beck-and-call'.

Long story short, we own this incredible property and when we leave, it will be back on the market as a rental.

Regardless, all I know is that Capri is a wonderland of gray rocky coastline, high stone cliffs with greenery that somehow grows atop of the stony surface, and tree-speckled hills surrounded by calm azure depths. Wafting around us is the fragrant aroma of citrus and olives intermingling with the salty perfumed sea. It is intoxicating. The smell often makes me hungry, which is why I have gained almost three pounds during our vacation so far.

Sadly, I take the last bite of my freshly baked, rosemary focaccia stuffed with feta cheese and perfectly-ripened Roma tomatoes. I wash it all down with an ice-cold glass of hibiscus tea sweetened with honey. Unashamed, I lick my lips and pat my belly.

"There!" Ando suddenly races up the landing leading my mother and father. *"Over there!"*

Frantically, he points to the scenic Mediterranean horizon.

"Do you see it?" he implores with enthusiasm.

Mom peers into the distance and lies.

"No... I don't see anything."

Disturbed by her comment, I glance in her direction not trying to disguise my irritation or confusion.

"It's right there," I educate, also pointing toward the massive dark shape against the horizon. "It's just sitting there, like a blob."

"I don't see anything, Selena!" Mom snaps then quickly apologies. "I'm sorry."

"Maybe it was a shadow of a cloud or an airplane or… something," Dad adds, joining the explanation.

We all continue staring in the same direction.

"Whatever it is," he gives a worried expression. "I don't see anything out there except blue sky and sunshine."

"You're joking?" I admonish, but he shakes his head no.

"Don't worry about it," Mom chimes in, her tone even keeled so as not to further excite us.

Every time my mother says, 'don't worry about it' I know that it is something worth worrying about. Again, I try to focus on the shimmering mass. I squint once… twice… then finally throw my hands up in the air in defeat.

"Fine, I'm going back inside," I huff, turning toward the villa. "It probably is just a shadow."

My mother says it is something benign, but in my heart, I know it is something else. Every cell in my body knows that it is something not of this world, something weird and *Sireny*. Something that will ruin our summer vacation, I am sure of it.

Great!

As fast as my legs can carry me, I make my way to my bedroom toward the back of the bungalow, overlooking the sea. The room is all white with soft, sheer white curtains, and an ornate cypress canopy bed dressed with white linen sheets that feel as soft as a cloud (or what I imagine a cloud would feel like if I had wings).

Why don't I have wings?

I have asked my mother this question before, but she just shrugged and said:

"I don't know, baby. The aunts do not like to talk about it. Whatever happened occurred on the day that I was born, that's why I don't have that memory. Don't mention it, okay? It will only upset them."

So, for the time being, I have never asked them why we no longer have the ability to fly, but I am positive it is an interesting story. One day, I fully intend to find out.

Still uneasy about the strange shape out at sea, I settle onto the padded seating in front of the open French-style window. From here I can see the entire harbor, otherwise called the *Marina Piccola*, which translates to 'little harbor', as well as the *Faraglioni*, which are limestone formations that jut out from the sea. The view from my window even allows me to see farther out into the bay on clear days.

Content for the moment, I close my eyes and begin to hum, a low tune with a few varying octaves… nothing special or complicated in my mind, just something to do to keep me occupied until we go out sightseeing.

The need to sing comes over me, like it often does, so I oblige the need, like I often do.

"Hmm... mmm... laa... laa... lee... la... la," I continue playing with the sounds, letting them fade at some points and then letting them grow at others.

I sit happily, imagining how lovely it is here and how much I would like to stay, and then it happens. An incredible sense of doom smacks me right in the face. My lungs have suddenly locked, and my gills have kicked in.

I can't breathe!

I do not know how long I writhe on the white-washed floorboards, but it seems like an eternity before Mom, Dad, and Ando come racing in.

"Selena!" Dad reaches me first. "Caramba! What's wrong?"

Mom's face is ashen, and Ando is crying as he holds my hand.

"It's her lungs!" Mom screams. "Selena! Concentrate on activating your lungs!"

I do. I try with all of my might. I try and... *Nothing!*

"Pick her up!" she orders my stepdad, who is dumbstruck and completely out of his element.

How can he not know what to do?! He is a marine biologist for goodness sakes! I am a fish for all intents and purposes! He should be able to fix me!

"Marina, what are you going to do?" he pleads but stays still.

"Get her to the window!" she orders more harshly.

"What?!" he cries, mortified, face turning as pale as Mom's.

"Now!" she shouts, then grabs me and throws me over her shoulder in a fireman's hold, then leaps out of the open window.

Without a parachute... without a life preserver... without her right mind!

As we plummet, all I can feel is the rush of air as we race toward the water. Suddenly, I flashback to last October when Amy and I had to jump from a balcony into the Caribbean to save her life.

I thought that was bad. This is so much worse.

"Brace yourself, honey!" my mother cries seconds before we hit the transparent surface.

The world becomes a loud, low rush of muffled currents deafening me and immediately I start to breathe.

Thank Zeus!

Mom is still holding me over her shoulder. I do that clickity-clackity language of the Sirens, and she slowly releases m, and then hugs me tightly against her chest.

"Mom—" I begin to clack something, but she hugs me even tighter.

"Are you alright?" she clicks too quickly, and I start to giggle because I translate it as, *'Are you albacore tuna?'*

"I'm okay," I inform with a relieved smile.

"Why didn't you activate your lungs?" she queries at a loss.

Dramatically, I give her a *Mr. Spock,* one eyebrow up the other down, which translates from *'teenager'* into: *Do you think I would if I could?*

Quickly, I take a few more deep breaths through my gills then motion to the surface. Mom shakes her head and points toward the exit of the harbor.

Yippee! We are going on an adventure!

It has been such a long time since Mom and I have spent quality time together. Lately, Ando has insisted on accompanying us wherever we go. Do not get me wrong, I love spending time with my brother, but sometimes I need to have *'girl time'* with our mother. When he and Dad have *'guy time,'* I do not want to join them.

"What do you think happened with my lungs?" I sputter in Siren, attempting to still catch my breathing rhythm.

Mom looks at me with a sympathetic expression. In fact, quite often, various family members have given me that same look at different times. I hope it is not a trend.

"Has that ever happened to you before?" Mom questions in Siren as she rests a compassionate hand on my shoulder.

"No!" I clack. "This was the first time and hopefully the last. Usually, it just takes a couple of seconds kick in, but lately, I can transition almost immediately."

Comfortingly, she smooths my hair back from my eyes, but the weightlessness of the sea only messes it up again. Similarly to when I was a child, Mom turns me around and with professional precision began to French braid my hair. In fact, she braids it so quickly that I barely have time to protest.

'There you go,' she smiles, communicating telepathically. *'Much better. Now, it will stay out of your face.'*

I grin at her motherly action.

"Mom?" I click.

"Yes, my love," she answers warmly.

"Has that ever happened to you?" I ask hoping that it has, needing some reassurance. "The lungs and gills not cooperating thing?"

To my disappointment, she lies again.

"No... it hasn't," she responds without looking at me. "It must have been a fluke."

"Mom—"

"We'll come back later," she responds, changing the subject. "After sunset."

Instantly, my mind wanders to the rest of our family members still at the villa.

"Won't Dad and Ando be worried?" I ramble as if I have lost control of my clickity-clackity tongue.

Suddenly, she pauses, cocks her head to the side like a bird then closes her eyes. A slow smile creeps over her face as she informs:

"It's done."

"What's done?" I ask as my brain tries to understand but does not.

Girlishly, she giggles, and it throws me off because she sounds exactly like me. It takes a few seconds for me to get the idea out of my mind that I am a replica of my mother in almost every way. There is no mistaking we are kin. Then another thought slams into me. Sirens do not age like humans. We go into a type of agelessness when we reach our early twenties. So, when I go into *'stasis'* my mother and I will look exactly the same, minus a small scar and her additional fifteen pounds that she gained while carrying Ando.

'I just told your brother that we're going exploring,' she states in my mind matter-of-factly. *'He'll tell your father.'*

"Oh," I whisper-click, still feeling a bit confused; hoping I do not have brain damage from the lack of oxygen for so long. "That was fast."

Mom only laughs and kisses my cheek.

"Are you sure you're alright?"

She keeps studying my movements and examining my pupils for dilation.

"I'm fine… I promise," I answer truthfully.

I hope she doesn't think I'm an idiot for asking this, I think.

"How do you do that telepathy-thing?" I ask in a slew of clacks, chirps and whistles, hoping she will tell me the secret.

"Like all skills, you just have to practice," she replies, winking playfully.

Knowing that she is right, I frown.

"I have practiced, but it never works," I meekly admit, doing an impromptu backflip followed by a handstand on the stony seabed.

"Then practice more," she utters with an impish smirk as she does the same, then continues into an underwater *pirouette* that turns into a *pas de chat,* which as I recall from my ballet lessons is a sideways leap while travelling. This ballet move is usually done in mid-air, until now. According to my former ballet instructor, Madame Chevalier, the dancer's legs are bent one after the other then brought up to *retiré* with the feet as high as possible, and the knees kept apart.

"You never told me that you studied ballet?" I grin, impressed by her graceful moves.

Mom blushes.

"Briefly," she admits with a smirk.

"When?"

"In the late eighteenth-century," my mother recalls as she does a quick *arabesque* then allows the current to move her along without effort. Knowing now that she is a professionally trained ballerina, I feel incredibly proud and a tad bit self-conscious. I, for a short time, also took lessons and am not glad to know that the scarring memory will literally be with me for an eternity. Admittedly, I was mediocre, but Mom's superb dancing skills make me jealous, so I try guilt on her instead.

"Everything comes easily for you," I pout, using the most puppyish expression I can muster and not crack a smile. "You could be a little more helpful, considering I almost died."

My mother, familiar with my dramatic antics simply laughs.

"C'mon," she says with several short clicks, taking my hand. "Let's go!"

CHAPTER TWO

The swim from Capri to wherever my mother is taking me is a beautiful route. From overhead, bright rays of sunlight pierce through the watery barrier separating the world above from the world below. The topography of the sea in Capri is nothing like Isla Flora, but it is beautiful nonetheless. Along the rocky seabed, there are orange Alcyonacea, pink Sea Pen, and copper-colored six-fold branches of Hexacorallia. Unfortunately, we only spy a few cuttlefish swimming leisurely through the bay, then to my delight, we finally spot a baby octopus suctioned to a rather large smooth stone. Startled, he glares at us then bravely shoots ink in our direction in warning.

"Where are we going?" I ask, trying to ignore my growling stomach.

"You'll see," she clacks with a knowing smirk.

"Is it far away?" I ask, pushing for more answers.

"Not too far," she reassures.

I try not to ask any more questions and just enjoy the new habitat, but my mind keeps wondering about our destination. Are we going to explore another shipwreck like we did in Isla Flora, or maybe scare some tourists—?

'No,' I hear Mom's voice inside of my head. *'We are not going to scare tourist.'*

Her tone makes me giggle.

"Mom," I plead. "Tell me where you're taking me, please."

"It's a surprise," she smiles.

"I'm not in the mood for surprises," I grumble brutishly.

Trying to keep the mood light, she gives in.

"If you must know, we're going to Anacapri," she finally reveals, eyes gleaming excitedly.

My brows arch to my hairline as I glare at her.

"What are we going to do there?" I question, full of trepidation at wandering so far away from our vacation home.

"You'll see," she grins, letting me know that all is well.

Those are her last words on the subject.

Slowly, we make our way along the coastline, each of us lost in our own train of thought. My mind is back on Isla Flora and Andrew which is not surprising. I cannot help but wonder if he is having fun with the rest of our friends or concentrating on getting a head start on our summer reading list required by our private school. I have already read two out of the three requisite books. I will probably start the third book on the flight home in order to pass the time. Mostly, I hope he is thinking about me.

"That's a good idea," Mom hones in on my thought which surprises me again. "And I'm sure he is."

Shocked at her intrusion, I nod my agreement, but remain silent, enjoying the peaceful journey, suddenly feeling the need to be more cautious with my thoughts.

As we swim, something moves several feet to our left, catching our attention. I recognize a few of the strange sea creatures in this area, one is an alien-looking cuttlefish and the other is an unusual looking fish with a body that tapers from a short, conical-shaped mouth and a large, blunt head to an elongated whip-like tail. Its body is greenish-silver on its back and sides.

"Look Mom!" I clack excitedly. "Aunt Ligeia taught me about that funny looking rabbitfish."

"Did she?" Mom grins. "Well, tell me about it."

Shrewdly, I smile accepting the challenge.

"It is a deep-dwelling fish with an unusual, yet distinctive appearance," I inform like a puffed-up peacock.

"It has another name," Mom reminds. "Do you know what it is?"

I think for a few seconds.

"It is also known as a ratfish," I say with a smirk.

"I'm impressed," she chuckles then points out a giant moray eel hiding in a rocky crevice, waiting for his next meal to swim by. It does not take long for an unsuspecting squid to cross paths with the stealthy predator. In less than five seconds, the eel has gobbled up his meal and the only thing left of the squid is a piece of its tentacle floating among the cloud of guts.

"So vicious!" I gasp indignantly.

"It's a part of life," Mom bluntly defends the violent act. "The eel has to survive too."

"I suppose," I scowl.

Steadily, we continue along our path to the opposite side of the island. It suddenly occurs to me that the currents in this part of the world sound differently than the ones in the Caribbean. Off the coast of Isla Flora the current is extremely smooth and low since the seabed is mostly soft sand. Here, the sea topography is incredibly rocky and uneven, so the current sounds hollow and bulky. The noises also seem to bounce off of the stony surfaces with more force than back home.

"Are you still hungry?" out of the blue, Mom asks.

Without hesitating, I nod.

Pointing ahead of us, she motions for me to follow then abruptly she turns and begins a slow descent at the drop-off. The water temperature immediately begins to fall, and goosebumps appear on my arms and legs. It does not bother me, just startles me.

Quietly, she clicks then disappears farther down into the dark chasm, but orders me to wait. It takes less than a minute for her to return carrying an armful of oysters, shells tightly closed. We make our way back to the reef where Mom pries them open and pulls out the slippery meat. Without wavering, she swallows it and hands me one to do the same, and eagerly I follow. The taste is exquisite; cold, salty, and sweet. We eat every last one, and it is the most incredible seafood snack ever.

With our bellies full, we continue our trip.

About thirty minutes later, we arrive at our destination.

"Why does this place look so familiar?" I ask, trying to recall as I examine the bumpy limestone exterior with an enthusiastic hand.

Mom smiles, her aquamarine eyes glistening.

"You'll recognize it once we're inside," she states confidently, leading the way. "The entrance is not that big, so be careful that you don't get cut."

"Okay, I'll be careful," I give her my word.

"This is one of my favorite places," she admits. "I hope you love it just as much as I do."

I feel another twinge in my chest, but the moment is so perfect with my mother swimming beside me, I choose to ignore it.

"Follow me," she states excitedly.

As if she has done this hundreds of times before, Mom motions to an opening just as she described: small, just six feet wide by three high, more or less, and I obediently follow.

"Is this safe?" I question our decision to enter into this enclosed space, but when we arrive on the other side I realize it was definitely worth the tight squeeze.

Mom laughs.

"Stop worrying so much and just enjoy the moment," she reassures.

"I've seen this place before."

My mind tries to recall. Finally, I remember.

"This is the Blue Grotto," I whisper like we are in church.

Inside the cavern, rays of sunlight pass through a subaquatic opening in the limestone and shine through the seawater, creating a blue reflection that illuminates the entire cave. The water is surprisingly cold, and the gently lapping of the waves against the walls is soft and melodic. I could easily fall asleep in here.

"How big is this place?" I ask, hearing my voice echoing against the stony walls.

"It spreads about one hundred and sixty-four feet into the cliff at the surface, and is almost five hundred feet deep, with a sandy bottom," Mom informs.

"It's so beautiful," I say with a smile. "Suppose someone finds us in here?"

Mom chuckles before notifying, "Today the sea is choppy and it's high tide. For humans, the grotto is only accessible during low tide when the water is calm, otherwise getting though the cave opening is almost impossible."

"That's good to know," I smirk as I dive down to the bottom to examine the sand. "It really is soft."

"Yes," Mom giggles, following me down. "The sand is like powdered sugar in here."

"Does the cavern always stay only partially filled with water?" I question, remembering the dry cave ceiling.

Mom thinks for a moment before answering.

"No, at the peak of high tide it fills completely," she educates based on her experience. "But for a Siren it doesn't matter."

I giggle knowing she is right.

"That's true," I agree with a pleased smirk.

My mother smiles brightly, as she remembers her childhood growing up with her human father, Marcus Antonius, a Roman sea captain. When Marcus died, she returned to the sea to be with her mother, Parthenope, and her aunts, Ligeia and Leukosia. She was sixteen, which is my age now, when she gave up her human life. Many centuries later, my mother returned to the land when she fell in love with my stepfather, Dr. David Marquez.

"As a child, I'd come here to think," she admits with a solemn sigh. "Mostly to sing."

"You can sing in here?" I give her a surprised glare. "Won't humans hear our call and follow it to their deaths?"

Mom winks.

"The grotto is naturally soundproof because of the limestone barrier combined with the fact that our Siren Song can't be transferred underwater," she admits nonchalantly.

Immediately, my brows hitch up to my hairline.

"What do you mean?" I demand, needing more of an explanation.

"We can't sing underwater so we can't influence anyone when we are submerged," she states matter-of-factly.

"Have you ever tried?" I grill, already guessing the answer.

"Yes," she says sharply then changes the subject by adding, "Sing something in here. The acoustics are incredibly pure."

Nervously, I probe.

"Are you sure it's alright? I don't want anyone getting hurt."

"I'm positive," she chuckles.

"Umm," I frown, debating with myself.

"Sing to your heart's content," my mother encourages. "This was my fortress of solitude as a teenager."

Mom turns her back to me in order to examine a marking on the cave wall.

My face beams and my heart begins to soar with anticipation.

"Okay," I grin. "Here goes."

"Swim up to the surface. We can't sing underwater, remember?" she reminds.

But for some reason, I do not. Instead, I stay where I am, submerged.

Needing inspiration, I close my eyes and think about the island and how it makes me feel at peace. I think about the sea and how it gives me joy. I think about my family and how I would protect them with my life. Then, I think about my new friends back on Isla Flora and how they know my secret, yet they still stay loyal to me. And, of course, I think about Andrew, the supportive teenager who waits for me back in the Caribbean.

I think of all of these things and begin my Siren Song.

"Hmmmmm… .mmmm… laa… laa… lee… la… la… " Just as before at the villa, I begin playing with the sounds, letting them fade at some points then letting it grow at others.

My mother suddenly turns to me with an astonished expression. Actually, it is not astonishment; it is more like shock and disbelief. Her eyes widen and her mouth gapes.

'*No!*' Mom shouts telepathically, rushing toward me, startling me. '*Not that!*'

"What—" I gasp as my lungs switch back on without warning.

Suddenly, the unreliable organ begins taking on water. Terrified, I start flailing my arms and legs as my body begins to convulse as my respiratory system realizes what is happening.

I'm drowning!

CHAPTER THREE

This is a nightmare! One horrible long-lasting nightmare! A nightmare that never seems to end!

All I can do is flail… flail and pray; pray that I go quickly and painlessly, but that does not happen. My lungs are burning from the lack of oxygen. My vision is blurry, too blurry for me to see inches in front of my face. Even my eardrums feel like they are about to burst.

'Great Zeus!' Mom shouts in my brain. *'Selena, don't panic!'*

Too late for that!

All I can do *is* panic. My mind is running on instinct alone. I push off the bottom and try to concentrate on getting up to the surface where there are several feet of air, but before I can make it that far, I feel Mom's embrace around my torso. She kicks off of the bottom hard and in one movement we are at the top. To my surprise, the area between the water and the cave ceiling is only a couple of inches now.

In agony, I gasp and sputter trying to gulp in as much oxygen as possible.

"It's the tide!" Mom informs loudly, sounding just as flustered as me. "We've gotta get you outta here!"

"Wait!" I plead, taking several more much needed breaths before we have to brave the practically submerged grotto exit.

"We can't wait much longer!" she says with a stern expression. "We have to go, *now!*"

Realizing the urgency of our situation, I take one last breath, filling my now empty lungs and nod that I am ready.

"Hold my hand!" my mother commands and I take it like it is my lifeline.

Much like a naval rescue diver, she leads me under and toward where the entrance used to be. Now, all I can see is the blue aura of the grotto surrounding me. At the moment, I am fully human with no gills, no webbing to help me swim faster, no Siren super hearing or strength. Thank goodness, my mother seems to be unaffected.

Our first attempt to get through the small opening of the grotto is unsuccessful, to say the least. The sea seems to have taken on a life of its own, creating currents that fling us from side to side like rag dolls in a washing machine. I feel my lungs begin to burn, yet I know I must stay calm. We try for the second time, but the agitation of the water batters me against the limestone, scraping my skin. For the first time since the mishap with Amy on Isla Flora, I wish for my scales to reappear. Unfortunately, I remain unprotected.

Thankfully, the third time is a charm.

As luck would have it, the sea calms briefly and Mom takes the opportunity to wrap her arms around my waist, holding me securely to her form, and with a few kicks with her webbed feet, we exit the cave. Now, all I need is to get to the surface.

It seems like an eternity before we exit the grotto and resurface on the other side, then up into fresh air. Frantically, I take another deep breath and hug my mother tight around her neck, suppressing the urge to sob uncontrollably, all the while, wishing that I was back on dry land.

"Wh-what happened back there?" I stammer, hoping to figure out why my body keeps acting so strangely.

"I'm not sure," Mom answers, but I do not believe her.

"Stop lying to me!" I snap then quickly apologize. "If you know what's going on with me, you've got to tell me because it's gonna happen one day when you're not around and I'll end up dead! Do you want that to happen?"

"No," she whispers in obvious pain at the mere thought of something bad happening to me. "Of course not."

"Then tell me… *please*," I beg, expecting she will put me out of this misery.

"Let's get onto dry land," she states more calmly. "Your lips are turning purple."

About twenty minutes later, we are sitting on one of the limestone crags drying off under the mid-afternoon sun, the summer heat warming my freezing body. What would be perfect is a glass of hibiscus tea and a hot bowl of soup.

"Well?" I urge with chattering teeth.

"Well, what?" she pretends to have forgotten.

"You promised to tell me," I remind rather abruptly.

When I think she will never reveal the secret, Mom takes a breath before blurting, "It is *The Calling*."

"*The Calling*... what's that?" I adamantly query with confusion.

With the mere idea of *'The Calling'* the hairs on my arms stand straight up, but not from being cold.

"Do you remember the strange dark shape from this morning?" she answers my question with one of her own. "The one only you, Ando, and I could see?"

"Yeah," I respond with a hint of sarcasm, earning me another glare.

"Only Sirens can see it," she reveals uneasily. "It is a beacon."

"A beacon for what?" I prod, stretching my legs out so that every inch of them are touched by sunlight.

Mom closes her eyes and stretches out her legs too.

"It calls us home," she replies with a soft sigh.

"Home?"

My mother answers without looking at me. This is something she does when she is discussing a disturbing topic. When we had *'the sex talk'* she did not look at me once and that conversation was quite embarrassing, yet in depth. This conversation feels just as uncomfortable.

"Eons ago, when Melpomene the Muse gave birth to the aunts and Yaya Parthenope, this is where she delivered. This is where our lineage started," she pauses trying to complete her thought. "At the very moment when Ligeia came forth into this world, Zeus, the father of the gods, protected her with a force field, for lack of a better description. The black-shifting shape is that force field. It surrounds and protects the very spot where *The Sirens* came to be."

"Ooooh!" Nothing else comes to mind to say.

"Every hundred years or so, it calls us back here," she says, motioning one leg outward.

"Where?" I ask feeling even more confused. "I thought that Capri was home… is home… you know what I mean."

She smiles all mysterious and unsettling.

"The actual birthplace of *The Sirens* is over there," she states, pointing toward the horizon. "No matter where we are, what continent, what ocean… it reminds us that we need to return to these waters."

"What happens if you ignore *The Calling*?" I question, already knowing the answer even though I can no longer hear my mom's thoughts.

"Our powers become wonky," she grins, touching my wet curls.

"But when I sang in the grotto, why did you yell at me?" I interrogate.

"That tune… those sounds are your answer to the beacon," she announces. "It is engrained in your deepest memory, that tune is you basically saying: *I am near, bring me home.*"

She sighs.

"Have you been having problems with your body doing weird things?" I probe in my most serious tone.

"Sometimes," she admits. "But I'm only half Siren. You are completely Siren. It will affect you sooner and stronger than me. Ando may only feel it a little, if at all."

"I wish I was more like you and Ando," I reply, feeling my temples beginning to throb.

"You, my sweet girl, are perfect just the way you are," she responds, carefully choosing her words. "I created you from my cells... my Siren cells. You are more amazing than I will ever be."

"Yeah, but I'm still just a stupid fish," I pout, breaking off a piece of the rock with one easy twist and throwing it into the sea.

Mom puts an arm around my shoulders and gives a gentle squeeze.

"You are my *special* little fish," she teases with a wink.

"Thanks a lot," I say all blushy.

"But you can't sing that tune anymore," she adds.

"But why do I keep singing it at all?" I ask still wrapping my mind around the entire supernatural explanation. "In my mind, I was singing something totally different, but it came out the same. I didn't even know what I was doing."

She frowns.

"How do I stop these things from happening to me?" I query, looking for a viable answer.

"For the meanwhile, until we can figure things out, you'll have to stop singing," she states quite sternly.

It is my turn to stare at her. What she is asking me to do is impossible! Ludicrous! Preposterous!

"Are you joking?" I respond with a smidgeon of a vexed attitude.

She shakes her head.

"I'm very serious," Mom replies as we continue to chat.

"You're telling me… a Siren… a Siren that is new to her *Sireny-stuff*… to stop *singing*?" I question with a mocking lilt.

"Yes," she states flatly, staring at me.

"Being here makes me want to sing all of the time," I longingly confess my problem. "I can't *not* sing. It's too difficult."

At a loss, my mother looks at me, her bright aquamarine eyes filled with compassion for my current plight. I understand that she only wants to keep me safe, but it is a ridiculous request. She of all people should comprehend that.

"You'll just have to try," she replies then closes her eyes once again and enjoys the sunshine.

"Mom?" I mumble, needing the opportunity to share my concerns.

"Yes, honey?"

"*Melpomene the Muse* is your grandmother, my great-grandmother," I say in a rushed jumble.

"Yes," she answers, eyes still closed, flawless olive skin drinking in each ray.

"And according to Yaya Parthenope in Grandpa Theo's journal, *Tethys'* son, *Akheloios*, was your grandfather, my great-grandfather."

"Right again," she gives another sigh.

"What happened to them?" I probe, wondering why it is such a taboo subject in our family.

My mother realizes that my curiosity is awakened and will not be put to bed unless some answers are given. The story might be hard to hear, but it still needs to be heard, to be diagnosed. In my opinion, keeping it a secret will only harm us in the end.

"I really need to know, Mom."

She sighs once more, the sound melancholier than before.

"That is a tale for another time, my love."

CHAPTER FOUR

As soon as we are back at the villa, I make a beeline to the refrigerator. In less than five minutes, I consume two chicken salad sandwiches on Ciabatta, half-dozen almond chocolate biscotti, and several glasses of water. Needing to refer to my grandfather's journal, I take a handful of red grapes to my room to snack on.

On my way down the hallway, I hear my father's voice.

"How was it today?" he asks with genuine exuberance.

"Huh?" I respond with wide eyes.

"You know... exploring... mother-daughter outing... alone," he says, sensing something is not quite right.

"Oh!" I respond, clearing my throat. "Umm... "

Dad studies my mannerisms intently, making me even more nervous.

"The outing," I repeat, forcing a cheerful smile.

My father's eyebrows hitch to his hairline.

"It was interesting," I mumble below my breath.

"Interesting?" he questions with a growing frown.

"Yup! Just interesting," I reply, trembling in my boots, actually in my bare feet. "There's nothing to report. Everything's great! Just great!"

I smile again trying to seem more authentic, but I can tell that he is not buying what I am selling.

Ruefully, his eyes automatically narrow.

"Are you sure?" he grills, reaching over and plucking several grapes from the bunch I am carrying.

I grin, feeling the growing perspiration above my upper lip that will surely give me away.

"I'm positive," I say my little white lie, and also pop a couple of the small, sweet fruit into my dry mouth.

"I see," he smirks, giving up his pursuit of data.

"Anything else?" I ask, praying there are no more questions.

He thinks for a moment.

"How was the Blue Grotto?"

"Huh?" I deflect again.

"Was it just as spectacular as in the travel magazines?" he asks with an expectant grin.

"Uh huh," I respond casually, glancing away, wanting to escape the third degree, not knowing what Mom has revealed.

"Could you please elaborate?" he chuckles, enjoying my uncomfortableness.

"It was *sooooo* much better than the pictures in the magazines," I grin again, fidgeting where I stand.

"I've been looking forward to visiting it," Dad reveals.

"Really?" I gulp, glancing around the space, avoiding his stare.

"Mom is going to take Ando and me sometime later this week," he beams, genuinely excited.

"Sounds wonderful," I reply, starting to walk away. "I'm sure you'll have lots of fun."

"Hey!" Dad calls after me.

Stopping suddenly, I almost trip over my feet, but I quickly regain my balance. I have to answer. It would be rude not to and besides that my stepfather's suspicions would be confirmed.

"Yes?" I squirm without turning around.

My body tries to give me away as I feel the heat creeping up into my neck. That has never happened before. I have never gotten so nervous that my *neck* blushes. *Ugg!* I would be a horrible undercover agent.

"Are you hiding something from me?" Dad chuckles.

His perceptiveness makes me cringe.

"Do you really want to know the truth?" I ask, slowly turning around.

Dad thinks for a moment, his dark eyes twinkling under the pendent lights. I can tell he is debating. Knowing what he knows about his mystical family members, he might not want to know. Or his scientific nature might kick-in and he may need to know. It is a toss-up.

"Never mind," he grumbles at last, shaking his head. "If someone loses an eye, will you tell me?"

I nod, rush back to give him a quick hug and a kiss to the cheek before heading back to my current mission: the journal!

Back in my room, I pull my suitcase out of the closet and retrieve the book from inside. The smell of timeworn cowhide instantly greets me. Inside, I thumb through the pages searching for the section that I need. At last, I see it.

On pins and needles, I start to read quietly aloud.

> *"It was in these days that Melpomene the Muse bore to Tethys' son Akheloios three sea nymphs named Parthenope, Leukosia and Ligeia. The ancient world came to know them as the Seirenes."*

Ugg! That is not what I want! Quickly, I search through the time-worn pages until I find the familiar words: The Calling. *This is what I need!*

> "Six months back on land and I am miserable. The Calling is getting stronger every day I remain here. Marina celebrated her first birthday today and Marcus grows more and more fond of us being together as a family, but the call of the sea is too strong to fight. Too powerful even for me to ignore. I cannot take her away from her father... away from the only home she has ever known... but soon I must leave."

"That's so sad," I whisper to myself as I devour the last grape.

"What's so sad?" Ando startles me, making me jump.

"Get out of here!" I bark, wanting to be alone, needing to be alone.

"What ya doing?" he asks in that cute, boyish voice of his, which usually makes me smile, but right now it just grates on my nerves.

"None of your business," I insult, turning back to my grandmother's account.

"Want a bite of my lemon?" he queries, holding out a slice of lemon dipped in honey.

"No, I do not," I pout, wishing he would leave.

"It's tasty," he insists, still holding it out to me.

"I said, no."

"You wanna play a game?" he continues, totally clueless to my irritated mood.

"Not right now," I reply emphatically.

"There's an X-box in the entertainment center," he informs with a grin. "Wanna play?"

"I said… maybe a little later," I state calmly.

"Dad is grilling steaks for dinner," he tells, licking his lips.

Totally disgusted, I grimace at the thought of hot meat or any type of cooked food. Instantly, my left hand goes to my belly as if to quell the nausea before it actually starts. I imagine this is how pregnant women feel during bouts of morning sickness.

"Can you ask if he can make some grilled prawns for me?" I request as an excuse for him to exit my space. "Ask that he barely cook them."

My brother gives me a sickened look and turns to leave, but then notices the open journal.

"What's that?" he says, pointing to it.

"Go away, Ando," I huff, closing the book.

"Not until you tell me what's going on," he answers as he folds his arms across his chest defiantly.

"It doesn't concern you," I blurt, just wanting to be alone.

Obviously annoyed, he uncrosses then re-crosses his arms and plants his feet like he has roots.

How can someone so small be so incredibly stubborn?

Unable to refrain, I roll my eyes at him.

"I'm not leaving, so tell me," he practically orders.

Feeling defeated, I sigh, long and loud.

"Fine, nosey!" I try to find the right words. "My body keeps doing strange things."

Sincerely concerned, he comes to sit cross-legged beside me on the floor.

"Like what?" he probes, his facial expression intense, his aquamarine irises larger than usual.

"Well, you already know about this morning when my gills turned on by themselves."

He nods.

"When Mom and I went exploring earlier, my lungs switched on when I was underwater."

His eyes grow wide like saucers.

"Are you okay?" he asks with a tremble in his voice.

Suddenly feeling angry at myself for taking my frustrations out on him, I give him a big hug. He is such a great brother. I do not know what I would do without him.

"I'm much better," I claim with a small smile.

"Good!" he smiles too.

"Have you been feeling strange lately?" I add, curious to a partial Siren's symptoms.

"I'm only a little bit Siren, so I don't have webbing yet. Mommy says I might never get it, but my gills are fine."

Wanting to be thorough, he thinks a little more.

"My head has been hurting sometimes," he informs like it is a secret. "It happens mostly at night."

I do not know why, but his confession concerns me. The idea of my brother being in pain actually hurts my heart. After all, I am the older sibling and it is my job to protect him.

"Have you told Mom or Dad?" I interrogate bluntly.

"Nope," he admits without hesitation.

"Why not?" I grill like Dad would.

"It doesn't hurt all the time," he states with a shrug.

I frown, showing my disapproval.

"Any other symptoms?"

"No… nothing," he pauses then adds. "I also have bad dreams sometimes."

My brow furrows at his comment.

"Bad dreams?" I question. "What happens in your dreams?"

He thinks for a minute or two while he consumes the rest of the lemon. I wait, trying not to rush him, but I am losing my patience. Finally, he swallows the last bite.

"Last night I dreamt of being in the sea, swimming alone. It starts out nice at first. There's a lot of fish and pretty coral all around me."

"That sounds good so far," I tell, nodding as I follow along.

"But then there's this dark stuff in the water and I can't see anything—" his words suddenly stop.

With my level of concern rising, my palms begin to sweat as I hold my breath waiting for him to continue. When he remains silent my blood pressure begins to rise. I can actually feel my heartbeat increasing., and I hope I do not faint.

"What happens next, Ando?" I press for more information.

Subtly, he clears his throat reminding me of myself when I am nervous or upset.

"I don't want to talk about it anymore," he blurts trying to stand up, but I stop him with a firm grip to his elbow.

"It was only a dream," I remind. "Tell me. Please?"

Anxiously, he looks towards the door, and I know he is debating if he should make a dash for it. Knowing that he is uncomfortable, I give him a quick hug. Calmer now, he takes a deep breath and continues.

"Then I see you and Mommy—"

"What are we doing?" I interrupt impatiently as my chest tightens.

"You're swimming really, really fast," he continues, his hands are slightly trembling.

His whispered words make my hands begin to tremble too.

"From what?" I drill for more details. "What are we swimming from?"

Again, my chest tightens.

"Sharks."

CHAPTER FIVE

Thank goodness the last three days have been normal. Absolutely, nothing fishy has occurred, which is a relief to my parents and to me. Ando, staying true to his laid-back nature, just blew off his bad dreams and decided to enjoy the temperate weather of the coast and the incredible beauty of the new place we are visiting. Several times, I have asked my brother to give me more details about the dreams, but he has refused every time. So, for the moment, I have decided to pretend he never brought it up.

Today, the family is at an outdoor concert on another island called Ischia which is approximately nineteen miles away from Capri, also in the Tyrrhenian Sea. Not surprising, Ischia is breathtaking with its rustic fishing villages, hill-top towns overlooking perfect vistas, and world-renowned vineyards. The twisting roads here also go on forever and where they come to an end, you can still continue hiking up to the many stony plateaus.

Currently, we are at the village of Sant'Angelo which is practically overrun by stunning pink and purple bougainvillea flowers on the southern slope of the island. It is also hard not to spot the gorgeous purple wisteria and vivid, yellow broom flowers that nestle among the island's quaint, white-washed houses adorned with brightly painted wooden doors. Even the sea is made more striking with the colorful sails of the yachts that dock at the narrow isthmus separating the small town from the outcropping of rock that rises out of the sea like fingers on a hand.

After a few hours of sightseeing, we decide to have a picnic in the town square while we listen to a local band performing traditional songs. I sway to the music trying my best not to sing along for fear of causing a riot or doing something odd. I can just imagine my scales popping out or my gills suddenly activating in the middle of the crowd of tourists and locals alike. That would be disastrous on so many different levels.

"Tomorrow, we'll visit *Castello Aragonese*," Mom informs with an excited grin.

"What's that?" Ando inquires, stopping briefly from chewing on one of his pieces of freshly baked almond wedding cookies.

Dad smiles, and then repeats what Mom told him earlier.

"It's this really amazing castle that was built on a humongous rock near the island back in four-seventy-four BC, by Hiero I of Syracuse."

"Did you know him, Mom?" I ask, realizing that anything is possible.

"We never formally met," she discloses. "But I would often spy on his people as they built it."

"Did you know anyone else who was famous?" Ando adds.

Mom thinks for a long while before saying, "I actually did know the Roman Emperor, Tiberius, sort of."

Her comment makes me pause.

"How did you know him?" Dad's brow hitches and the vein by his left temple suddenly begins to throb.

Mom laughs and kisses him on the lips.

"It wasn't like that," she blushes at her husband's lewd implication.

"How was it then?" he probes, hugging her around the waist, the action makes me miss Andrew even more.

"Back when I was very young, during Roman times, the grotto was my sanctuary. I would often go there late at night to think and to sing. It was my way of connecting with my mother and aunts even though we were not together. Somehow, the Blue Grotto comforted me."

"Didn't your dad worry about you going there by yourself?" Ando asks as he swallows the last morsel of food in his mouth.

Mom just smiles and answers.

"No, my love. He knew what I was, remember?" she smiles as she recalls her life before motherhood. "He understood that part of me would always have the need to be in the sea, no matter how much I tried to suppress it."

We all look at her sadly, knowing how much she gave up to be with Dad. It was a great sacrifice that would always gnaw at her soul. It was also one of the most selfless things for anyone to do, especially for a creature who was specifically created to be a servant of the oceans. One day, I know I will have to make a sacrifice too.

"Wow!" Ando exclaims as he reaches into the basket of food and takes out a bottle of water.

Thirstily, he gulps it down.

"You'd never let us do fun things like that," he pouts.

Mom laughs and pulls him close, giving him a sweet kiss to the top of his head.

"Nope, no swimming off on your own, my little cuttlefish," Mom instructs in a firm, no-nonsense tone.

"Okay," he promises, but knowing my little scamp of a brother, he probably has his fingers crossed behind his back.

At last Mom continues.

"In twenty-seven A.D., the emperor relocated from the capital to Capri. My father, being a high-ranking member of the Roman Navy, had him over once for a very elegant dinner party. I was allowed to eat with the rest of the guests even though I was only six at the time. I actually got to sit right beside him at the table."

"Was he nice?" Ando beams, his mouth still full of water.

"He was a pompous jack—umm… jerk who smelled of wine and pickled herring," she blurts, and shrugs her shoulders.

"You've never told me this," I chastise her playfully.

"I haven't thought about it in years, decades," she acknowledges.

"What happened next?" Dad's interest is piqued.

"One day, not long after the party, I swam to the cave, but when I arrived, Tiberius was using it as his own personal swimming hole," she frowns, picturing the scene in her mind. "He even had the audacity to proclaim it as a marine temple."

All three of us gasp in horror at the idea of Mom's haven being swarmed by religious zealots.

"How did you get back at him?" Dad smiles as he waits for her confession.

Mom bats her long ebony lashes coyly, but her entire face reddens.

"We know you got even with him, so just spill it," my stepfather probes with enthusiasm.

"Several days later, when my father was out on business, I swam out to the grotto to sing somewhere private where no one could hear me. When I got there, it was decorated with several statues of the Roman sea gods, Triton and Neptune, as well as sitting areas around the edge of the pool."

I frown.

"So he just claimed it for himself?" I exclaim in disbelief.

Mom nods with a sigh.

"What did you do about that?" Dad questions with a raised brow, knowing too well his wife's temperament.

She only smiles.

"I did nothing," she finally outright lies.

"C'mon," I encourage. "Tell us."

After a few moments of silence, she finally answers.

"Well… let's just say that the next time Tiberius went swimming, all three statues were missing." She laughs wickedly. "They were recovered from the floor of the grotto in the early nineteen sixties."

"Where are they now?" my brother stops eating to ask his question.

"They are now safely on display at a museum in Anacapri," Mom informs with a hearty chuckle. "Maybe, next week, I'll take you there."

"Was he surprised that the statues had disappeared?" I blurt, loving the fact that my mother has a wicked sense of humor and is not opposed to playing pranks.

"He was speechless," Mom answers with a saucy wink.

We all burst into suppressed snickers.

"Did he leave after that?" I inquire with a hearty snort followed by a giggle.

"Unfortunately, no," she admits. "But every night, when the grotto was empty, I would leave signs—"

"What kind of signs?" Dad interrupts with a grin.

"Rotting fish, dead seaweed, things like that," she sneers. "One time, I left an old whale bone with the word *'Death'* carved into it."

"You're kidding?" I chuckle.

"Nope," she laughs again. "Eventually, he and his servants believed the grotto was haunted by some evil water sprite and decided to find another swimming hole and temple."

"Good going, honey!" Dad praises his sassy wife.

"I agree," I chime in.

"Me too," Ando finally agrees as he takes another breakfast pastry, we bought at a nearby café a half-an-hour before.

As we continue our conversation, the next band comes onto the stage to warm-up. According to the sign on the platform, they are a local rock band. Apparently, they are an all-male band of five young men in their late teens or early twenties. All of them are adorable.

It does not take long for them to set-up their equipment, tune the various musical instruments, and do a quick warm-up. Eagerly, the entire crowd of spectators which range in age, ethnicities, and races are all waiting in anticipation for the performance to start. Even the baby in the stroller beside us with her parents is sitting up as though she knows what is about to happen. I giggle at the fact that this will be her first concert... probably.

"Good afternoon, ladies and gentlemen, boys and girls!" the main singer announces in a thick Italian accent with great enthusiasm causing the crowd of onlookers to cheer wildly. "We are *Le Sirene Urlanti*!"

Mom and Dad look at each other with sickly expressions.

"What's the matter?" I query, curiously. "Why do you look so pale?"

"Did you hear the name of the band?" David mumbles.

"Le Sirene Urlanti?" I repeat. "What about it? What does it mean?"

Mom swallows hard.

"*Le Sirene Urlanti* translates to 'The Screaming Sirens'," she reveals blankly.

Dad immediately jumps in as the voice of reason. A job he is extremely good at. Maybe he has gotten too good at it.

"I'm sure it's just a coincidence," I also try to reassure even though the vein on my left temple is beating like a bongo drum in a Cuban salsa band.

"*Mi chiamo Matteo*, my name is Matteo," he clarifies. "Enjoy the show!"

With that, the band immediately begins to play an upbeat tune that they wrote themselves, no words only instruments, but the song is fast paced and makes you want to dance, so we do. Mom and Dad dance together while Ando and I do the same. Everyone around us is dancing too. It is fantastic!

"This is a cool song!" Dad shouts over the music so we can hear.

Mom nods in agreement, but continues to dance, moving in perfect timing to the beat. Ando and I do the same, but I keep hearing words in my head that would go perfectly with this particular beat.

'Fight the urge to sing,' I suddenly hear Mom's voice inside of my head.

'Don't do it, Lena,' Ando also joins in.

I nod.

'I'm trying my best,' I think, knowing they are prying.

'We can leave if you want to,' Mom says telepathically, alarmed for my welfare.

Without hesitation, I shake my head. If I am to live in both worlds, I will eventually have to learn to control my Sireny ways. If I cannot, how will I be able to function with humans without harming them? This is the best test of my willpower.

"I'm fine!" I answer truthfully aloud, glancing around at the many people having fun. "I can handle this."

Both Mom and Ando nod, and my brother gives me a thumbs-up.

"I know you can do it, Lena!" he replies encouragingly, but this time verbally.

I have to admit that it is with difficulty that I hold back the need to sing knowing that every man here, excluding my brother and stepfather, will be turned into mindless zombies all attracted to me. There would be rioting, which would lead to people getting hurt and it would be on my shoulders. After what happened at the Winter Concert on Isla Flora, I do not want to take the chance of someone getting hurt, or worse.

The song that follows is slower and more seductive in rhythm and for some reason speaks to my inner Siren. Mom and Ando must sense my overwhelming desire to accompany the musicians, but as I promised, I suppress the desire to burst into song. Matteo, the lead singer croons a hard-hitting rock ballad that is both romantic and fierce. For a young singer, he has immense stage presence and his voice... *Dear Father! His voice!* Sweet harmonic perfection mixed with raspy undertones that make every hair on my arms stand on edge.

Damn, I want to sing!

But I don't.

Instead, I grit my teeth until my jaw aches, but I keep my promise. I hold back my Siren Song until it fades into the dark crevices of my mind. It slides back into the place where it is safe, where people are safe from it.

I can do this!

When the song ends, everyone, including me, fills the square with thunderous applause.

Dad glances over at me.

"How's it going?" he inquires, his expression optimistic.

"I'm having fun!" I proclaim loudly.

"Okay!" he states, giving me a huge smile.

When the third song begins, I realize that I am humming along without even realizing it. Now, it is time to leave. I have no doubt that if I stay, the concert will end badly by no fault of the band.

"We need to leave, now!" I exclaim, raising my voice so my family can hear me over the instruments.

"Of course, sweetheart," Dad replies without any questions.

"Are you up for something to eat?" Mom asks, gathering our belongings. Dad takes the picnic basket from her along with the trash that needs to be thrown away. Ando continues to dance to the song currently playing, but starts to walk at the same time. He reminds me of a marionette dancing as if he is controlled by unseen strings.

"I can always eat," I reply jokingly.

"What are you in the mood for?" Mom probes, taking my stepdad's free hand in hers.

"Pizza!" Ando jumps as he expresses his food wishes. "And gelato!"

"We'll see what restaurants are enroute to the hotel," Dad answers, herding us like a flock of geese.

"There is a family-owned café not too far from here," my mother educates. "Everything there is amazing."

"Sounds like a plan," Dad smiles at his wife. "Okay Clan Marquez, let's go!"

Happily, we leave the concert, thrilled that I have kept my promise and embraced my humanity. Proud of myself, I take the blanket from Mom and lead the way back to the hotel's shuttlebus parked nearby. Giddy with relief, I smile.

I truly can do this!

The day has been perfect so far; clear blue skies, warm gentle breezes with that alluring scent of sunflowers wafting across the land, wild songbirds sharing their summer songs, and the calm turquoise waters surrounding all of it. Even the food tastes more delicious in Italy for some strange reason. I think about asking Mom if there is a reason for that, but decide against it since I do not want to ruin her time with the family. After all, she deserves some peace of mind too.

"Does anyone want the last piece of chicken?" I nod in the direction of the white platter in the middle of the dining table of the family-owned restaurant overlooking the Ischia harbor. Everyone stares at me for a moment.

Finally, Dad answers.

"Go ahead."

"You're acting like you haven't eaten anything all day," Mom scolds in her maternal way. "Slow down, Selena, before you get a stomachache."

"Are there anymore potatoes?" I ask, ignoring her and scratching a sudden itch below my chin. Glancing around at the dishes laid out on the table, I notice that the bowl once filled with oven roasted spuds is now empty. Not even a sprig of rosemary remains. My stomach grumbles its complaint.

"No," Mom announces softly, so the other restaurant patrons will not overhear. "You ate the last of them a few minutes ago, along with the bread and the fruit tarts."

"What's wrong with you, Lena?" Ando watches me devour my poultry as if I have not eaten in days.

"Nothing," I reply, continuing to scarf my remaining bite of the moist, grilled chicken. "May I have some more?"

"I think you've had enough," my stepdad informs, taking the check to the cashier to pay the bill.

Still ravenous, I glance over at the table beside us and notice their spread of food. In the center of their neatly laid out dishes is a platter of grilled swordfish steaks lightly drizzled with herb vinaigrette. There is also a basket of garlic bread that has barely been touched.

"Pardon me," I boldly call to the family sitting around the table nibbling daintily on their food. "Are you finished with your fish?"

Shocked, they stare at me.

"Pardon me?" the mother huffs with a blank expression.

"If you are, may I have it?" I beg, completely serious.

Terribly embarrassed, my mother jumps in.

"I'm so sorry," she smiles sweetly. "She's joking. Please, go back to your meal."

Starving, my mind begins to drift to other sources of food.

"There's a fruit stand in the marketplace," I remind, grabbing my lightweight cardigan and purse as I stand to leave, the itchy sensation growing stronger and more annoying. "Can we get some—"

"*Selena!*" my mother interrupts on a whispered scolding. "What is going on? You're not acting like yourself."

Unable to respond, I stare blankly at her as the itch races to my nose. Without thought, I begin scratching… scratching harder… scratching in vain.

"I'm a growing girl," I begin, but am sidetracked by nausea that appears out of left field.

Suddenly, I feel my stomach lurch. In a panic, I push away from the table and race to the ladies washroom, passing confused eaters, not caring what anyone thinks. Right on my heels, Mom follows to make sure I am alright.

As soon as I enter the ladies' room, I dart into a stall. The spaces between my fingers and toes are itchy, along with my face, neck and scalp and I cannot help scratching until the areas are almost raw. It is the vilest feeling I have ever experienced in my entire life!

Oh! No! Not now! Not here!

"Are you okay?" my mother probes, knocking on the bathroom stall door.

"No!" I gasp for breath. "I'm five states away from okay!"

"Did you eat too much?" she queries in a worried tone.

"I don't think so," I gasp. "I still feel hungry, but my stomach is upset, and I can't stop itching!"

"How long have you been feeling like this?"

I pause, not knowing what to say, the truth or another lie. I decide the truth might be best at the moment. So, I take a deep breath before answering.

"Since the first day we got to the Mediterranean," I admit, meekly. "But even more so since we got to this island... to Ischia."

"Why didn't you say anything?" Mom questions with alarm.

Crap! I shouldn't have said anything!

"I didn't want to ruin your vacation," I explain, hoping she will understand.

She taps her foot in agitation for a moment, upset and hurt that I did not share this with her.

"Let's go back to the hotel," she insists in a calmer tone, waiting for me to exit the stall, but I cannot.

"Not yet!" I exclaim, leaning against the door in case she decides to use her Sireny strength and bust the door open.

Maybe if I stay super still and pretend that I do not hear her, she will leave and I can rectify my *'problem'* on my own. At the moment, I am more embarrassed than anything else and I want to prove to myself and my family that I can handle being a Siren. I do not want help. I want to figure these things out on my own.

"Selena," my mother's voice hardens. "Come out, now."

"I can't," I whisper, wanting to cry. "I can't come out."

There is a pause that seems to last forever.

"Why not?" she interrogates with growing irritation.

Hesitantly, I unlatch the door and peek out.

"Is anyone with you?" I demand uneasily.

"It's only me," she reassures in a hushed tone.

Taking a deep breath, I open the door the remainder of the way revealing my predicament. In the back of my mind, I pray that no one enters the restroom and sees me in this condition. There would be no way to explain how I look at the moment.

"*Holy crap!*" Mom gasps loudly then quickly glances toward the entrance, probably thinking the same thing that I am.

All I can do is stand with clasped hands looking pathetic.

"Your webbing and scales!" Mom's voice raises an octave. "They are showing!"

CHAPTER SIX

Thank goodness for Dad and Ando!

Together they convince the owner of the bistro to let us leave through the back door, use his truck to get back to our hotel, and also to borrow his wife's long, yellow raincoat so that I can cover myself. I do not know how they managed it. Ando probably did most of the talking. No one can resist my little brother's cute voice, those endearing aquamarine eyes, and sweet dimples that he inherited from his father.

"What is going on?" Dad raises his voice as he runs a frustrated hand through his dark, brown locks, with his even darker irises glaring at Mom.

"I have no idea," she tries to convince, her worried eyes darting between me and the rapidly moving road.

"Marina?" Dad huffs. "Why is she covered with scales?"

He stares at me in the rearview mirror.

"She's not in the water," he reminds, unable to believe his eyes.

His wife frowns.

"I am telling the truth this time," she declares and I believe her. "I don't know what's wrong, David. I'm just as confused as you."

Ando continues to stare at me. He moves closer to where I sit with my head in my hands on the seat beside him. Filled with curiosity, he leans over and pokes the webbing on my hand with his index finger.

"Wow!" he exclaims as he continues to ogle my webbing. "I've never gotten my webbing. It's so... flappy... and... squishy."

Boldly, he reaches toward me again, but I slap his hand away before he can touch. Determined, he tries again.

"Let me touch it, Lena," he whines and giggles at the same time.

Irritated, I smack his hand away harder.

"Stop it!" I admonish moving farther away.

"Let me touch it just once more," he continues.

Unable to argue any more, I allow him to touch the sensitive skin that helps me swim faster in the water. However, on land, it does absolutely nothing. It simply hangs there, mocking me.

"It feels like frog skin," my brother reveals with one more poke.

"Dad!" I shout. "Tell Ando to stop bothering me!"

Suddenly, Dad pulls over to the side of the road and gets out to pace, stopping long enough to say, "Ando… for heaven's sake… *Dios Mio!*… leave your sister alone!"

His pacing starts again.

"We were doing so well," he talks to himself. "So well."

"David, let's go to the hotel," my mother urges, appearing nervous and who could blame her. After all, her teen daughter currently looks like an alien.

Reluctantly, he stops, but continues to stare into the back seat… at me!

"Is there anything we can do to make it go away?" I ask, feeling the tears welling.

"I have no clue," Mom sulks, throwing her arms above her head.

Finally, my father orders: "Call the aunts."

Mom's eyes widen in shock.

"What?" she questions with a confused glare.

"I said call Ligeia and Leukosia," Dad repeats.

"I haven't heard from them since we got to Ischia," Mom reminds.

There is silence.

"Can't you contact them from anywhere with your telepathy?" he asks, taking a soothing breath.

"Apparently, they can block me," Mom grumbles below her breath.

David throws his arms over his head and begins a minute long rant in Spanish that makes everyone in the vehicle blush. When he stops, he seems less agitated. No one speaks.

"Combine your strength with the children and use that Sireny-fishy-mythical telepathy-thing and call them."

Mom silently debates.

"I'll try," she gets out of the SUV and stands motioning for Ando and me to join her. "Ok, clasp hands... good... now concentrate. We're going to amplify our thoughts... just think about the aunts... how they look... how they act..."

We stand holding hands at the side of the road for almost thirty minutes without any luck. I can only imagine what passersby are thinking. *Crazy tourists.* That is what *I* would be thinking if I were in their shoes.

"Maybe, we have a bad connection," I say like we are on cell phones.

"Take a break," Mom sighs. "We'll try again in a few minutes when we are at the hotel."

Needless to say, it does not work. Ligeia and Leukosia refuse to answer. Finally, my parents send us to bed and retire themselves. What a disaster.

Why do these things always happen to me?

A few minutes past midnight, I begin to drift off to sleep. In my dream, I am swimming along the rocky shoreline of Capri. All around are brightly colored fish darting in and out of the branches of coral, their forms shimmering as moonlight breaks through the water like hundreds of spotlights landing on their scales.

Below the surface, everything is intensified… colors are brighter… scents are stronger… emotions are more extreme. Happily, I chase a medium-sized grouper through patches of seaweed. Unfortunately, he gives me the slip by dashing inside of a small cleft in the seabed.

It is at that moment when a school of Bluefin Tuna appear, glowing as moonlight illuminates them from above. Tickled pink, I swim as fast as I can toward them, causing them to scatter in different directions, but to my delight they almost immediately reform their tight grouping. I do this several more times until I get bored.

Then I hear them.

"Come with me… into the sea… in the ocean's waves we'll play."

Almost instantly, I catch sight of them, Ligeia's crimson locks that shimmer like flames appear first, followed by Leukosia's long, golden mane, then I see their infamous hypnotic aquamarine eyes. My heart melts when I see their faces. But that happiness does not last very long.

"What is going on?" Leukosia scolds without even a hug.

"I'm broken," I click then clack my condition.

"I see," she sympathizes in Siren.

"What am I doing wrong?"

Before she can respond, I hear Ligeia's no-nonsense voice in my head admonishing.

'You are trying to be human and you are not,' she states flatly.

Like a toddler needing its mother, I rush toward her with my arms out to hug her, but she quickly darts out of the way.

"Where are you, Selena?" Ligeia interrogates as if it is a question on a test.

I grin.

"I'm in bed at the hotel," I purr, thoroughly enjoying this ethereal, yet vivid dream.

"Are you sure?" Leukosia joins, her voice like an angel's.

Confidently, I nod.

"I'm in bed enjoying a lovely dream."

"Is that right?" both retort with narrowed eyes.

"Yup!" I answer with a giggle. "I've missed you both so much."

Finally, they let me hug them. They feel so *real*.

"Selena—"

"Wait," I interrupt. "Let's just enjoy the water. It's so warm tonight. So calm, so perfect."

"Selena—" Ligeia begins, but I halt her with a raised palm.

"Let's go to the Blue Grotto and sing... sing until morning... or until Mom wakes me up."

'Selena?' I unexpectedly hear my mother's voice in my head. *'Where the hell are you young lady?'*

Suddenly, I am confused.

"I'm in bed," I remind, wondering why she just does not walk over to the adjoining room and talk to me.

'Don't lie to me!' she practically growls. *'Your father and I are worried sick!'*

There is a long pause before she speaks again.

'David is pacing and cursing in Spanish!' she warns. *'You're going to make him have a stroke!'*

What? That makes no sense.

'Where... are... you?' she snarls inside of my head.

"I'm in bed sleeping... wait..."

Speedily, I swim toward a nearby spiny branched coral and run my finger over it. Immediately, it begins to bleed.

What the hell?

Slowly, I raise the same finger to my lips and lick the tip. I taste copper.

Oh, my gracious!

"Where am I?" I ask, turning to Ligeia.

She rolls her eyes then finally replies.

"You are in the harbor."

Stunned by the news, my eyes widen and my mouth gapes open.

"No, I can't be," I reply, shaking my head in disbelief.

"Sing," Leukosia orders.

In shock, I respond.

"I can't do that!" I huff. "I'll cause a disturbance in the bed and breakfast!"

"I said… sing," she repeats with an irritated tone.

"Fine… you want pandemonium… I'll sing," I state petulantly and with as much haughtiness as I can muster.

Determined to set the record straight, I open my mouth and nothing comes out. Not even a peep. I try again, but this time with more passion and manage to create a stream of bubbles.

Still no sound.

At last, it dawns on me.

I really am in the harbor!

Holy crap!

This cannot be happening! How in the world did I end up in the harbor surrounded by boats and fishing traps?

The last thing I remember is climbing into bed. Ando was already asleep on his double bed and I had been eating a late-night snack of canned sardines and saltine crackers that Mom bought from a small grocery store near the main square. I had just brushed my teeth, settled into bed, and began watching an old episode of *Green Acres* with English subtitles on the hotel's satellite television system.

(Don't judge me!)

'I don't know what's going on with me, Aunt Leukosia,' I release the words in a rushed jumble that is a mixture of English, Italian, and Siren then realize that I used my telepathy.

Curiously, she studies me, yet remains silent allowing me to rant.

"Something is wrong, but my mother doesn't know how to fix it," I continue in Siren.

Still, she continues staring at me.

"Please help me," I plead, not knowing what to do next.

"Of course there is something wrong," Ligeia agrees rigidly with a stream of annoyed clickity-clacks as she braids her hair to keep it out of her face.

"Are you hungry all of the time?" Leukosia grills.

My stomach acids begin to churn as it growls very loudly, making, both aunts gawk at me.

"Starving is a better word," I confess, placing both hands over my abdomen.

"Here," Leukosia says handing me a still squirming baby tuna. "This should help."

Registering her command to eat it, I gag.

"No way!" I reply with a shake of my head. "No way! No how!"

"Eat it!" Ligeia shouts a clack.

"I can't... I won't!" I loudly clack back, feeling my innards rolling.

I feel the acid churning my stomach as it growls even louder than before.

"I'll get sick!" I bluster with disgust. "Can't we cook it or something?"

My stomach answers with another tumultuous growl.

"No," they answer in unison. "Trust us."

"It's disgusting!" I bellow, wanting to swim to freedom. "It's alive!"

"We are Sirens," they both say together.

I huff, yanking on my soaking wet pajamas.

"I know what we are!" I snap rather loudly, earning me a fierce clack.

"No!" they shout in my mind. *"You do not!"*

Stubbornly, I state, "I don't even like sushi!"

"Eat it," they request much calmer.

Wanting them to stop ganging up on me, I take the small fish from Leukosia's webbed hand. I pray that the thing will stay down, but something tells me that it will. Horrified, I close my eyes and take a small nibble.

"Just eat it… pop it into your mouth and swallow!" they both snap as they make a chewing motion like they are feeding a baby.

Completely disgusted, I do as they command and take the entire fish into my mouth. Then I wait. We all wait.

"How was it?" Ligeia asks with a raised brow, and I think for a few seconds before answering:

"May I have another?"

I have learned the hard way that there is no debating with the aunts. After my *'snack'* they convince me to go on a *'road trip'* with them to see something that they deem as important. Try as I might to dissuade them, they still insist that the trip is necessary. It has come to my attention that arguing with the aunts, especially when they are together, is a battle I will lose every time. From my observations, they have a demigod-like stubbornness that has no weaknesses. Whoever is against them will always give up. It is just easier to do so.

"Where are we going?" I query as we swim toward the windward side of the island.

"There is something you need to know about your heritage," Ligeia informs as she swims beside me; her red braid trailing behind her like an incredibly long, thick rope.

'Your mother has forgotten her history lessons,' again the two voices merge inside of my head.

"What does that have to do with anything?" I probe, feeling my blood pressure rising.

"You need to understand your past, so you can figure out your future," they clack then click.

Overwhelmed by the conversation, I stay perfectly quiet, wishing I could blend into the background.

"Come with us," they command as they swim ahead, leaving me alone staring after them.

"Wait!" I call. "You didn't tell me why my body keeps doing these strange things."

"That dilemma will be answered soon," they insist. "Come on, young one… follow us."

Gasping for breath, I race to catch up to the sisters, who speed through the water like torpedoes that have been launched. Leukosia's blonde mane reminds me of a sail fluttering in a hurricane.

"How much farther?" I click loudly, knowing that they can hear me even though they are so far ahead. Apparently, our clicks and clacks can travel an extremely far distance underwater. It is kind of like how dolphins and whales communicate with their pods across the open sea.

"It is just up ahead," Leukosia informs with a regal wave of her hand.

As she proclaims this, both Sirens abruptly stop. Finally reaching them, I halt also, wondering what is so important. As we float weightlessly under the sea, I begin to feel strange. My mind becomes calm, clear and focused as my instincts suddenly kick-in. I think the water is too murky in this area and my eyes instantly switch to Siren-mode. Everything around me is crystal clear and I can see for miles away.

'What's happening?' I whisper with my mind and am shocked when The Sisters hear me. *'I have telepathy? Holy cow! I have freaking telepathy!'*

Completely amused, my aunts muster smiles.

Wanting to try communicating with someone farther away, I say to myself, *'Ando... Ando... can you hear me?'*

'Lena,' my brother's small sleepy voice comes through loud and clear. *'I'm trying to sleep. Get outta my head.'*

'Sorry,' I respond with an ecstatic giggle. *'Go back to sleep.'*

Next, I try something different. I command the webbing between my fingers to go away, but the ones on my toes to stay. Without hesitation, it happens. Then I switch them, several times I do this enjoying the control that I have over my body. Then I imagine activating my scales, but change my mind remembering how itchy they are.

'Call to the animals in the sea,' my aunts encourage with gigantic smiles.

With my telepathy, I call out to the closest pod of dolphins, specifically the alpha of the group. Within a few minutes, I see a smooth, gray male swimming toward me at top speed. He comes within touching distance and allows me to stroke his skin. He even opens his mouth and lets me touch his tongue. I laugh. It feels very tongue-like. Thanking him with a few clickity-clacks, he turns and swims away.

'Control the sea,' Ligeia orders with a boisterous belly-laugh.

Unsure if I can successfully do the task, I take a deep breath, say a prayer, and concentrate as I race to the surface with the sisters right on my heels. Up above, the water is barely moving. As I break through the surface, I activate my lungs and without hesitation my gills retract and my lungs begin to breathe the fresh night air.

'Control the waves, Selena,' again they speak as one.

They make it sound so easy.

Not wanting to disappoint them, I close my eyes, focusing on making the water roll and it does. Larger waves begin to come in from the deep; large angry waves that resemble a giant wall.

Whoops! I don't want those kinds of waves! Immediately, I ask them to be more gentle… more manageable. And they become much smaller. Then I request that the water be still and once more, the surface transforms to glass.

"Oh my!" I yell-clack as I swim around The Sirens, then dive below the surface to reemerge in a spray of mist as I leap out of the water like a Great White Shark catching a seal as it shoots out of the water. The speed is exhilarating.

"How is this possible?" I ask my aunts breathlessly in Siren.

They laugh before answering.

"Look down."

I do, but do not understand what I should be looking for.

"I don't see anything," I reply anxiously.

"Look harder," they encourage, their excitement evident. "The answer you seek is there."

This time, I really look, I look with my soul. I see it or rather I *feel* it. Feel the pull of something extraordinary… something powerful… something that cannot be explained in conventional terms.

"Wait," I mumble, plunging to the bottom. "I think I see something."

More determined than ever to find the cause of my newly found control, I dive down and grab a handful of sand. Among the tiny grains is a small piece of black glass, which I then race back with to where Ligeia and Leukosia are waiting. Surprisingly, where the glass touches my skin I can feel a slight static electrical charge as if I have just walked across carpet and touched a metal doorknob in the dead of winter. It does not hurt, it just tingles slightly.

"What is this?" I enquire as I inspect the smooth, two-inch fragment.

They smile.

'It is the source of your power,' they inform from inside of my head at a mere whisper and in my spirit, I know that it is true.

Unable to take my eyes off of the innocuous fragment of glass, I turn it over in my palms several times inspecting it, studying it; searching for flaws in its smooth surface, but finding none.

It is just glass!

"I don't understand," I say to my aunts as we swim back to the Ischia harbor at a leisurely pace. "How can *this* be the source of my power?"

They pause for a moment, pondering the question. Abruptly, they stop moving, only their long hair seems to be affected by the movement of the sea. A large compass jellyfish, also known as a *Chrysaora hysoscella*, passes between them and they do not even notice when it touches their skin. From my studies, I know that this type of jellyfish has an extremely painful sting level and just the slightest touch can cause itching and burning and can also scar the skin for up to three weeks. Any normal person would have instantly felt its painful sting, but not these two characters.

At last, they speak.

"A better explanation is it helps channel our abilities and makes them keener, more precise."

My science knowledge springs forward.

"Like an antenna will boost the signal on the television set?" I state quizzically.

They glance at each other with a strange look on their gorgeous faces.

"We suppose so," they respond robotically, not quite comprehending the word *antenna*.

I look at them hovering a few feet off of the stone-covered seabed. I mean really watch them, their facial features particularly. Every curve, every beauty mark, every aspect of their perfectly formed porcelain-like, olive complexion is the same. Exactly the same. The only difference is the color of their hair and the timbre of their voices.

"What is a television set?" they probe cocking their heads to the side mechanically.

"You know, it is like a flat box that has moving pictures on it," I educate, using my hands as I speak.

Of course, they watch me in a haze.

"How can a box be flat?" they grumble.

"Actually, it really isn't flat," I correct myself.

"We do not comprehend," they inform mechanically. "What are *'moving pictures'*? Pictures cannot move."

"Umm… they are shows followed by commercials," I add, hoping that something will click.

"Commercials?" they ask as they blink several times. "What are *commercials*?"

"Well," I try to gather my thoughts, "commercials are advertisements for stuff."

"What type of *stuff*?" they ask still bewildered.

"*Stuff*... you know," I say moving my hands around like I often do when I am frustrated.

They repeat, "What type of *stuff*?"

"Knickknacks," I blurt.

"Explain... *knickknacks*," they reply, beginning to move closer and invading my personal space.

I have come to realize that the aunts are not familiar with the concept of *'personal space'*. I once tried to explain the idea, but they only looked at me like I was *Cerberus* (in Greek mythology, *Cerberus* is a three-headed dog that guards the gates of Hades to prevent the dead from escaping).

"Knickknacks are things you don't really need," I try to inform.

"If it is not needed then why obtain them?" Leukosia grumbles.

"I don't know," I reply honestly.

"What else can you receive from the tele-vis-ion?" Ligeia chirps.

I think for a moment as my brain searches for the correct words to use.

"You can see ads for clothes, jewelry, cars, food, travel, movies—"

"Moo-vies," they annunciate slowly, feeling the word rolling around their tongues.

This causes me to chuckle, earning me a look of disdain.

"Never mind," I snicker to myself.

I have so much to teach them… my two ancient aunts.

Still wrapping my mind around the magnitude of this lowly piece of glass, I question the wisdom of these two *'women'* and wonder if they recently found a shipwreck filled with casks of aged rum. Suddenly, their words no longer make sense.

"So… this little piece of whatever it is will make me stronger?"

"Yes," Ligeia responds firmly.

"Especially when you are alone," Leukosia interjects sadly.

"Oh," I state only half comprehending.

"When we are together," they say as one, "we are able to channel though each other. We are like fingers of a hand. Each individually possesses immense power, but together we are… *more*."

Now, I understand…

… Sort of…

… Maybe.

Curiously, I turn the piece of shiny onyx material over and over in my hand, studying it; feeling its smooth exterior and its rounded edges, created by time and movement of the currents. It still tingles in my palm.

"How can it amplify my abilities?" I utter, wondering if it is radioactive and if I keep it, will my entire body become contaminated, or will I sprout another head? They look at each other, debating… I think. Each speaking to the other, but shutting me out of the conversation, which is quite rude in my opinion; I think I need to teach them about human manners one of these days.

"It is volcanic glass created when Mount Vesuvius erupted," they answer rigidly.

"Why does it affect us this way?" I wonder aloud.

More Siren language occurs between the two before they answer.

"When Poseidon, created our mother… " more clacks and clicks and a few sounds I have never heard before follow before they continue. "… he used the sand and mud surrounding Ischia to mold her form then asked his brother, Zeus, to breathe life into her vessel."

"That's sort of romantic," I coo with a longing sigh, picturing Andrew.

Ignoring my comment, they talk some more then reply, "The volcanic glass is part of our chemical makeup, for lack of a better explanation."

"Oh!" I clack as understanding bludgeons me over the head. "It's in our DNA!"

Speechless, they stare at me with confusion then turn to each other, blink several times then turn back.

"It deals with our cells and other much more complicated factors. We learned about it in biology class," I educate the pair.

"It is what makes us... *Us!*" they exclaim together.

"*Exactly!*" I squeal, creating a stream of bubbles.

"So... because of its existence within our cells, we can connect through it to harness the power of every drop of water on the Earth," this time only Leukosia replies.

"We are all interconnected," they say with large toothy smiles.

Ah ha! Now, it is clear. *Somewhat!*

Not too long after our Siren briefing, The Sisters deposit me at Porto Ischia. Reluctantly, I climb out of the bay to return to the bed and breakfast located in the middle of the town center, just a half mile walk away.

Suddenly, I turn back toward them as they silently bob in the calm water.

"Will you be staying for a while?" I ask, missing them already.

"We shall see," they clack then click then clack again.

My chest tightens.

"Will I be able to talk to you?" I pout like my brother.

They both glance at my closed fist where I clench the newly found glass shard.

"You will be able to communicate with us no matter where we are in the world," they inform with a grin.

"Alright," I acknowledge with a half-hearted smile. "Please, don't go too far, okay?"

Just as before, they nod their answer, then faster than a strike of lightning, they disappear below the dark waters of the bay. My heartbeat instantly quickens as my chest does that now familiar tightening. Without my permission, a lonely tear rolls down my cheek and I brush it away with an angry swipe.

The Sisters are gone, and my soul misses them already. It misses them like the flowers miss the warm spring showers. I understand the emptiness Yaya Parthenope must have felt being away from her sisters and the sea. It is like someone cutting out your heart with a spoon.

    Now, I get it.

CHAPTER SEVEN

I do not know what time it is when I finally wake. The curtains in our room are pulled closed so that the space remains dark and cozy. Slowly, I sit up, letting the soft cotton sheets slide down my torso and pool at my waist. Still groggy, I look over at my brother's bed, but it is empty. On the nightstand between the two beds is a note in Mom's handwriting that reads:

Heading downstairs to the restaurant for breakfast.

Meet us when you are dressed.

Love Mom!

Breakfast! That's what I need!

Swiftly, I shower, brush my teeth and hair, get dressed, and find footwear. On my way out, I happen to notice that the suitcases are already packed and waiting near the door for the bellhop to take them downstairs. I forgot that we are returning to Capri today. I will miss Ischia, but I will have wonderful memories until the next time I visit.

"Good morning, sleepy head," my family greets me as I sit at one of the white-washed dining tables at the bed and breakfast.

Functioning on limited sleep, I grunt my acknowledgment which only makes them joke more.

"We thought you'd never wake up," my stepfather teases.

Curiously, he studies me when I do not respond.

"Are you ready to tell us how you got out of the hotel and into the harbor last night?" my mother questions.

Great question!

"I'm not sure," I admit, swallowing my uneasiness. "I went to bed and thought I was dreaming, but I guess I wasn't."

In true David form, he smiles, silently reassuring that he will not give me away to the gypsies… at least not today.

"Did you have fun with the aunts last night?" he asks, changing the subject.

Feeling somewhat self-conscious, I nod as I reach for the oversized bowl of Carbonara, helping myself to a large portion of the steaming pasta. The smell is mouthwatering. I hope I can keep it down, but according to my aunts, I can process cooked food as long as I also indulge in raw food, especially raw seafood, on a regular basis. On the swim back to Porto Ischia, they schooled me on the dietary restrictions of a *'fledgling'* Siren when it comes to processing cooked food. Surprisingly, I was quite impressed at their precise instructions.

"Selena?"

"Yes, Dad?"

My stepfather pauses to formulate his next question.

"You know you can tell us anything, right? Like how you got out of the hotel."

Unfortunately, all I can do is frown.

"I'm not sure," I repeat with all sincerity. "I honestly don't know how I got into the harbor."

Hearing my stomach rumbling in protest, I survey the items on our table. Today, the cook has made garlic bread specked with parsley, crunchy almond biscotti suitable for dipping into coffee, a bowl of fresh fruit salad, the Carbonara of course, and two pitchers: one containing water, the other lemonade. Unable to resist, I take in a deep breath of the heavenly aroma.

At the other tables, casually dressed patrons are enjoying their complimentary morning meal. The tantalizing fragrance of hot baked bread, pungent cheeses, spicy cured meats and the unmistakable scent of brewing coffee wafts through the impeccably kept eating area.

Outside, a perfect view of the turquoise depths of the Porto Ischia Harbor bids us good day.

"What time did you finally go to bed?" Dad asks as he finishes a cup of frothy cappuccino.

Not wanting to appear ill-mannered, I suppress a yawn.

"I'm not sure," I admit, sleepily. "I think the sun was rising. I didn't bother to check."

Ando finishes chewing his bite of pasta before asking, "What were you doing? I saw the light from the laptop."

"I was doing some research," I confess as I reach for a slice of bread.

"Research on what?" he pushes, obviously curious.

"More like… who," I convey, resting my elbows on the table then quickly removing them when I realize my mistake.

"Who, then?" Mom's interest is showing too.

"The aunts mentioned Poseidon last night, so I wanted to know more about him," I reply, my mind swimming with unanswered questions.

Dad's face lights up. He, like me, loves the subject of Greek mythology. Now, that I know it actually is true, I adore it even more.

"Who is Pose-I-don?" Ando tries to pronounce the word but has difficulty.

"Poseidon," I repeat slowly so he can wrap his mind around the sound of it.

"Who is *Poseidon*?" he smiles when he repeats it correctly.

Wanting to sound well-read, I clear my throat before answering:

"According to lore, Poseidon was the Olympian god of the oceans, rivers, storms, flood and drought, earthquakes, and horses. He was also considered to be the sovereign leader of the various sea gods and goddesses. It was believed that he controlled every facet of the seas. Later, the Roman equivalent to him was the god, Neptune," I finish, feeling rather scholarly.

"Honey, do you know all of this?" Dad interrogates as Mom just stares at him making him chuckle, and then he mocks playfully. "Of course, you do. Siren one-O-one."

"Is he really the king of us?" Ando asks with wide eyes.

Mom frowns.

"Sort of," she responds, brushing his hair from his eyes. "It's... complicated."

My father smiles before adding, "Seems like 'The Sisters' gave you quite a tutorial."

Ando glares at me before asking, "Why didn't they call for me? I miss them too."

"I know," I reply, giving him a smile. "But they will be close by. They promised. I'm sure they'll visit again."

"When?" my brother beams brightly, showing his dimples.

"Soon," I promise, ruffling his neatly combed hair.

"How are they?" my mom questions eagerly as she pours herself a glass of cold lemonade from the pitcher on the table; beads of condensation race down the smooth surface to dot the crisp white tablecloth.

I giggle.

"They are great!" I reveal. "Just as *'Sireny'* as ever."

That makes us all laugh. Anyone who has ever known a Siren understands this reference. Tia Ligeia and Tia Leukosia are set in their ways, to say the least, and they question everything, and I do mean *everything*. They are quick to judge and even quicker to condemn. Especially humans.

"Did they fix you?" my brother rejoins our conversation.

"Yes," I smile. "They gave me some advice."

I pull out the fragment of glass from my shirt pocket.

"And they gave me this."

Mom and Ando beam.

"Did they explain what it does?" my mother asks hopefully,

"They did," I say with a grin. "They were also quite disappointed with you, Mom."

Mom's brows hitch to her hairline.

"Why are they upset with me?" she gasps dramatically.

I pause, enjoying having the upper hand for once.

"They said that you didn't remember your history," I add, taking a manageable bite of garlic bread.

"Which part of our very long, very complex history were they referring to?" Mom smirks, her hand holding the glass hovering in midair as she waits for my reply.

"Oh… just about the very large deposit of black volcanic glass that surrounds Ischia," I poke, enjoying making my mother squirm.

"Well, I—" she starts to defend herself then suddenly stops. "I did forget. I'll never live it down."

Dad and Ando stare at both of us.

"What does it do?" Ando prods, breaking the uncomfortable silence.

"According to the aunts, we, Sirens, are composed of high concentrations of said volcanic material," I smirk at her expression.

"Hmm… " she hums to herself as she blushes. "It's true."

I lean back in my chair and clasp my hands in my best Marlon Brando *Godfather* impersonation.

"Also, that because of this high concentration of volcanic glass, combined with me ignoring *The Calling*, plus my order… from you… my own parental unit… to *not* sing… *at all*, is contributing to my lack of control."

The entire family watches her blank expression at my revelation with wide eyes.

David leans over and takes it from my hand.

"Are you sure we shouldn't get rid of it?" he queries, studying it like the scientist he is.

"Nope," I grin. "It will help me focus my energy and abilities, thus giving me back my control."

My mother still appears concerned.

"I'm sorry," she apologizes at last. "I should have remembered the adverse effects the glass would have on you. The aunts were right."

Just as I am about to let her off of the hook, pun definitely intended, one of the hotel staff heads towards our table carrying a covered dish of something that smells amazing. Slowly, the woman approaches. As she comes closer, I can see her salt-and-pepper hair, and gleaming brown eyes surrounded by thick black lashes. She appears normal, but the only thing that disturbs me is the odd expression covering her highly wrinkled, grandmotherly face. Wordlessly, she rests the long platter on the table between us.

"Thank you," Dad speaks first. "But we didn't order anything else."

The woman simply stares at him and smiles. Slowly, she turns to me, then Ando and lastly, Mom. Like a statue, she stands motionless with that same elusive smile resembling the *Mona Lisa*. Every hair on my arms is standing at attention. Something is not what it seems with this woman. Without warning, my palms begin to sweat and from the look on my brother's face, his are doing the same.

Finally, the lady speaks. The words are fragmented and mumbled, but full of emotion… the only word I truly hear is *seirína*.

My mother's face turns pale.

"Let's go!" Mom practically jumps out of her seat and grabs Ando and me by the hands. Her palms are sweating too. *"Now!"*

Wordlessly, the woman reaches across the table and removes the lid covering the dish. My stomach growls again as the contents beneath are revealed… a large uncooked Atlantic Bluefin Tuna, just like the ones I saw last night. There is a gaping hole where its guts should be. My eyes widen in disbelief. As we rapidly gather our belongings, I hear her call after us that same word…

"Seirína!"

Glancing over my shoulder to keep a watchful eye on the waitress, Mom and Dad rush us in the direction of the front desk to pick-up our already packed suitcases then out of the establishment's front door. Ando's little legs can hardly keep up with Mom's almost galloping pace.

"Slow down, Mommy!" my brother pleads breathlessly.

"Not until we get to the boat!" she apprises with a snap.

Terrified at the entire situation, I inquire as I speed walk beside her, "What language was that?"

"Ancient Greek," Mom replies as she quickens her pace.

I am almost jogging to keep up with her now.

"What did she say?"

"*Seirína*," Mom repeats in a hushed tone, looking behind us to make sure we are not being followed.

I still do not understand the significance of the word, but then again, my studies of world languages with Ligeia and Leukosia are few and far between. Mom rarely has time to sit and teach me or Ando, even though she is fluent in every single language that exists, as well as several that are used by only mythological beings.

"What does it mean?" my father whispers as we race toward the harbor.

"Siren!"

"Damn it!" Mom swears as she paces the width of the boat that is currently taking us back to Capri, her cornflower blue sundress fluttering gently around her ankles as it is tugged by the salt-kissed breeze. "Where are the aunts? Why can't I contact them?"

"I'm sure they're alright," I try to reassure. "They like doing that *'mysterious-Siren-thing'*."

"Who was that lady?" Ando asks as he looks over the railing of the chartered vessel that races through the Bay of Naples, a pod of dolphins at its bow.

"I'm not sure," my mother huffs her frustration. "Why aren't they answering?"

"Do you want me to try?" I question, coming to stand beside her.

"Please," she sounds like she is about to burst into tears.

Ando also joins us, adding his strength to ours, but there is still no connection with the two stubborn Siren sisters.

"Maybe, they're out of range," Dad adds his two cents, but shrinks at Mom's icy glare.

"That's not possible," his wife replies, her eyes now concentrating on the horizon.

"The sisters explained that we are always linked, no matter where we are," I inform David, knowing that he cannot truly understand our physical and mental connection.

For Sirens, being cut-off from each other is literally torture. On many occasions, I have felt that extra surge of power when we are all together: Ligeia, Leukosia, Mom, Ando and myself. Imagine tapping into the world's most powerful energy source, feeling that current strengthening your body and mind. Every part of you coming to life as this unseen entity transforms you into something... *More!*

It is remarkable.

Formidable.

Addictive.

And when it is gone...? Unbearable.

"They're still not responding," my mother announces as she sits beside her husband, and he immediately takes her hand in his.

"What can I do to help?" my stepfather inquires, his white polo enhancing his naturally tanned skin.

Our mother smiles, a slow depressed smile that hurts my heart.

"Nothing, honey," she sighs. "Just you being here is all that I need."

"Maybe we really should return to Isla Flora," David suggests.

Mom shakes her head.

"Not yet."

"How did the old woman know what we are?" I probe with a whispered tone so only my parents and Ando can hear.

Mom just shrugs her shoulders as she rests her head on Dad's shoulder.

"I don't know," she whimpers fearfully. "I honestly don't."

CHAPTER EIGHT

A few hours later, we are back at our villa in the *Belvedere of Tragara*, still trying to contact Ligeia and Leukosia. As the three Sirens of the family stand with clasped hands concentrating on the task of speaking to the aunts, my father is busy sipping a shot glass of *Limoncello*, an Italian liqueur prepared from locally grown lemon rinds, which is predominantly made in Southern Italy.

"Still nothing," Mom growls low in her throat as she releases our hands. "I don't understand why they haven't answered."

Agitated, she sits on the sofa then stands and then repeats until I am almost dizzy watching her nervous ritual.

"Don't panic," Dad soothes as he takes another small sip of the vibrant yellow drink.

"Panic is the only logical thing to do," she informs, grabbing the glass and taking a sip as well.

"It was just some creepy old lady," I remind, trying to calm everyone. "Why are we so scared just because she said *Siren*. For all we know you misinterpreted."

She glares at me but says nothing.

"It's been years since you've spoken Greek," I continue. "Remember, you said so yourself."

Mom seems a little more at ease as she hands my father back the now empty shot glass.

"That is true," she sighs, releasing a held breath. "My language skills *do* need more practice."

Filled with relief, I nod.

"A misunderstanding," I giggle. "That's all it was."

Ando's forehead creases and his eyes narrow.

"How do you explain the gutted tuna?" he interjects with a smug glare.

"Be quiet, Ando," I reply, shooting him my own warning stare.

Thankfully, he remains silent.

For the rest of the day, we keep to the villa spending time as a family. We decide to play board games and make homemade pizza for dinner. Mom makes the best pizza with her own dough recipe, along with red sauce and fresh mozzarella that she also makes from scratch. She even cooks it on the grill to keep it authentic. Dad and I help by cutting the mushrooms, onions, and peppers, while Ando helps by arranging the thin slices of prosciutto on the lightly sauced partially cooked crusts.

We have quite an assembly line going and a lot of pizzas to grill since my parents alone can eat two whole pies by themselves. I can devour at least one whole one. Ando lately can eat almost as much as me. That is another great perk of being a Siren: you do not need to be concerned with having a slow metabolism (usually).

Lately, with me, it is hit or miss when it comes to what my stomach will accept.

Dinner cooks in less than five minutes and before long we are all settled around the outdoor dining set eating and conversing.

"This is delicious," I announce, taking another slice.

Mom nods her head in agreement.

"Why does everything taste better here?" I question with all seriousness.

Dad only smiles since his mouth is full of the heavenly creation.

"I have no clue," my mother replies as she too reaches for another wedge of pizza.

The only sound from my brother is, *Mmm*, which makes all of us giggle.

"Who taught you how to cook, Marina?" Dad questions as he takes a sip of his iced coffee sweetened with condensed milk.

Mom just smiles mischievously.

"Was it someone famous?" he probes again, wanting but not expecting an answer.

Mom blushes as she reaches for another napkin to wipe her prosciutto flavored lips.

"It couldn't have been the aunts," Dad states with a hearty laugh. "They hate cooked food."

Finally, my mother answers.

"When I was growing up, my father had a housekeeper named, Sofia, she was from Naples," Mom confesses with a smile. "She taught me everything I know about cooking."

"Was she nice?" Ando asks, swiping his greasy lips with the back of his hand.

Mom beams and gives him a quick hug along with a much needed napkin.

"Sofia was one of the nicest people I have ever had the pleasure of knowing," she states, her eyes beginning to well with unshed tears. "I think about her almost every day."

My curiosity rises as I ask, "Did she know your secret?"

We all stop eating, waiting for Mom to respond, but she never does. Instead, she stands and excuses herself from the table, leaving us staring after her with befuddled expressions. It does not surprise us though. Mom is an extremely private person who would rather listen than talk.

I think it is a Siren thing.

🦉

After dinner, I convince my parents to let me take Ando for a swim to the grotto. Ando, as expected, is thrilled at the thought of having an adventure with just the two of us. Just like when we were back home on Isla Flora.

"I want you to keep in contact," our mother reminds as she gives me a hug then my brother.

"We will," we both answer at once.

"Don't forget," Dad reminds with a stern expression.

Ever since he found out that he is married into a family of Sirens, he has become even more protective. He lectures of safety and staying together, reminding us of the dangers that may come with this dangerous, yet provocative 'designation'. I have a sneaky suspicion that the mood ring he bought for me last Christmas is actually fitted with a GPS tracking chip.

I would not put it past him.

"Look after each other," he states sternly. "Ando, listen to your sister. Selena, don't be too bossy."

My brother and I both nod.

"Be aware of your surroundings," he adds without falter. "Just because you are Sirens doesn't mean that you are invincible."

We nod again.

"Your Mom and I are getting old and we won't be able to make more of you—"

"Hey!" our mother interjects with a blushy grin. "Speak for yourself, Marquez. I could make babies for the rest of eternity if I wanted to."

David laughs while my brother and I grimace at the thought of them making another baby. Yuck, Yuck, and triple Yuck! I am certain Ando feels the same.

Satisfied with his advice, Dad hugs us then takes a step back in order for Mom to do the same.

"We won't be reckless," we answer in unison once more without even thinking about it.

Mom sighs as she clasps her hands together, trying not to hug us all over again.

"If you get into any trouble, I can reach you in a heartbeat."

"Mom," I whine, "I've got it covered."

"Are you wearing your keepsake?" Dad exclaims in his fatherly tone.

Reaching into my swimsuit top, I reveal the marquise-shaped, black volcanic glass that hides beneath. On our way back to the villa, we stopped at a nearby jeweler to have my new *keepsake* made into a charm. I made sure to add it to my sterling silver chain that also houses the black pearl that Dad gave me when we first moved to the Caribbean. I promised myself, and my parents, that I would never take it off.

"The sun will be setting soon," Mom informs, peering out the large living room window. "It's better if you wait until then."

Both Ando and I nod our agreement.

Impatiently, we all wait until we see the sky begin to transform from a soft powder blue to teal then finally, a canvas of navy blue with splashes of twinkling white stars. Ando squeezes my hand and I do the same to his.

I cannot wait to show him all of the wonders that are hidden below the waves.

Shortly after, my brother and I are safely in the sea on our way to the Blue Grotto. Tonight, the water is lovely. Just the right temperature, not too hot, not too cold.

'What's that?' Ando asks telepathically, excitedly, pointing to a purplish-blue, oddly shaped cephalopod.

I try to suppress a snicker but fail miserably.

"That's a cuttlefish," I instruct in Siren, feeling quite proud of my Ichthyology knowledge taught to me by my stepfather, the marine biologist.

He frowns.

"Mommy calls me her little cuttlefish," he grimaces. "They aren't very cute."

I call to the slowly moving creature and it immediately swims towards us, its eight arms moving steadily.

Ando reaches out for it.

"Be gentle," I remind as he touches the animal's head, right between two large eyes sporting W-shaped pupils along an elongated body, with two tentacles furnished with suckers used to secure prey.

"He's so smooth," my brother giggles.

The cuttlefish responds wordlessly.

She says, 'thank you,'' I translate with my thoughts, filling with pride.

I click several times, thanking her and she reluctantly resumes her journey toward the nearby coral reef.

"How do you do that, Lena?" Ando clicks and clacks.

My brother watches the six-inch marine creature swimming away with a huge toothy grin.

"Practice," I reply, immediately reminding myself of Mom.

Ando reaches over and examines my new glass charm.

"It's because of this," he says, holding it in his palm. "You can do everything more easily now… because of this. The aunts never came to see me. They never gave me a charm. They just like you."

Suddenly, I feel guilty and try to comfort him.

"Come on." I ruffle his hair. "You know that's not true."

Disappointed and hurt, he does not look at me.

"They more than like you, little man," I wholeheartedly reassure.

"It doesn't seem like it," Ando pouts, making me feel worse.

Finally, I answer.

"I don't want to make Mom and Dad worry, so we better get on our way. I can't wait to show you the Blue Grotto."

After several silent seconds, he gives me another huge smile.

"Okay!" he grins, halting my forward motion with a hand to my forearm. "Wait!"

"What?"

He crosses his arms across his small chest.

"We haven't checked in since we've been gone."

"You're right," I agree. "One moment."

Not even having to close my eyes anymore, I contact our mother, giving her our location and letting her know that all is well. I know she will relay the message to our dad. The idea makes me smile at how much I can do now.

"All set," I advise. "Mom is well informed."

Taking his much smaller hand in mine, we swim the route Mom and I did several days before, all the while chatting, pointing and enjoying the beauty of the sea.

On the way there, we see a few Nurse Sharks, but we do not bother them, and they do not bother us. A vision of Ando's nightmare suddenly flashes inside of my brain causing my brother to pull his hand out of mine.

'No, Lena!' he bellows in my head. *'I don't wanna think about that nightmare again!'*

"Tell me if you've had anymore dreams of me or Mom," I urge aloud.

Stubbornly, the little brute shakes his head *No*, yet takes my hand once more.

Well... I tried.

Deciding to let it go, I refocus on getting us to the grotto. It takes a few more minutes for us to reach the cave. Immediately I notice that the tide is high, but for Sirens, as Mom says, it does not matter. Glancing to my right, I notice Ando's face is already beaming.

"Are you ready to go inside?" I question, knowing he is.

'C'mon, Lena!' he squeals in my mind. *'Stop stalling!'*

Unable to help myself, I laugh out loud; creating hundreds of bubbles that quickly rise to the surface then burst as they touch the edge of the waterline. The night seems magical and I am glad that I get to share it with my brother.

Bursting with anticipation, I reach for his hand again, but suddenly stop.

"The entrance is narrow," I state with a frown.

He acknowledges with a rapid nod.

"I'll check it out."

He nods again.

"Wait here."

Leading the way, I enter the grotto first, making sure that nothing dangerous is inside. After a quick examination, I call for Ando, who swims past the rocky entrance and hovers underwater beside me. Inside, the cave is now being illuminated by bright beams of moonlight that have replaced the sun's rays.

It is a spectacular sight.

"It's dark in here," my brother verbalizes his anxiety.

"Turn on your Siren vision," I advise using my most sisterly tone.

"Wow!" Ando exclaims in a boisterous double-clack.

I cannot help grinning.

"It's so cool," he click-clacks his excitement.

"Do you like the pretty blue?"

His aquamarine irises are glowing in the darkness.

"It's like looking through blue sunglasses," he gasps with a broad grin. "Is it like this during the daytime?"

"During the day, it's brighter, even more… blue," I answer as I continue to admire how the light illuminates the ceiling even at night.

"Can we go down to the bottom?"

"Sure, follow me," I encourage playfully.

At the grotto's floor, we take our time playing with the soft sand and digging to see if our mother had buried anything else there. We both laugh at the idea of Mom as a precocious six-year-old, hiding Emperor Tiberius' statues in the sand.

"I wish I had brought one of my toy cars with me," Ando huffs his regret with short whistles, clacks, and clicks.

"Why?" I ask in Siren, surprised at his comment.

He giggles before informing, "So that one day I can come back with my own kids and dig it up."

My heart clenches and I cannot help wanting to hug him, so I do.

"How cute," we both hear an unfamiliar voice from above. "You two are so adorable."

What the hell?

CHAPTER NINE

Startled, I grab my brother's hand and slowly back away from that side of the grotto. On the ledge above, I can hear whoever it is pacing the lip that surrounds the edge of the naturally formed pool. Its steps are sure-footed, but barely there like a woodland creature that walks through a leaf-covered forest floor with the most minimal of sound.

In this predicament, all we can do is wait.

'Lena!' Ando shouts in my head, almost deafening me. *'Who's that?'*

I shrug my shoulders as I place my pointer finger to my lips imploring him to be quiet.

'I don't know?' I answer truthfully, mind-to-mind. *'No one comes here at night.'*

Ando moves closer.

'Could it be one of the aunts?' he whispers inside of my head.

'I don't think so,' I admit with wide eyes. *'That voice is not familiar.'*

"Yoohoo!" it teases. "I know you are still down there, little guppies."

Little guppies?

Distracted and needing my regular vision, my Siren-sight switches off, but now the lack of light in the grotto renders me useless. Immediately, I feel bile rising up my esophagus and I have to use all of my will to keep it contained. As we crouch low still remaining at the bottom, I contact our mother.

'Mom,' I whisper with my mind. *'We're in trouble.'*

'Animal?' Mom suddenly questions.

Steadying my thoughts, I manage to advise:

'No… not an animal… at least I don't think it's an animal.'

'What do you mean?' the several-century-old Siren interrogates at the most inconvenient moment.

'Someone is in the cave with us,' I reply, trying to remain still, hoping that whoever or *whatever* is there will not see us either.

'Where's Ando?' Mom queries frantically.

'I'm here,' my brother interrupts.

'Stay close to your sister, understood?' she orders.

'Yes, ma'am,' he assures.

'Don't worry, Mom. I'll keep him safe.'

"I can hear you," the voice replies to our unspoken thoughts.

What?

"That is right, young ones," it states out loud proudly. "And I can see you."

I gulp my fear, hoping to keep my brother from freaking out too.

'Lena...' his voice is trembling inside of my head.

Our mother's voice chimes in once more.

'I'm on my way,' she soothes in a frantic tone. *'I'm calling the aunts.'*

'They're not picking up,' I remind, my internal voice shaking too.

Another pregnant pause.

'I'll be there in ten minutes!' she promises. *'Try not to panic.'*

'What should we do until then?' I ask, still discombobulated at the eerie predicament we are in.

Silence again.

'Try to get out of the cave... into open water,' Mom suggests.

'Alright,' I take a deep breath through my gills. *'Hurry!'*

Ando tugs on my arm then clicks, "Should we make a run for it now?"

The unseen figure laughs, the sound of it rattles my nerves even more.

"You can try to *make a run for it*," the voice is smooth and pleasant, which makes me wearier. "But I will still catch you."

Both my brother and I swallow hard. Whatever this creature is, it can hear our thoughts as well as understand Siren. I have no clue what to do next.

'Who are you?' I ask telepathically, trying to distract it while I come up with a plan of escape.

It giggles, childlike and innocent.

"Who am I? *Who* indeed?" it ponders the question.

Nervously, I rephrase.

'Would a better question be... what are you?'

It remains silent, and then abruptly, it speaks.

"I am the rain..."

What?

"... I am the mist that sprays as the ocean meets the land..."

Ooookay.

"... I am the salty breeze that tickles your nose..."

Crazy much?

"… I am it all."

'Huh?' Ando and I both respond nonverbally, more confused than ever, to say the least.

Grabbing my brother's hand, I call to my webbing and kick hard off of the floor of the grotto, so hard in fact, that I create a force so powerful that it feels like an explosion under our feet. All of my focus is aimed at the cave's narrow entrance. Seeing the clear moonlight on the other side of the water, I allow myself to release my held breath. But before we can exit, Ando and I slam into something solid.

"What the hell is going on?" I yell in a stream of clicks, clacks, whistles and squeals as my body bounces off of something hard… something invisible.

"Lena!" Ando shouts too, banging his small fists against whatever is in our path.

Doing a backflip, I kick the object with both legs as hard as I can.

Nothing happens… nothing at all.

Again, I kick, but this time I feel a sharp pain dart up the bones in my feet into my legs.

Ouch! Ok. That's not working.

"Let us talk," it says in a creepy timbre. "We have a little time before Marina gets here."

'How do you know our mother's name?' I gasp.

The entity pauses.

"I know all. See all. Remember all."

Once more, Ando and I kick and punch at the unseen barrier blocking our way out. How I wish Mom was here. Or the aunts would come to save the day like they usually do. Unfortunately, it is just my little brother and I against this *thing*.

"'Thing'?" It huffs as its voice fills with indignation. "I am no... 'thing'."

As it pauses again, I look out and I am relieved to see not only our mother racing toward us, but also Ligeia and Leukosia! Ando and I begin pounding closed fists against the shield again, hoping that this time it might break or at least weaken.

Unfortunately, it does neither.

"Let us out!" I shout at it in Siren, my ire growing more substantial.

Ando's eyes light up as he sees our family approaching. Impatiently, he starts to shout too; all the while, flailing his arms and legs like a cowboy strapped to a bucking bronco at the rodeo.

'Mom... Ligeia... Leukosia!' He pounds with all of his strength. 'There's something blocking the entrance to the grotto! We can't get outta here!'

'Move away!' all three commands at once, their voices melding into one inside of my mind. Without hesitation, The Sisters and Mom grasp hands and close their eyes and the invisible barrier starts to violently shake. Ando and I obey as they combine their abilities in order to draw power from the sea.

All around us, the grotto walls are vibrating, the movement so intense that I pray the entire cavern does not collapse on top of us. The grotto water heats until I envision us as lobsters inside a stockpot of boiling liquid. I want to call my scales, but Ando has none yet, so I endure it with him. It is then that we hear a loud crash, followed by a forceful bang, and finally the water returns to its normal temperature.

As the invisible wall disintegrates, the Sirens rush inside. Mom gets to us first, her scales up and ready for battle. Ligeia enters next, her rage unmasked and terrifying. Even Leukosia is transformed into a fierce sea monster with eyes glowing and teeth bared. *The Three* ready to unleash their wrath on this new foe.

Ando looks around the cavern and yells to the faceless entity.

"My family is gonna kick your butt!"

Ligeia shouts first.

"Where is it?"

Leukosia is next.

"I hear it!"

Finally, Mom screams into the cavern sending another sonic boom around the space, uncaring if it topples down.

"Show yourself! Coward!" she snarls, and I am suddenly afraid to be near her.

"Catch me if you can, Marina," it laughs.

Mom freezes.

"How do you know who I am?"

"My... my... my," it sneers. "So much like your mother."

Wait! It knows Yaya Parthenope?

"Selena looks exactly like her too," the thing's voice lowers and I feel all of the hairs on my arms stand on end.

It giggles like it is playing some sort of game.

"Whoever you are, you better get out of here unless you want to get turned into sushi!" Mom threatens brazenly.

"Whoever?" it purrs then snickers. "Not whoever... " it pauses again as if deep in thought, "... You can call me *Amphitrite*."

CHAPTER TEN

I have never swum so fast in my entire life. By the time we reach the opposite side of the island and to our vacation villa, all of my muscles burn. My lungs feel like they have been stretched on a rack, while my brain throbs from thinking too much.

After showering and changing into my pajamas, the entire family gathers around the dining room table to discuss the day's events with a platter of ham and cheese sandwiches and a carafe of cold honey-sweetened hibiscus tea. Thank goodness, even with the hullabaloo we just experienced, Mom, Ando and I still have our appetites.

Dad, on the other hand sits with his mouth gaping as the information soaks into his brain.

"This person... *creature*... called you by name?" he asks as we all huddle around the dining table at the vacation home, trying our hardest to get rid of that ominous cloud hovering above our family.

"Yes," Mom sits beside him and leans her head on his shoulder. "It was spooky."

Quickly, I chew then swallow my mouthful of food.

"Whatever it was… " my mother sighs, "… the children said that it can read minds and understands the Siren language."

Dad frowns but does not respond.

"Are you sure you're alright?" Mom asks again. I think she feels responsible for us being in harm's way, but we all know that this could not have been foreseen.

"Mommy!" Ando hugs her tightly, trying to comfort her. "I was very brave, and Lena kept her cool!"

Mom laughs.

"I'm sure you were extremely brave," Mom praises encouragingly, placing a quick kiss to his forehead.

Unable to remain still, Dad begins his ritual pacing and every few seconds, he sighs and runs his hand over his neat beard.

"This being told you its name was… what again?" he asks, trying to get an understanding.

"*Amphitrite*," I mumble at first then increase my volume. "It said to call it Amphitrite."

Dad turns to his wife and asks, "Is that name familiar to you?"

"Not at all," Mom denies sincerely.

"Do the aunts know who it is?" he continues.

"I'm not sure," Mom replies, brows furrowed. "But they definitely left in a hurry."

"Yeah," Ando agrees. "They didn't even swim back with us. It was strange."

The only thing I can do is nod in agreement. The aunts were acting strangely, even more than usual. They knew something about the entity, but they would not divulge it.

Later, while everyone is asleep and the moon rests high in the sky, I creep out of my room, down the dimly lit hallway, tip-toe past my parents' room and make my way to the living room; specifically, to the glass doors that lead from the living area out to the patio overlooking the *Marina Piccola*.

"I'm a Siren for heaven's sake," I mutter under my breath. "I can do this. Don't be a chicken."

Mentally, I psych myself up, trying to do what I need to do before someone hears me.

"Lena!" Ando startles me, causing me to jump out of my skin. "What are you doing?"

"Shh!" I admonish, grabbing him by the arm and moving him onto the patio, closing the glass doors behind him so our parents will not hear. "You're going to wake Mom and Dad."

He studies me before speaking.

"You're going back to the sea? Tonight?" he growls. "Amphitrite is still out there."

"I have to," I admit without hesitation, the finality of my words igniting my irritation.

"Wait!" he pleads. "I'll go with you."

"No!" I snap, and then hug his small body. "I'm not putting you in harm's way. I can't protect both of us."

"But—"

"But nothing," I interrupt, putting my foot down.

Kneeling, I look him straight in the face... eye to eye.

"Amphitrite is strong, way stronger than either of us," I drill into his stubborn head. "I have to face it alone. I need to know how it knows Mom, how it can speak Siren, and how in the world it can read our thoughts."

"Ask the aunts first," he pleads, tugging on my elbow.

"Suppose they won't tell me the truth?" I state, my mind made up regardless of what he says.

Ando thinks for a moment. I can see the gears turning as he ponders the question. This is never good. My brother has an extremely analytical mind. I always tell him that he should become a lawyer when he gets older. No one would be able to beat him when it comes to knowing how to outwit your opponent.

At last, he smiles.

"The aunts never lie," he reports with a well-informed grin.

"Yes, they do," I counter. "They never reveal anything."

He shakes his dark locks, aquamarine eyes glowing with the newly found revelation.

"They don't lie... they just don't give information freely," he states more firmly, giving a smirk.

"Huh?"

Frustrated, he sighs then huffs then growls.

"They... never... lie," he repeats, using hand gestures to emphasize his point.

I sulk knowing that he is right.

"They are logical and honorable," I agree. "To lie would go against everything they believe in."

"Exactly!" my brother exclaims.

"Mom lies," I remind out of the blue.

Ando rolls his eyes.

"Mom is half human and she lived with Grandpa Marcus for part of her life, she's not the same as the aunts."

That makes sense.

"You know what?" I give him a big smile.

"What?"

"You are really smart," I sincerely compliment.

Slightly embarrassed, my brother blushes and I know he knows that it is true.

"Okay," I agree, returning to the former situation. "I'll find the aunts first, then if I can't get the four-one-one from them, I'll find this… whatever it is and ask it my questions."

Ando thinks for a moment.

"Contact the aunts and let them know you're coming to see them," he says, getting directly to the point.

"Why?" I question. "I'm sure they won't answer."

"Even if they don't, they won't want you swimming alone, especially since Amphitrite knows about us," he educates like an expert.

"Good point," I agree with a deep breath.

My brother gives me a quick hug.

"You better go now, before they wake up," he orders like a little Napoleon.

"If I'm not back before dawn, send the cavalry," I state, giving a small smile that does not reach my eyes.

Unfortunately, he does not find my comment amusing; not at all.

Gathering my courage, I move toward the railing that separates the edge of the patio from the four-hundred and ninety foot some-odd drop down the side of the cliff to the choppy waters of the harbor.

"It seemed so easy when Mom did it," I admit to my brother who looks like he is about to puke.

"Are you positive you wanna do this?" he grills with a shaky voice.

Taking another cleansing breath, I respond.

"I need to talk to the aunts."

I do not know why I make the sign of the cross, but I do. I also say a quick prayer and wish I had time to draw up a will. Unfortunately, I do not own much: a few hundred dollars in my savings account from my Sweet Sixteen party, a couple of gold and silver necklaces, and my collection of vinyl records that once belonged to Grandpa Theodore that he left me since we both loved singing along to them. Other than those things, I do not have many valuables.

"Be careful," Ando warns, giving me a thumbs-up and showing a brave face.

"Remember... by dawn—"

"Don't worry," he interjects supportively. "I'll send the cavalry."

Unable to stall anymore, I climb onto the railing and make the mistake of looking down.

"*Ay, Dios!* Please watch over me," I pray to God in Spanish as I see the sharp rocks that mock me waiting for me to make my move.

"Watch out for the rocks," Ando prompts as I glance down.

Duh!

"I bet no one has ever jumped from such a high spot before... except Mom," my brother chuckles, making me more nervous.

"I know," I growl, hoping that he will get the message and be quiet.

"It's kinda cool," he giggles.

"Ando?"

"Yes."

"Be... quiet."

"Okay."

"Just remember to leap out," I tell myself.

Wait! I am not as strong as Mom, and I am not used to these waters. I need a running start!

Steadily, I climb back down and walk toward the house.

"Did you change your mind?" Ando questions hopefully.

"Nope," I huff. "I need some more space."

Ando looks confused.

"More space for what?" he asks, wrinkling his nose.

Counting each step, I stop at the doorway leading inside, say another quick prayer then sprint toward the balcony railing. Without any further hesitation, I jump into the air using the railing as a push-off. The rush of wind hits me as I plummet to my death.

No!..No thoughts of dying.

On my way down, I cannot hear anything else except the vacuum that I am in. I do not even hear the waves battering the coastline anymore. Below, I see the surface quickly approaching and grimace at the thought of hitting the rocks instead of the sea. Within a few feet, I switch on my gills and webbing and I am surprised that I make only a minimum splash when I enter.

My mother would be very proud.

Under the rough sea, the water below is surprisingly calm. There is a stronger current tonight, but nothing I cannot handle. Once more, I close my eyes and send the call out to my aunts, this time I hear Ligeia's voice.

'I am surprised that you did not kill yourself,' she admonishes with an impressed tone. Usually, when I do something right she tells me that *'It is acceptable'*. Tonight, she must be in one of her rare good moods.

'I need to talk to you… face to face,' I demand, forgetting my place as well as her temper. Her hair is not the only thing that is fiery.

'Meet me at the Faraglioni,*'* she gives in without any negotiation, surprising me.

'The stacks in the harbor?' I verify, not wanting to end up in the wrong location in an unfamiliar sea.

Capri, unlike Isla Flora, is full of hidden caves and underground tunnels that are practically everywhere. There are so many strange sea creatures that for some reason defy the rules of nature. Everywhere you turn there is something poisonous and unafraid of young Sirens.

'Yes,' she answers much too sweetly.

'I'll be there in a few minutes!' I reply psychically, becoming excited. *'Don't go anywhere!'*

'Do not worry,' she purrs. *'I will be waiting for you.'*

As I am swimming out to meet my aunt, I hear my mother's voice in my head. No, I do not mean figuratively, quite literally. She is communicating with me telepathically.

'I know you are going to see Ligeia, so don't lie,' she warns, her tone clipped.

'I'm sorry,' I apologize, hoping that she will be lenient with my future punishment. *'But I have to.'*

There is a long silence as if she has hung up on me and I wait, holding my breath, anticipating what she will say next.

'You know you're going to be grounded for the next week, right?' Mom finally informs confirming my penance.

Sadly, I am getting used to being grounded. At first, I would be bored out of mind, but now, I do not mind so much. As a matter of fact, I have gotten to read several wonderful books and I have even learned how to don socks.

'Yes, ma'am,' I acknowledge, knowing that I deserve being on restrictions.

'Where are you meeting Ligeia?' Mom asks, wanting to know where I will be in case I run into any trouble or trouble runs into me.

'The Stacks,' I answer honestly, feeling better that she knows my destination.

'Be safe,' she reminds in her motherly way. *'If there are any problems—'*

'I know,' I interrupt her sentence. *'I will call.'*

'Make sure that you do,' she insists, causing me to smile. *'Selena?'*

'Yes, Mom?'

'If there is danger, any danger at all… I want you to leave,' my mother asserts. *'No superhero antics. Do you understand?'*

Silently, I debate.

'I'm serious young lady,' she emphasizes in her most no-nonsense mom-voice.

'I promise... no superhero stuff.'

The sky tonight is cloudy, the small crescent-shaped moon barely lights the looming shadows below. As far as the eye can see, the sea is awash in black. Looking up, there are no stars to help brighten the night.

Suddenly, the hairs on my arms are alerted.

"Tia Aunt Ligeia?" I call to the shadowy silhouette on the largest of the famed limestone stacks that decorate the *Marina Piccola*. "Ligeia! I'm here. Sorry it took longer than expected, but I ran into a chatty squid."

"Over here, dear," she whispers, but I hear her like she is right beside me.

Dear?

"The moon is just a sliver tonight," I make small talk as I retract my webbing, activate my lungs and commence the short climb up the side of the stack. "It's difficult to see—"

I stop in midsentence as the little bit of moonlight reveals my aunt. But it is not Ligeia. It is someone else, someone that sounds like my aunt, but is definitely not.

"Good evening, little guppy," it smiles as it greets me. "So glad you could make it."

CHAPTER ELEVEN

Backing up a few steps, I try to put some distance between the thing and me, but my foot slips, nearly tumbling me into the awaiting sea. I could dive into the water and attempt to swim away. That is an idea; however, something tells me that this creature could catch me without breaking a sweat, so I guess I will stay where I am at and hope for the best, but plan for the worst.

"Who are you?" I ask trying to steady my voice but failing miserably. "Come into the light so I can see you."

Slowly, the figure emerges from the shadows. She is gorgeous with long reddish-blonde tresses, long enough to cover all of her exposed body, milky jade eyes set in flawless, alabaster skin; skin so fair that it mimics translucent seafoam on the crest of a wave or the petals of the skeleton flower after it rains.

Averting my eyes, I ask as nicely as possible, given the circumstances, "Could you put on some clothes?"

The woman laughs.

"You are not human," she scoffs. "Why should you be shy?"

Needing to defend myself, I respond.

"I grew up among humans and until a few months ago, I believed I was human," I snarl. "So put some damn clothes on!"

Her face darkens and I fear what she might do to me, so I quickly add: "Please."

Thank goodness her face returns to normal, and she smiles before replying.

"As you wish."

As I watch, the long strawberry-blonde tendrils begin to shimmer and reorganize until they transform into an elegant ankle-length, charcoal-gray toga, the exact color of the sea tonight. On her feet, a pair of simple white sandals that I have seen in historic pictures appear. Her complexion, much like the aunts, is flawless and glows as if lit from within. In this state, the being is even more alluring, yet still mind-numbingly terrifying.

"Is this more to your liking?" she giggles, smoothing the fabric with her palms.

"Yes. Now... " I slowly nod as I repeat, "... who are you?"

"We met at the grotto," she smiles as she speaks. "Did you forget me so soon?"

"Amphitrite," I recall with a shiver making her grin. "I remember you held my brother and me prisoner."

She thinks for a moment.

"Prisoner… " she smiles as she speaks, showing two perfect rows of teeth. "Such a harsh word. If I wanted you as prisoners—" she steps closer and looks down her nose at me, her six foot frame towering above me, "—you would be."

She snickers.

"Your brother, what is his name? Fish-bait?"

I actually hear myself growl.

"Go near my brother and I'll kill you," I reply through gritted teeth.

"Oh my!" she scoffs. "Such a good big sister, but there is no need to threaten. I mean you no harm."

Suddenly, I feel my blood pressure skyrocket.

"I doubt that!" I snap, wanting to run, but standing my ground instead, and then I remember my conversation with my mother.

Didn't I promise to flee if there was any danger?

"It does not matter," Amphitrite grins like we are having the most delightful conversation. Immediately, my brain focuses on her and not my mother's warning.

I have to find out what this creature knows about my family tree.

"Are you listening to me, little guppy?" she jibes jovially.

Her softly spoken words make my palms sweat and my stomach heave. Fearful, I try to contact Mom and the sisters, but before I can finish the thought, the being points at me. Her irises are glowing like neon bulbs.

"Ahh... ahh... ahh," she reprimands, shaking her finger as she scolds me. "None of that. Do not send any messages to your family members or I will gut you where you stand."

Instantly, I stop my actions, knowing quite well that she means what she says.

"Then why did you trap us in the cave?" I grill, swallowing hard.

"I only wanted your undivided attention," she discloses adjusting her dress as she very gracefully sits on the stalagmite surface. "I remember your mother when she was your age."

"You knew her?" I gulp. "How?"

"Well... we never truly met, per sè... I saw when she frightened the flounder out of that imbecile, Tiberius," Amphitrite belly laughs, the evil yet intoxicating sound makes my upper lip perspire. "Even as a child, she was amusing."

"I'm glad she entertained you," I retort, off-handedly.

"You remind me so much of her... of Parthenope and Melpomene," she concludes with a snarl.

Now, she has my undivided attention.

"You knew my great-grandmother, Melpomene?"

"Of course," Amphitrite exhales loudly. "I know all."

Looking down at the water around the base of the stack, I probe.

"Where's Ligeia?"

"She will not be coming."

"What did—"

Instead of replying, Amphitrite waves her hand at the sea in a circular pattern and to my surprise, a thin whirlpool appears, a whirlpool so deep that I see the exposed seabed below. Waving her slender hand in the opposite direction, the swirling water returns to its natural state.

"Close your mouth, dear," she commands, obviously pleased with herself.

At her rude remark, my face reddens with anger.

"Is my aunt alright?"

The being gives me a sideways glance like she is bored.

"Do not worry child," she placates, making me feel worse. "I simply intercepted your call to her."

"You can do that?"

She laughs and actually blushes.

"Of course I can do that," she reconfirms with a twinkle in her jade orbs.

"What are you?" I ask again.

"I am Amphitrite. Daughter of Nereus and Doris," she answers as if I should know this already.

"Okay," I respond like I really do know who she is. "Why did you trick me into meeting you here of all places?"

Ignoring me for the moment, she gathers up her extremely long hair and begins to braid it… just like Ligeia did before. I am mesmerized by her fluid movement.

Her strength…

Her demeanor…

Yet most of all, her self-confidence.

"I want us to be… *friends*," Amphitrite coos.

"Huh?"

"Friends," the 'woman' repeats. "You do have friends, do you not?"

"U-umm," I stammer. "Y-yes."

Amphitrite offers me her hand, but of course I do not accept it. Slowly, she lowers her arm, looks me up and down then grins.

"I want you and I to be good friends."

Shocked at what I am hearing, I can only glare at her.

"Would you like that?" she continues, still wearing that mysterious expression.

"I don't understand," I reply, staring down at the water, wondering how fast I would need to swim to get away. "Why would you want us to be friends?"

Reading my mind, she scoffs.

"You would need to swim faster than Apollo's chariot... swifter than winged Pegasus... more rapid than Great Zeus' thunderbolts to escape my clutches."

Geez! This chick likes to hear her own voice. Could she just wrap it up already?

Glaring at me, she replies to my unspoken comment.

"Did you learn sarcasm from human beings as well?"

Bored now.

"What do you *really* want, Amphitrite?" I hear my voice raise an octave as I grow annoyed at her presence. "I know that friendship isn't your endgame."

Again she smiles, but it does not reach her eyes.

"Tell me where the *Spílaio Seirínon* is," her words rush out in a jumbled wreck, and I blink awkwardly, frightened to tell her that I do not understand Greek.

Afraid to move, afraid to breathe, I simply stare at her.

"You are pathetic," she leers, reading my thoughts, making me feel like a piece of lint. "Did your mother and aunts teach you anything?"

Amphitrite suddenly stands, causing me to jump back a foot, almost making me lose my balance and tumble feet first into the harbor.

"Tell me what *Spílaio Seirínon* is?" I plead, needing to understand.

"Where is the Siren Grotto?" she demands at the top of her lungs.

"I don't know," I answer honestly. "I swear."

Believing me, she frowns.

"Then I have no need for you."

Before I realize what is happening, she grabs me and throws me into the sea. Thankfully, my gills instantly appear along with my webbing. Unfortunately, she throws me so hard that I slam against the rocky seabed before I can steady myself. Then I feel my form spinning and realize that I am trapped inside one of her whirlpools. Trying my hardest, I attempt to swim through it, but there is a strong vacuum holding me in place. Desperate to escape, I try again and again until I am exhausted.

Think, Selena! Think!

Suddenly, I remember the volcanic glass charm hanging from the chain around my neck. Desperate, I say a little prayer, right as I visualize the waves growing higher and higher, the swells so tall that they slam against the stack and knock her off. Anything would help since the witch is currently kicking my ass.

Although I cannot see what is happening on the surface, it must have worked because the whirlpool dissipates, releasing me from its grasp. Swiftly, I kick off the bottom of the seabed and propel myself through the water. I flee, never looking back until I am back on solid ground.

Needless to say, when I return home, both parental units, along with my little brother are waiting. My mother's face is red and that is amazing, since her skin is olive in appearance. Obviously, she responds first.

"What in the name of Gaia were you thinking?" Mom yells, causing the windows to shake. I try to speak, but she raises her hand to shush me. "Obviously, you weren't thinking!"

"Mom—" I manage, but immediately get cut-off.

"You promised me that if there was any danger… any at all… you would—"

"I know… there should have been no superhero moments," I interrupt her this time.

"Exactly!" my mother sharply growls. "What were you thinking?"

"She said she could have stopped me," I whimper, reliving the memory of the scary goddess.

"And you believed her?" Mom interrogates with narrowed eyes.

Without hesitation, I nod.

She is now pacing and mumbling to herself in clicks and clacks as she waves her arms around in overemphasized gestures. Fearful of what is coming next, I brace myself mentally and hope for the best.

"You were going to be grounded for a week, well now it's two!" Mom barks as she points a quivering finger at me.

"Marina?" Dad interrupts hesitantly.

"What?" she snaps at my stepfather.

"Calm down," he implores. "She's a teenager—"

Mom turns on her heels and makes a beeline toward her husband.

"I know she's a teenager, David, but she's a Siren first and foremost... a teenage Siren with a death wish apparently!" Mom laboriously sputters. "How could you? How could you disobey us? You could have been killed by that... that—"

"Marina... *calmate, por favor,*" Dad soothes in Spanish.

"I will not calm down!" she responds in English, taking a deep breath. "For the next two weeks you are not allowed to leave the villa grounds. Is that clear?"

"Yes, ma'am."

Mom turns to Ando.

"Did you know your sister had left the villa?"

Ando remains silent, but the guilty expression on his face is all that is needed to convict him.

"I told her not to do it, especially since she was jumping off the pat—" he confesses, and then realizes what he has said and suddenly shuts his mouth. Both Dad and Mom glance at each other then turn back toward me. I know my goose is cooked. Ashamed, I bow my head and simply stare at my bare feet.

"You jumped off of the patio?" they both question with shocked faces.

"Yes," I admit in a hushed tone, still looking at my feet.

"That's almost five hundred feet down!" Dad scolds and begins to tap his foot, while the woman who gave birth to me stares at me with an open mouth.

"You did it, Mom... remember?" I remind hoping to gain some sympathy, but 'Sympathy' never comes. 'Sympathy' is on an airplane heading out of town, just like I wish I was.

"Selena, Capri was my home for sixteen years," Mom explains as calmly as possible. "I know this sea better than anywhere in the world and I would dive off of these cliffs on a daily basis. You just got here and have no clue about the dangers you face on this island.

"You think this is a game, but it's not. *Amphitrite* is out there and she knows what we are and doesn't care if she provokes us." Mom pauses and takes a deep breath. "*'To follow a Siren is to follow death,'* remember? This thing is following us and isn't afraid. Do you understand what that means?"

I shake my head but remain quiet.

"That means that it is more powerful than us," she schools with a concerned countenance.

"Selena," Dad jumps in. "Go to your room, right now."

Nodding, I turn and speed walk down the narrow, white-washed hallway, turning briefly to give my brother a hopeful smile.

"Fernando David Marquez," I hear Mom sigh just as I turn the corner. "You will be joining your sister here on punishment for the next week. Is that clear?"

"Yes, ma'am," he says in a small voice, and I wish I could hug him.

CHAPTER TWELVE

True to their word, our parents make us stay at the house while they go sightseeing, tour vineyards, deep-sea fishing, sailing, and souvenir shopping. I think they did it on purpose to make their children feel even worse than we already do.

Unfortunately, their plan worked.

"Hurry, Lena!" Ando whines, rubbing his grumbling stomach.

"I am hurrying," I chuckle, reviewing the steps of making our meal without causing a house fire.

"Are you sure you know how to cook?" he quibbles with a cynical stare.

I stick my tongue out at him and he returns the gesture.

"I've seen Mom and Dad do it," I reply with a confident tone. "It doesn't look difficult."

"Lena?"

"What is it now?" I huff, trying to keep focused on all of the components of the meal.

His eyes are wide as he points to the stove.

"The water is boiling over!" he shouts as he jumps up and down like a jackrabbit.

"*Ugg!*" I roar as I lower the temperature of the burner under the large stockpot.

"What do we do next, Lena?" Ando asks, readying himself for my instructions.

"Get the ziti from the pantry," I order my brother who has volunteered to be my sous chef.

Obediently, he trots to the walk-in pantry and retrieves a box of the pasta as I continue to stir the marinara sauce that I made from a recipe in one of the cookbooks in the library.

"Here ya go," he tells, handing it to me.

"Thanks," I reply with a smile.

"It smells great!" he responds as he sniffs the air. "Do you think Mom and Dad will like it?"

"I hope so," I answer, taking a small spoonful of the bubbling red sauce, blowing on it to cool it down then tasting. Proudly, I hold out the spoon to Ando who also gives it a taste. "What do you think? Good?"

"*Molto bene!*" he replies in Italian with an over-exaggerated hand flourish.

"Not too spicy?" I wonder, remembering when the spice jar of crushed red pepper flakes flowed out quicker than expected.

"Nope," he states confidently, taking another spoonful.

"My hand slipped when I was pouring the chili flakes," I confess, blushing.

"I like spicy," he reminds. "So do Mom and Dad."

Nervously, I taste it one last time before I lower it to a simmer. Quickly, I add some salt to the pasta water, just like I have seen Mom and Dad do, then the pasta. According to the package directions, it should only take about ten minutes for *al dente*, which is Italian for firm to the tooth. I pay particular attention to the time since I hate mushy pasta.

"Would you like some grated parmesan cheese to sprinkle on top?" I ask, thinking that sounds extra tasty.

"I'll get the grater," Ando replies as he goes to the cabinet that houses that utensil.

Thoughtfully, he takes it upon himself to carefully grate the pungent, hard cheese on the device, being careful not to cut his knuckles. He only eats a few tablespoons of the cheesy goodness before he puts the remainder of it into a small ramekin and places it on the kitchen counter where we will be eating. My stomach also begins to complain.

"Okay," I announce wiping my hands on the apron I borrowed from the linen closet. "Dinner will be ready very soon. Go wash up."

Ando nods and heads toward the hallway bathroom to wash his hands. Checking the digital clock on the stove, I make sure to make note of when the pasta will be done. As I wait for my brother to get back, I start washing the dishes in the sink, wiping down the granite countertops, and making sure that nothing has spilled on the cobalt and white ceramic tiles. My parents always clean as they cook, so I guess I will do the same.

Next, I drain the pasta, adding a pat of butter the way my stepfather likes to do it, and grating some more fresh Parmesan cheese into the steamy noodles and stirring it all together. Following my mom's lessons, I also sprinkle some of the pungent *fromage* into the bubbling meat sauce. Next, I spoon some of the sauce into the pasta, give it a toss and put it all in a lovely serving bowl I found in the cabinet. The final thing is ladling even more of the red sauce on top of the bowl of ziti then giving it another toss and a last sprinkle of Parmesan and chopped parsley for garnish.

Quickly, I set the table, so we can eat as soon as Ando returns, which should have been already.

"Hey!" I call down the hallway. "Time to eat!"

There is no sound, except for the faucet running.

"Stop playing in the water," I reprimand.

Still no answer.

"Ando?"

Resting the dishes down on the beautiful hand-carved dinette, I turn off the burners and head to the bathroom to see what he is doing.

"The food is gonna get cold and I'm gonna be super mad at you—"

To my horror, the bathroom is empty, but the faucet is running. Immediately, my stomach starts to churn.

Where is my brother?

All of my fears have come to life, losing someone I love. I can only imagine what my parents will say. They will not ground me; they will just sell me to the gypsies like Mom threatens when I am acting *'too big for my britches.'*

Whatever that means.

"Ando!" I yell, racing down the hallway to his bedroom.

Flinging open the door, I dart inside. The room is filled with fading sunlight and the fragrance of blossoming sunflowers. I open the closet and even search underneath the bed. Not a sign of my little brother.

"Damn it!" I swear then scold myself for doing so.

Stay calm… No need to panic… Yet.

"Fernando David Marquez!" I yell his full name like a parent would, the sound of my voice echoing throughout the empty villa, making me uneasy. "Where are you?"

The only answer I get is the rustling of branches against the stucco of the outside wall.

"You had better not be hiding from me!" my voice wavers as I continue to search.

Silence batters my ears as the uneasiness grows from a sapling to a mighty Sequoia.

"Please come-out, come-out wherever you are," I prompt like when we would play hide-and-seek; hoping that I will hear his silly giggle from behind the couch or one of the potted plants.

"The ziti is done," I remind, knowing how my kid brother loves to eat. "C'mon out, you win!"

More silence.

Closing my eyes, I picture him in my mind and call out to him. All I hear is the beating of my own racing heart. My stomach somersaults again and I race to the toilet just in time to release a stream of acidic foam. Feeling sorry for myself, I sit beside the throne with my head against the cool surface praying to the porcelain gods to help me find my brother.

The aunts! That's it! I'll call for the aunts!

Again, I repeat my ritual and try summoning the Sirens, but some sort of interference keeps blocking my signal. Taking a full breath, I concentrate harder, but no answer. Maybe he is outside playing with the British family's little boy renting the villa beside us.

Yup! He's probably in the front yard.

As fast as my bare feet can carry me, I run out front hoping to see him playing soccer with his new friend or climbing the towering Bald Cypress in the middle of the yard.

No Ando.

On shaky legs, I circle the entire villa only to find a pair of mating Blue Lizards which inhabit the Island. Their intense blue scales resemble both the sea and the sky of Capri, and if I was not hunting for my brother, I would have stopped to take a picture of them and sent it to my friends in Isla Flora.

Once again, no Ando.

Down the street, I spy a group of old men carrying a bocce ball set while having a passionate debate in Italian. Needing to question them, I race back around to the front yard once again. Maybe they have seen Ando, and at this point, I am willing to try anything. Boldly, I stop one of the men.

"Have you seen a little boy?" I plead, but they just look at me with quizzical expressions. "He's six, dark hair, eyes like mine, inquisitive... damn it... he's my brother."

"*Scusami?*" the burly man with the thick sideburns replies with confusion.

"Umm... " I try remembering the Italian lessons David gave us; he says Spanish and Italian are very similar, and they are both languages *de amore*... of love. I just need to communicate with these men. I try again and hope I do not botch-it up.

"*Hai visto un ragazzino?*" I say shakily.

"Ahhhhh!" they all reply at once then begin to speak very rapidly in Italian. What I am able to interpret is either, 'No, we haven't seen him' or 'No, he's no potato of mine'.

I decide on the former interpretation.

My mind is racing while my heart is having palpitations, and I am pretty sure that I am about to have a coronary. Needing to calm down, I inhale then exhale slowly, then repeat the process until my mind clears.

I'm so stupid! I berate myself. *I need to call my parents*!

Hoping they will not kill the messenger; I try my stepfather's cellphone. It rings several times then finally he picks up.

"Dad!" I yell into my phone.

"Don't shout, please!" he barks. "You're going to deafen me."

"I'm sorry," I apologize as I walk toward the neighboring villa to check with the British couple's son.

Jeez! What's his name? Oh! Henry... Henry Martinson.

Over the phone, I hear the sound of a tugboat's horn and realize they are probably near the harbor. Next, I hear my mother laughing in the background, right before my stepdad inquires.

"What's wrong, Selena?"

"It's Ando!" I blurt then pause to fill my lungs with much needed oxygen.

"Be calm." Dad's voice instantly fills with concern as he commands. "What happened?

"He's gone!" I sob into the phone.

"What do you mean he's gone?"

"We were making dinner... it was almost done so I made him go to the bathroom to wash his hands—"

"Sweetheart, take a breath before you faint," he instructs and I do, but it does not help. "Slow down."

"Alright," I agree, feeling the tears beginning to flow harder.

"Ok... tell me," his voice is stern, but comforting.

I start by explaining.

"The faucet was on, but... but... he wasn't there," I tell, almost choking on my own tears.

"Did you check his room?" Dad questions tranquilly.

"I did that before I called you," I inform in a rush.

"What about outside on the patio?"

"Yes," I feel the tears landing on my black, V-neck t-shirt. "I checked there and now I'm outside, but I can't f-find h-him!"

Mom must have grabbed the phone because I hear her frantic voice blurt: "Don't leave the house! We're almost there!"

"Okay," I whimper, feeling sick to my stomach.

It takes only five minutes for the rented, black Range Rover to pull into the driveway. Filled with relief at the sight of them, I sprint to my stepdad first, hugging him tightly around the waist, feeling another wave of salty tears begin anew. Next, I turn to Mom, who is now holding me tight and whispering soothing words into my ear. I inhale deeply, taking in the fragrance of her lightly applied perfume. The scent has always given me solace. Even right now, when things are so chaotic, I immediately feel my muscles relaxing.

"Try to focus, Selena," she urges, wiping my tears away with the palm of her hand. "When was the last time you saw your brother?"

"We were going to surprise you with dinner," I explain through the tears. "But I sent him to clean up before you got here."

"Calm down, sweetheart," Dad tries to soothe my frayed nerves.

"I heard the water running and told him to stop playing in the sink," I sniffle; my eyes are burning now. My parents' faces are terse and tense as they listen to my account of the events leading to this point. "He didn't answer so I thought he was playing around..."

I start coughing and crying again pathetically.

"What happened next?" they both urge.

My temples are now throbbing, and I feel a little dizzy.

"I checked his room, the patio area, inside the house... I even checked next door, but no one is home!" The sobbing suddenly lessens as I apologize. "Please... don't be mad at me! It's not my fault this time! We never left the villa! I promise!"

Mom smiles as she informs, "I believe you, my love—"

Just as she utters those words, we see Ando walking up the paved road, a confused look on his small, tanned face, his new mustard polo smudged with dirt. Our parents run to him, taking turns hugging and kissing his face, but he just stands lackadaisically, looking curiously around like a lost puppy.

"Ando!" I shout, waving at him, but he does not seem to notice.

Slowly, carefully, I walk in their direction on legs that feel more like spaghetti than supernatural appendages. I have never been so thrilled to see my kid brother. I will never be mean to him again (well… mostly). Thankfully, I am not the only one shaken-up; Dad looks like he is about to faint and that is not like him at all. He is the rock of the family in comparison to the overly sensitive, fish-people in the household; however, right now, his hands are trembling.

"Fernando!" Dad roars. "You are not allowed to leave the villa, *comprende*?"

He ends in Spanish, his accent doubling when he is upset, and he only speaks *Spanglish* when he is off kilter.

"Ando! Are you okay?" Mom exclaims, kneeling in front of him, not caring that her new jeans are being stained with dirt as she examines him for cuts or bruises. "Don't you *ever* disappear like that again? Do you understand?"

He only nods his head; his bizarre behavior makes my skin crawl.

Dad's voice is finally returning to normal as he questions, "Where were you, son?"

"I was with the lady," he responds then blinks like he is sleepwalking.

"What lady?" Dad grills, looking around the street. "I don't see anyone."

Ando looks at me and cocks his head robotically.

"You know… the lady from the restaurant," my brother still looks dazed.

"The lady from which restaurant?" Mom queries as she glances at Dad who looks just as worried. Several seconds pass before Ando finally says, grinning:

"You know, the nice lady from the bed and breakfast in Ischia… the one with the fish."

CHAPTER THIRTEEN

How could this have happened?

I have asked myself this question more times in the last hour than I would care to admit. My brother and I followed the rules and kept inside to the safety of the villa. Never once had we ventured outside for any reason.

How could this have happened?

"How's Ando?" I ask, peeking around the doorway of his bedroom. He looks so innocent and small, tucked into bed with only his round face showing and the top of Alfredo's furry ears above the covers. My heart tightens again, as it often does when dealing with my little brother. Mom frowns, the sleeplessness in her eyes obvious. In her hands is a large mug of dark liquid that might be coffee based on the smell of it. As if to soothe herself, she inhales the wafting steam that rises then suddenly disappears out of sight.

"He seems to be fine," she tells on a loud exhale. "But…"

I hear the concern in her voice.

"But, what?" I repeat, waiting for more.

"He claims he can't remember what happened," my mother lowers her voice so not to wake my exhausted sibling.

"He can't remember?" I repeat as the pit in my belly grows, similar to a sinkhole that is about to swallow a car.

Slowly, she shakes her head as she gently closes the door with her free hand.

"The last thing he remembers is washing his hands before dinner then—"

"Then?" I encourage, waiting on the edge of my seat.

"Then nothing," my mom huffs. "Except walking up the street toward the villa."

"What do you think happened?" I whisper, trying not to think the worst.

Mom only shrugs, but I can tell that her mind is racing a hundred miles a minute. I can only imagine that her maternal instincts combined with her Siren vengeance are in overdrive, and I pity the creature that may have harmed my brother. I am certain that my mother will show no mercy.

"He's a Siren," I remind with pride, like it is the cure for everything horrible in this weird world.

Mom's face darkens, causing me to cringe before she even speaks, and I hear a crack of lightning and an angry roll of thunder over the villa roof. The pitter-pattering of fat raindrops against the windowpanes warns of the growing storm outside. Recalling that the meteorologist spoke of a cloudless night, I know that my mother's emotions are clearly to blame for the negative change in the weather.

"He's a little boy first and foremost... my little boy and I will kill anyone who dares put a hand on him. *Anyone!* Human or otherwise."

Her words send a chill up my spine. I have never seen her so enraged. So Siren-like. It scares me.

"Will he be safe tonight?" I question nervously.

Mom nods.

"Dad is staying with him," she informs as I catch a glimpse of David's form sleeping at the foot of the full-sized bed. His legs from the knees down are hanging over the edge. He looks very uncomfortable. He did not even change into his pajamas.

"Is he afraid that Ando might disappear again?" I question, feeling the same way.

My mother nods, too choked-up to respond verbally.

Truthfully, we are all on edge. Not knowing what happened to Ando during that span of time is driving us insane. Did the old woman do something to him? How did she take him from a locked house? Where did she take him?

All questions that need to be answered but cannot be... for the moment.

"How did the aunts take the news?" I inquire, knowing that their reaction will be volatile, to say the least.

"The aunts are patrolling the harbor," Mom educates with a small smile. "They wanted to be helpful. They are feeling a bit guilty for not protecting him."

I know that what she says is true. Out on the horizon, bands of rain pelt the sea until it churns like white water rapids dumping over a cliff. What else can I say? Sirens are emotional entities. No PMS needed.

"It's not their fault," I interject, taking my mother's hands in mine. "No one in their right mind would ever go against our kind."

"Exactly!" Mom huffs. "No one in their *right mind* would."

Screaming awakens me from an already tumultuous sleep.

"No!" Ando screams out. *"Stay away!"*

Mom and I storm into the dark room just in time to see Dad hugging his son's much smaller body.

"Shh!" our father soothes, brushing the sweat-drenched strands of hair out of Ando's wide-awake eyes. "You're okay. Shh! Everything is okay."

"What happened?" Mom questions, her hands shaking as she joins them on the bed.

"Nightmare," Ando whispers as he tightens his grip on Alfredo, tears rolling down his heated cheeks.

"Tell me about it," our mother encourages. "Sometimes bad dreams go away when you talk about them."

Ando shakes his head. The only comfort he accepts is from Alfredo, who is covered in my brother's perspiration. If it was not for the gnarly-furred teddy bear, Ando would not sleep at all.

"Why won't you tell me?" she beseeches more firmly as she takes his sweaty hand in hers.

"Because," he whimpers sadly.

"Because why, son?" Dad joins.

"Because… because I just can't."

"Coffee?" Dad offers as his wife enters the kitchen at a few minutes past seven in the morning.

Mom kisses his cheek before answering.

"You read my mind."

Dad chuckles; eyes red-rimmed and puffy.

"Maybe I'm becoming a Siren too," he jokes, trying to lighten the mood as he hands her a steamy mug of *café con leche*.

His sleep-deprived spouse gratefully accepts.

"Hungry?" he adds, too exhausted to construct complete sentences.

Mom nods enthusiastically.

"What are you in the mood for?" her husband manages a thin smile.

"Whatever is easy," she coos, takes a big gulp of the hot brew and sighs.

Dad grabs the extra-large Teflon frying pan and turns it on low as he goes to the refrigerator for the carton of eggs and the container of butter. Next, he grabs the loaf of white bread from the bread box. He moves so confidently that it makes me giggle.

"Why are you giggling at me?" he lightheartedly scoffs as he blushes.

"I don't know," I fib, turning red too. I do not want to admit that I am happy to have him as my stepfather. I do not know what we would do without him.

"Stop looking at me," he admonishes playfully, throwing the dishtowel at my head.

"Okay," I laugh again.

"Come help your old man make some food," he orders like a general.

Happily, I come to his aid, taking over the task of cracking several brown eggs with some salt and pepper, and a tablespoon of milk into one of the lovely cobalt-blue mixing bowls. David gets another pan to cook some bacon he found in the freezer. Quickly, he thaws the package in some water in the sink. Before long, the entire kitchen smells wonderful.

"I'm hungry," Ando's voice startles me as he enters the roomy kitchen, his teddy bear accompanying him.

"Good morning, little man," his father greets first.

Thrilled to see her son alive and well, Mom walks to him and kisses his forehead making him smile. Not wanting to crowd him, I stand by the granite kitchen island waiting for the frying pan to heat up to scramble the eggs. I wink at him and he winks back.

"Hi, sweetheart," Mom greets, kneeling to look directly in his eyes. "How did you sleep?"

"Okay," he replies with a sleepy tone.

"Any more nightmares?" I add, hoping the answer is no.

Regrettably, he nods and tightens his grip on Alfredo the Bear.

"Daddy and Lena are making bacon, eggs and toast," Mom informs with a genuine smile.

"Mmm," he responds like his usual self.

Somehow, that is all that is needed to cheer us up.

"Get away from me!" my brother's eardrum-piercing screams wake me from a sexy dream starring Andrew and me.

"Holy crap!" I cry out as I search for my robe and slippers.

This is the third night in a row that phantom dreams have haunted his thoughts. He always wakes in terror, but within seconds he forgets what the dreams are about. Mom and Dad have not left his side, hoping that their presence will put him at ease; unfortunately, it has not. In fact, I think they have made it worse.

"Baby?" Mom coddles softly, wiping the sweat from his brow. Dad sits beside her, holding his hand, whispering caring words in Spanish.

I look at the three and turn silently to go back to my room, feeling utterly useless.

Why are days only twenty-four hours long? There should be some way to add a few more hours to the Earthly time cycle. In the near future, I will find a way to do that. Maybe one day I will meet Gaia, Goddess of the Earth, and suggest doing just that.

Yeah! Sure! That's going to happen!

Last night, I woke to strange clunky footsteps in the hallway. Next, David's low whispers could be heard, but not understood. I swear I even heard Ando's small voice as well; however, when I rolled out of bed to check, the hallway was empty.

When I finally fell back asleep, I kept tossing and turning trying to get comfortable. Unfortunately, try as I might, I was the young lady whose noble identity is proven through a test of her physical sensitivity like in Hans Christian Andersen's fairy tale *The Princess and the Pea*.

Tired and irritable, I tumble out of bed this morning and stumble to the washroom in a zombie-like state where I fumble into my robe. Now, all I want to do is go right back to bed, but instead I make my way to the kitchen.

"How's Ando today?" I ask, needing better news.

"He only woke once last night," David informs with a tired yawn.

"That's good," I respond, knowing that my parents and brother have not had a good night's rest for almost a week.

Mom and Dad glance at each other. Their eyes narrow like they are silently communicating. Dad growls and gets up to refill his coffee cup. My mother simply appears overwhelmed.

"What's wrong?" I probe, wondering why they are keeping me out of the loop.

Silence.

"What aren't you telling me?" I question again.

This time my stepdad speaks first.

"He's been sleepwalking," he reveals with a loud exhale.

The hairs on my arms immediately stand on end and my stomach lurches.

"Ando's never sleepwalked," I state, scratching my head.

"We know," they answer in unison.

This is not good!

"Good morning, everybody," my brother greets as he rounds the corner with Alfredo in tow.

"Hey, buddy!" Dad responds happily, his face instantly brightening at the sight of the half-awake six-year-old with the sleep-tousled hair and the droopy expression.

"Good morning, baby," Mom smiles too, her eyes crinkling on the sides due to her lack of slumber. "How are you feeling today?"

"I'm okay," Ando yawns as he informs us.

Sleepily, he looks down at his favorite teddy.

"Alfredo is a little bit tired, but he wants breakfast," my sibling replies as he rubs the sleep out of his eyes.

At my brother's request, Dad jumps up.

"Does Alfredo want some pancakes?" our father gleams with a wink.

Ando giggles.

"Pancakes with blueberries?" my brother adds.

"Coming right up, son," Dad chuckles as he goes to the fridge to retrieve the pint of blueberries.

Needing a break and a well-deserved evening out, my parents gather the last of their belongings. Mom has reluctantly agreed to go on a date night due to some heavy negotiating on Dad's part. I think we all need a night of boring and peaceful.

"Are you sure you'll be alright with your brother tonight?" Dad asks as he helps our mother into her black cardigan.

Rolling my eyes, I answer.

"We'll be fine," I state with confidence. "I promise."

"If you need anything... anything at all," Mom interjects. "Just call us."

"I will," I grin at her protective nature.

"Ando?" our father says, getting my brother's undivided attention.

"Yes, Daddy?" Ando replies as he smiles, showing the gap where he recently lost a tooth while biting into a rather large, juicy apple.

"Do not leave the house under any circumstance," Dad orders. "Do you understand?"

Ando nods.

"Not even on the patio?" Ando pries mischievously.

David frowns.

"Not even on the patio," our father clarifies without humor.

Ando nods again as he throws his small arms around Dad's waist then Mom's.

"Listen to your sister," Mom states firmly, yet lovingly.

"I will," my brother promises.

"Don't worry so much," I plead with a grin. "We are going to watch television and make snacks."

Mom nods then turns to leave then turns back. She reminds me of a puppy chasing its tail. If she continues, I am sure she will become dizzy.

"Call us if—"

"I know... I know... " I interrupt, rolling my eyes one last time.

An hour later, my brother and I are lounging on the sofa watching an Italian soap opera. Its characters are overly dramatic, but fun to watch. It reminds me of the American soap operas Grandpa Theo used to watch when he was alive. He would always make us popcorn while Ando and I sat beside him on the couch, looking at the actors doing weird things. It was fun.

Tonight, after gorging ourselves on homemade pork tacos that our mom made before they left for the opera, we decided to watch a local show instead of one on cable. Ando, who was eager to watch television, almost immediately fell asleep beside me with Alfredo tucked under his head.

"I'm not supposed to leave the house," my little brother mumbles in his sleep as he rearranges himself on the cushions.

I remain quiet, hoping he will go back to sleep.

"They're not here… " he babbles and returns to his former position.

"Ando?" I whisper, trying to get him to wake, but his eyes remain closed.

"Ok… " he finally says after several very long minutes.

"Ando," I repeat, this time louder and he still does not respond, but then he does the strangest thing. He bolts up into a seated position, swings his short legs over the edge of the cushions and begins walking to the front door.

What the hell!

"Ando!" I cry and then command in my most parental tone. *"Wake up!"*

Seemingly lost in his own mind, my brother robotically unlocks the bolt, turns the knob, and pushes the ornately-carved barrier open with a smooth motion. Instantly, my eyes widen. Glancing around the living room, I search for my cell phone, but cannot remember where I had it last. In the few short seconds I pause, Ando is already down the street, barefoot and on a mission. No time to find the phone, I pull on my sneakers and race after his swiftly moving form.

Around the bend he goes with feet that seem to know the path to his destination, even though the rest of his body does not. Hurrying, I debate what exactly to do. Unable to keep pace, I find myself lumbering behind although still within seeing distance.

Scared beyond belief, I decide to fall back just a tad in case trouble arises, all the while willing my legs to go faster. As we continue out of the *Belvedere of Tragara,* he makes a left at the small grocery store at the corner of our street, and then continues up toward the rugged hills above the town. My palms immediately begin to sweat as I diligently follow his path.

Where is he going?

It is dark out here away from the lights of the villas and surrounding shopping areas. Overhead, gloomy rainclouds hide the semi-rounded moon; its dim rays unable to disperse the shadows that follow us along our trek.

How I wish that our parents had not gone out for the evening. For once, I would like to have a dull night of watching television and scarfing junk food.

After twenty or so minutes, Ando stops in the middle of the dusty, unpaved, tree-lined path high above the town of Capri and waits. Heaven help us if something evil jumps out of the bushes. Quickly, he races into the heavily wooded spot where the bushes are taller than me, definitely taller than him, and then, he is gone.

"Ando!" I shout not caring who or what hears. "Fernando, if you don't answer me this instant—" I think for a second or two, "—I'm gonna kick your butt!"

Nothing.

It is only now that I realize the woods are thick here and the ground beneath me is covered with twigs, broken branches, and decaying leaves. All around, the heavy fragrance of wet bark and honeysuckle wreak havoc with my sense of smell, and I realize what a dangerous position we are in.

No scary Latin father.

No scarier Siren mother.

No terrifying Siren aunts.

Just us. Two untried baby-Sirens, alone in the woods.

"I'm not joking!" I shout again, slapping a mosquito that dares bite my arm while I am in panic-mode. "Answer me! *Right now!*"

Something scurries across my path causing me to scream.

"Ando!"

"*Shh!*" a silky voice admonishes instead, making me jump out of my skin.

Terrified beyond my wildest dreams, I raise my hands in front of my body like I am Bruce Lee in *Return of the Dragon.*

"Who are you?!" I growl, taking two steps back.

Several yards away, in the shadows, all I see is a short, plump figure cloaked by a dark hooded jacket. Man or woman, I cannot tell, and then slowly, it smiles at me and says:

"Come inside my dear. We have a lot to talk about."

The vein in my right temple is pounding so loud that it drowns out the even louder palpitations of my heart. Even my palms betray me as they begin to perspire profusely, and if my feet had a mind of their own, I would be halfway home by now. Unfortunately, the rest of me—the stupid part—stands waiting for the next shoe to drop.

Apparently, Sirens are not the sharpest tools in the shed.

"Who are you?" I question again, trying to keep myself together, but failing miserably as the being's delicate voice seeps into my cerebellum and starts to sedate my senses. "Where's my brother?"

"Do not fret, my pet," it says with a serendipitous drawl. "He is perfectly fine."

I seriously doubt that!

"I swear to the gods, if you've harmed him in anyway—!"

Unable to control them, my hands clench into tight fists, ready to throw down if necessary.

"Come inside," it requests sweetly. "Come inside where it is safe."

Confused, I glance around the area.

"Come inside, where?" I snap, sweat dripping from my brow onto my shirt. "There's only wo—"

As I stare into the darkness behind the being, the air begins to shimmer and bend. Then the soft breeze morphs into a blustery wind tunnel that almost lifts me off of the ground. As if it is alive, my wildly whipping hair assaults my unprotected eyes stinging them, and now in panic mode, I lash at the strands to keep them out of the way in order to keep my companion in view. However, as I continue to stare, a small building suddenly appears out of nowhere.

What the—

Cautiously, *it* steps back, motioning to the small door leading into the even smaller house. The rounded entrance reminds me of a *Hobbit's* door. Remarkably, the structure itself is rather charming and quaint.

"Ando is safe," it answers, the cloak still hiding the upper part of its face.

Feeling the need to deliver a warning to this potentially dangerous creature, I quickly think-up a lie.

"My parents will be home soon—"

"No, they will not," it interrupts with an omniscient chuckle that further antagonizes my jagged nerves. "The opera does not finish until eleven."

"How do you know that?" I ask, cocking my head to the side.

It laughs. This time the sound is light and airy like the clinking of champagne glasses on New Year's Eve. If I was not so unnerved, it would have been the most pleasant sound I had ever heard, and being a Siren that says a lot.

"I have my ways," it answers, motioning me inside.

Nervously, I wait as I signal for it to enter first, unwilling to turn my back on it. Suspiciously, I follow, my defense on high alert. If we were in the ocean, I would be extremely confident right now. I know that I could defend myself as well as Ando, but here, on land, I am not so sure, yet I decide to take my chances. Obviously, I have clearly got height and an age advantage over the much smaller entity and that makes me feel better. More reassured, I decide to bide my time until I form a more lucid plan of escape.

"Tsk, tsk, tsk," it nonchalantly soothes. "No need to formulate plans to get away."

My mouth gapes as it sighs.

"I would never harm you or your brother."

Shocked at its reply to my unspoken words, my eyes instinctively narrow as I continue to study the covered figure.

"I don't believe you," I firmly condemn, but I can already feel my apprehension diminish even though I am trying to hold it in place.

"Selena," it speaks, and the tone sounds so wonderful... so parental that I almost believe it. *Almost.* "Please, step inside. It is not safe out here."

Steadying myself, I gulp down the extra-large lump in my throat.

Instinctively, I glance around the area hoping not to see anything out of the ordinary. However, one thing ensnares my attention: a lone dandelion; its soft fluffy seeds full and delicate as they cling to its base. As I watch, somehow now completely enthralled by the lovely weed that stands alone like a watchful sentinel guarding the unassuming cottage, a gust of wind races by causing all but six seeds to be blown away. Mesmerized, I stare as each individual seed drifts up and away, getting smaller and smaller with each passing second. Never do they get pulled back to Earth, but instead rise into the dark heavens. Bizarrely enough, the thought that they might never land disturbs me.

As usual, the hairs on my arms immediately stand up, but the stranger's words bring me back to reality.

"What do you mean: *'it's not safe out here'*?" I question, stepping closer to the cottage entrance.

Like a wise old owl surveying the woods for its dinner, it pauses. Expertly, it scans our surroundings and sighs deeply. I think I even hear the faintest melody in my head as I stand next to it.

"Amphitrite," the *'person'* whispers, and the tone makes me shiver.

"You know Amphitrite?" I gasp, feeling that lump returning as my breathing labors.

To my surprise, it nods briskly, but the cloak hiding its face remains in place.

"She and I go way, way back," it admits in a perturbed voice that makes me calm a bit more. After all, the enemy of my enemy is my friend or so the saying goes. Hopefully, it is true.

"Lena?" I hear my brother's voice calling from inside the cute cottage.

"Yes!" I answer, feeling a sense of relief wash over me. "It's me! I'm here!"

"Please," it pleads. "Come inside."

Still uncertain, I pause for another minute.

"I just want my brother back is all," I remind. "If there's any funny business—"

"No funny business," it interrupts, and I can hear the amusement in its voice.

Somehow, I believe it.

Graciously, it leads me inside. Taking slow, careful steps, it waits like a butler welcoming me, but I stop at the doorway. I cannot help but give an appreciative nod and I know it has me under its spell.

CHAPTER FOURTEEN

Inside is not what I expected.

Although the cottage looks tiny from the outside, it is rather large inside with oversized, rectangular windows encompassing the entire circumference of the house that allow the picturesque cypress grove to become framed art. The surfaces of the walls are stucco and painted a soft powder-blue and decorated with various framed landscapes which are quite pleasing to the eye.

That is when I see him; my brother, all smiles and giggles. With a carefree demeanor he waves at me, turning my attention away from our unusual host. If I could smack him and not get in trouble for it or grounded for another week, I would.

"Come in, Lena," my sibling encourages with a smile... a wide-awake smile. "Don't be afraid."

Easy for him to say!

Reluctantly, I step further inside, closing the door behind me. That feeling of dread appears again as I glance nervously around then to Ando, who is currently sitting at the dining table enjoying a snack of chocolate biscotti and a glass of water. He seems quite content at the moment.

"Are you alright?" I probe in a bit of a stupor at his carefree attitude.

"I'm fine," he informs with a grin as he takes another bite of his cookie then sits, olive-complexioned legs swinging since they are too short to reach the floor.

Filled with curiosity, I take in my surroundings.

The main area acts as the living room housing a floral-print sofa/loveseat combo, and a tree stump base, glass-top coffee table anchored by a handwoven multihued carpet that must be worth more than the entire cottage. To the left, there is the designated space for the small dining table and four hand-carved mahogany chairs. Adjacent is a cramped, yet neatly kept galley-style kitchen with open shelving and 1950's era appliances, which is next to a long row of windows facing a bountiful garden of fruits and vegetables, some of which are not even native to this region.

Caught off guard at recognizing several of the unique plants from television culinary shows and documentaries that my parents love so much, I take a closer look. According to experts, these things could never grow in the soil of the Mediterranean.

"Are those... papayas... a-and dragon fruit?" I interrogate similar to a customs official. "My goodness, is that durian fruit and cacao?"

It nods as it goes into the kitchen and begins to fill a small copper teakettle with water from the tap. My eyebrows hitch automatically at the sight of the exotic fruit growing carelessly outside.

"Those don't belong here... on Capri, I mean," I inform rather accusatorily.

"I know," it says with a soft giggle, placing the kettle on the stovetop on high heat.

My interest is now standing at attention as I allow myself to wander around the space examining its contents, stopping once again to stare out of the window at the breathtaking garden.

"How did you get them to grow here?" I lawyerly cross-examine, holding back the desire to go outside to study them.

Nonchalantly, it shrugs and moves to the cupboard to retrieve two expensive cream-colored gold-rimmed teacups that I have seen in several expensive bridal magazines.

"Sit with me, Lena," my cheesy brother requests and I oblige, suddenly feeling more at ease.

As I sit on the comfortable dining chair beside Ando, the kettle lets out a high-pitched whistle announcing that the water is ready. As gracefully as a classically trained ballerina, the being flits and flutters to and fro; gathering ingredients from the cupboards and drawers. Unable to contain my glee, I giggle. It is like watching Odette in *Swan*

Lake, mesmerizing as well as enchanting. Who knew that making tea could be so captivating?

"Ando, are you finished?" it asks thoughtfully.

Appearing to be satisfied, my brother nods as he shoves the small piece of biscotto into his mouth.

"It is more comfortable in the living room," it announces daintily. "Let us relocate."

Seeing no reason to object, I follow a few feet behind.

"Please sit," it gently requests, and I obey immediately.

What is happening to me?

"Here you go, dear," it says, resting the elegant teacups on the coffee table as it sits on the sofa, cloak still in place.

I cannot help but look inside the drinking vessel.

"What is this?" I question, taking a long tentative inhale of the steaming caramel-colored liquid.

"Just Earl Grey tea," it admits as it takes two sugar cubes to sweeten the brew and adds it to our drinks.

Drawn to the intricate teacup pattern of hand painted flowers and mourning doves all outlined in real gold, I very carefully run my finger over the slightly raised etchings. The contrast between the smooth porcelain and the decorative pattern feels strange against my skin.

"This china is lovely," I admit with a grin, wishing that one day I will have a set just like it.

"Thank you," it responds then tastes the steaming liquid and nods with approval.

"Did you buy it?" I question boldly, not caring if I offend.

Without hesitation, it answers.

"No, I did not," it admits, and I can hear the smile in its voice. "It was a gift from the Swiss artist who created it."

My eyes narrow as I scan the room wondering if everything is *'one of a kind'*.

"Oh," is my only comment.

"How is the tea?" it asks with that charming lilt.

Giving it a sip, my eyes widen.

"It's the best thing I've ever tasted!" I say truthfully, licking my lips then eagerly draining my cup.

It laughs, and the dainty melody makes me smile.

"Would you like some more?" she offers, and I nod with a grin, wondering why I am feeling so comfortable now.

What witchery is this?

"Are you a witch?" I blurt, unable to control my tongue, suddenly filled with excitement and energy like my drink was spiked with something.

On the verge of laughter, it shakes its head making the hood sway, and for an instant I glimpse a patch of flawless olive skin and a beautiful *human* smile.

Taking another glance around the room to keep my mind focused, I notice the stunning *Steinway* piano tucked away in the corner with a piece of sheet music resting on top of it. Forgetting where I am, I quickly walk toward it, hypnotized by the shiny surface that reflects my excited features.

"This is beautiful," I whisper, touching the smooth surface of the Upright, but it does not quite resemble today's pianos.

"It is a prototype designed by Henry Steinway a very long time ago," it answers my unspoken comment proudly.

As if recalling the event, it pauses then sighs happily.

"It's amazing," I compliment in awe, wanting to sit on the bench, but deciding to remain standing instead.

"I agree," the being nods, jostling the hood with the movement.

"It looks old," I add, hoping not to offend.

"It is," it agrees with a chuckle.

This time, I run both of my hands over the exquisite instrument enjoying the smooth surface against my palms. The wood is cool to the touch and perfect in every way. I also notice that there is no dust, so it must be played quite a bit.

Before I can ask, it answers.

"Unfortunately, I do not play."

That surprises me, but I dismiss it.

"How long have you had it?" I wonder aloud.

"Hmm," it contemplates. "About one hundred sixty years... give or take a month."

Stunned, my eyes widen, and Ando stops chewing long enough to say: "Wow! You must be really old."

Filled with amusement, it laughs jovially and the heavenly sound travels down my spinal column and filters into my extremities filling me with a similar emotion: Joy! Pure... unadulterated... *Joy!* The sensation is completely overwhelming in a pleasant, yet odd sort of way. The entity laughs this time; the kind of laugh that warms you from the inside out. It is a laugh that could easily warm the coldest heart or so it seems. If I could find a way to bottle it and carry it around with me always, I would.

"I am... extremely... old," it confesses with a frivolity that would come from a much younger person in my opinion, but somehow fits this wistful soul.

There is a long pregnant pause lingering over the room, a pause that hurts my ears so much that I clear my throat in order to break its spell over us.

At last it speaks again and I struggle to trap the sound in my memory.

"Do you play?" It questions as it turns in the direction of my gaze.

My cheeks redden.

"Unfortunately, I don't," I blab. "But I've always wanted to."

Unexpectedly, it stands.

"Come, give it a try," It encourages.

Backed into a corner, I shake my head.

"I took a few lessons, but my playing always sounded like cats mating on a hot tin roof," I gulp as my stomach takes a nosedive like a jet whose engine has given-out.

Reassuringly, it motions me to take a seat on the padded bench and for some inexplicable reason, I cannot say no.

"Okay," I blush, not wanting to humiliate myself.

"Close your eyes," it orders sweetly, and I do. "Now, place your fingers on the keys."

"I feel silly," I giggle with embarrassment.

"Shh!"

"Sorry," I blush even more, but gently rest my hands on the keys, careful not to jostle them.

"Pretend the keys are an extension of your fingers… good, now play."

"I can't," I huff, recalling the last time I attempted to play.

I was seven and had been taking piano lessons for approximately six months with a private instructor, Mrs.

Vincent. She was a kind and patient teacher, but I could never get my hands to do what they were supposed to do. Every time I touched the piano, my fingers would be replaced by ten, plump hotdogs, minus the buns.

At my first piano recital, I walked onto the stage, sat on the bench, placed my hands on the keys, took a cleansing breath and played the most God-awful piece of music in the history of recitals. Halfway through the song, I bolted and hid backstage until my mother and stepfather tracked me down. I have not played the piano since, and I promised myself I never would again.

"You can do this," it states firmly. "All you have to do is *believe*."

Determined to break my cycle of shame, I think of my favorite nursery rhyme, *Twinkle, Twinkle Little Star*, but my fingers sound like cucumbers against the wooden keys.

"I can't do this," I pout, tears welling.

"Stop thinking so much... feel the music inside of you... you are a Siren... channel your inner fish!" it replies playfully, yet with a sense of command.

More at ease, I laugh and try again, but it is horrible; worse than when Ando got ahold of David's bagpipes. We stumbled upon it when Dad temporarily moved out of the house when the whole Siren fiasco blew-up.

I cringe from the sound.

"I'll never be able to play," I huff like an errant child.

"Again," it states firmly, ignoring me.

Then I feel the soft touch of its fingers resting on my shoulders, light and barely there. Something deep inside of me awakens, yawns, and stretches as I place my hands more comfortably on top of the keys. I let my fingers loosen, take a deep breath and listen to the space inside of me where there is only my love of the world... my love of my family... my love of my friends... my love for the sounds of the sea, and then I play.

The sounds that leave the piano are beguiling and sensuous; exquisite and clearly defined. Soft and fluid in some parts; loud and boisterous in others. It lifts to the heavens and my heart fills with joy. The joy that only a being, such as a Siren, created by music and magic would know, could possibly comprehend.

"Now... *Sing!*" It pleads, giving my shoulders a gentle squeeze of encouragement.

Forgetting about the consequences, I allow my voice to join the notes of the piano. The two slither against the other like a mating dance. Twisting into corkscrews. Turning on its heels. Pivoting. So graceful... so elegant.

Just as softly as when it touched me, it removes its hands, leaving me empty once more.

"That, my dear, is *your* Aria," it claps ecstatically. "This Aria is made for only you."

"I don't understand," I whisper, fingers still touching the keys.

"It is your most beautiful Siren-song ever," It explains. "Not even another Siren can repeat it or recreate it."

"How do you know this?" I ask, wondering if its words are true.

"Trust me," it begs. "All of the happiness and love that it evokes will never fail you. Never desert you. Reach for it when times are at their darkest and it will show you the way home."

Slowly, even more confused, I turn to it and ask:

"Who are you?"

Unhurriedly, it removes its hood revealing a face much like my own.

Almond-shaped eyes as blue as the sky on a cloudless afternoon with specks of chocolate, violet and aquamarine embedded in them. With hair as black as the volcanic glass pendant which hangs around my neck, highlighted with crimson and gold streaks and high cheekbones, surrounded by unblemished olive skin.

"To many I am known as Melpomene the Muse," she pauses. "However, you can call me Great-Grandmother."

Miles beyond shocked, my eyes dart open as my mouth drops to my chin.

"You c-can't be our great-grandmother," I ramble, bolting to a standing position almost causing the piano bench to fall to the white-washed, planked floor. "S-she's... *she's dead!*"

The older, yet still enchanting woman gives a dazzling smile followed by a light-hearted chuckle.

"Timeworn... but not dead," she reveals.

Maneuvering around the seat, I make my way to where Ando sits with his plate of biscotti and firmly take his hand in mine.

"C'mon!" I command, starting to feel the hairs on my arms standing up. "We're getting out of here, *now!*"

Remaining in her original position at the piano, the woman speaks.

"Your mother's name is Marina," she says in that slow, pleasant tone that makes a person want to follow her like rats following the *Pied Piper*.

"You knowing our mother's name doesn't prove anything!" I snap, backing toward the entrance.

"She was born right here in Capri," she continues.

My little brother and I are almost to the door.

"It was a cloudy night," the woman continues, her voice with a faraway sound, eyes partially closed as though she is recalling a memory. "In the Blue Grotto."

Mom had never mentioned that.

"And when Parthenope delivered, the clouds disappeared revealing a full moon... the fullest most exquisite moon that ever graced the heavens and the choppy sea immediately calmed to hardly a ripple."

I pause, hand on the glass doorknob.

"That is why she named your mother *Marina*," the woman's features beam with nostalgia. "Because from birth, she held dominion over the sea. Not even Ligeia, Leukosia, or Parthenope had that power until they were much older."

Opening the door, I nudge Ando outside and quickly follow, still facing our opponent.

"Ask Marina," she says as she repositions the bench and closes the lid to protect the well-worn keyboard. "Ask your mother."

"Stay away from us," I order then quickly and harshly slam the door.

Outside, the wind is gathering strength as my emotions continue to grow. The clouds are coming in from the sea and an aggravated roll of thunder announces its approach. Nothing makes sense. Hooded entity... mythological Muse... my long-lost Great-Grandmother... whoever she is, I can feel our connection. Taking a deep breath, I will the sky to remain closed until we get back to the villa.

"Lena?" Ando speaks softly, his expression worried as he glances up at the night sky and then back at me.

"What is it?" I mumble, wishing we were home already and praying that I can hold back the oncoming storm.

"Do you think she's really who she says she is?" he questions with a confused yet hopeful glimmer in his bright eyes.

I shrug, unsure of the answer.

"Our great-grandmother is dead," I huff, walking out of the thick cypress grove.

Ando struggles to navigate the branch-cluttered ground, so I pick him up.

"Ugg!" I moan as I heft him up.

"What?" he snaps self-consciously.

"No more biscotti for you!" I admonish, feeling my arms tremble under his weight.

"Lena," he states, ignoring me. "Suppose she is our great-grandmother."

I stare at his innocent face.

"She's not," I respond. "She can't be. The aunts would have felt her presence… " I pause. "… Wouldn't they?"

This time he shrugs and kicks his legs to be let down when we are back on the semi-paved road.

"We have to tell Mom and Dad," I state, releasing his hand.

Glancing at his dive watch, he pleads.

"Not yet."

"Why?" I question, staring at him.

"Because."

"That's not a good answer," I respond, stopping in mid-step.

"Lena, just trust her."

"Why?" I ask again. "Why should we trust her?"

Ando thinks for a moment.

"I… I like her," he admits, looking into my eyes, aquamarine to aquamarine. "I trust her."

"How can you trust someone who can control your actions?"

He pauses again.

"You trust her too," he accuses with a smug stare.

"I don't!" I huff, beginning to walk toward town.

With determination, he hurries to catch up. When he is beside me, he gently touches my arm, stopping me once more. His face is unyielding.

"Don't tell Mommy and Daddy," my brother orders.

"*Grr!*" I growl, not knowing what else to do. "I just need time to think."

He nods his head, the action filled with satisfaction.

Why does he have to be so stubborn?

"They need to know," I try to reason.

"She wouldn't lie," my brother insists with a scowl.

"Even if she is Melpomene, why would she abandon her children... grandchild... us?" I huff, feeling angry.

Ando frowns.

"She has her reasons," he defends.

"How do you know that she has her reasons?"

He says nothing.

"I can't tell you," he maintains.

"Did she confide in you?"

Again, he shakes his head.

"I c-can't tell you how I know."

Battered by frustration, and the need to shake my brother like a maraca, I stomp my feet, ball my fists as I ramble in Siren; clicking, clacking, whistling and chirping like a lunatic bird. To my surprise, Ando just stands wordlessly looking toward the bright lights of the belvedere, his mind on something else.

"Why are you being so secretive?" I add, trying to reduce my blood pressure while standing at the side of the deserted road.

Finally, he speaks.

"If I tell you, promise you won't freak-out," he requests, his arms folded across his chest.

Wanting to be a good sister, I ponder his demand.

"Alright," I agree nervously. "I promise."

Several seconds pass as he stands… internally debating.

"I've seen this all before in a dream," his voice lowers.

CHAPTER FIFTEEN

We enter the villa right as my cell phone rings.

Crap! It has to be our parents checking on us.

Immediately, my brain locks-up as if it is a laptop low on memory. Ando begins to look under the sofa while I rummage through the layer of magazines currently covering the coffee table.

Where is it?

Thankfully, Ando finds it on the seventh ring under the sofa cushion.

"Hello!" I bark into the device, quite out of breath.

It is our father.

"How's it going?" he inquires with a hopeful smile in his voice.

Uneasy, I glare at my brother, hoping he will take the phone from me, but being a smart kid, he just stares at me like a raccoon in headlights. This is one of many problems connected to being the older sibling. I always have to deal with our parents.

"Uh… it's going well," I fib, playing with the hem of my *I Love Capri* t-shirt. "How was the opera?"

There is a short pause as I hear our mom's voice in the background. She sounds so happy that I wish my brother and I never left the villa. Although, I am not at fault, I am just the unfortunate sap that had to follow him and keep him safe. God forbid something was to actually happen to the little rug-rat, it would be my hide.

David chuckles before he answers, and I grimace at the thought that my parents are being frisky.

Yuck!

There should be a law against such disturbing things.

"It was terrific, but it was packed," Dad mumbles, trying to regain his waning composure.

"Oh, that's great!" I try sounding excited, but it sounds too shaky.

Suddenly, he pauses, and I know that he suspects some adolescent chicanery afoot.

"What's going on?" he grills flatly.

"Nothing," I reply with a nervous giggle betraying myself.

Without warning, Ando takes the phone.

"Hi Daddy!" he pours on his childish charm which usually throws our parents off of our scent when he/we are doing mischief… usually.

"Hey, little man!" David's voice is loud enough to hear even though my brother is holding the cell phone to his ear.

"Are you on your way home?" Ando innocently checks, his cheeks heated as he bites the corner of his lower lip.

"We are going to make a quick stop at the café for some dessert and coffee," David informs cheerfully. "Would you and Selena like something?"

Ando hits the mute button.

"Dad wants to know what we want from Caffè Augusto?"

Quickly, my mind mulls over the menu. We have visited the café several times since we arrived on the island. Everything we have tried there has been tasty.

Taking the phone, I make my request.

"I'd like a latte macchiato please, and Ando wants his usual."

My brother nods gleefully.

"So, one latte for you, and a Nutella panino for your brother?" Dad repeats like a veteran waiter.

Proud that my sibling has used his power for good not evil, I grin.

"Yes," I confirm, still grinning.

"Okay," Dad smirks. "We'll be home in about an hour. And Selena...?"

My palms start to perspire.

"Yes, Dad?"

"Whatever you and Ando are up to… get your stories straight before your mom and I get home," he lays it all out with finality.

Nervously, I chuckle, playing it off.

"I love you," I coo, hoping they will have mercy after I explain the night's events.

To my surprise, he laughs.

"I love you more," Dad pleasantly replies and I can imagine he is shaking his head the entire time.

Quickly, I hang up the phone, exhaling the breath that I have been holding.

"That was close," I say after a loud exhale.

"Lena?" Ando tugs on my arm.

"Yes?" I respond, looking down at his bleak countenance.

My upbeat spirit takes a nosedive after looking at my brother's furrowed brow and watery irises as he stares at the cellphone still clenched in my palm.

"Do you think he knows that we left the villa?" he queries with a small shaky voice.

Unsure, I shrug, suddenly exhausted. Meeting the being who claims to be our great-grandmother would be tiresome for anyone, but after all of the trouble with Amphitrite I feel like I have been run over by a tractor.

All I want to do is rest my weary brain.

🦉

Trying to relax, I sit on the loveseat and turn on the television, Ando sits beside me with Alfredo squeezed between us.

"Lena?"

"What now?" I respond, trying to find something worth watching.

"I need to ask you a question," he announces dryly, his face expressionless.

My brows furrow.

"What sort of question?"

Blankly, he stares at the television screen, avoiding eye contact, his cheeks heated.

"Do you think I'm... *weird*?" he mumbles below his breath, and I have to strain to hear him.

Pausing, I turn. The look on his face is sad and concerned. All I want to do is make him feel better.

So, I say, "Our entire family is weird."

He grimaces at my flippant response.

"But Lena," he continues. "I have dreams about the past and the future."

I weigh my retort and finally remind.

"Our ancestors were mythological creatures. Our great-grandmother is a Muse who gave birth to Sirens who are being accosted by the queen of the watery domain." I roll my eyes and poke his belly with my finger. "We're all *weird*."

"What about Dad?" he probes with a thin grin. "He's human."

I think for a moment then smile.

"He's strange too," I giggle as I ponder how odd my stepfather is also.

"Why do you say that?" Ando asks, filled with curiosity.

Amused by the thought, I chuckle heartily.

"Because he knows about our crazy dysfunctional lineage and still loves us," I remind, giving him a playful elbow nudge.

Much happier, he giggles and pats Alfredo's head, right between the ears.

"Lena?" he speaks, looking straight ahead.

"Yes?"

Uneasily, he shifts in his seat.

"Do you think it's strange that I have these dreams?"

"No," I say too quickly revealing my angst.

Being an observant kid, he pouts.

"Tell me the truth," he insists, looking directly at me.

Even though I want to change the subject, I give in because I know that he is relentless. I decide to go with the truth and hope he takes it with a grain of salt.

"It freaks me out a little," I admit, not looking at him for fear that he will realize how much his gift truly frightens me.

"I don't want to dream anymore," he mutters, grabbing Alfredo and hugging him tightly to his chest.

Putting my arm around him, I soothe.

"Do you know that you are the strongest person I know?"

He blushes.

"Let's find some cartoons," he proclaims, smiling from ear to ear and I do.

About an hour later, our parents arrive at our vacation home, still giddy with joy from their evening out. It is a good sign when Mom pinches Dad's butt and he grabs hers back. At last there is hope that we might not get grounded until we are at the age when a nursing home might be required. Being Sirens that may be an extremely long incarceration.

"Here you go," my mother announces, handing me the ice-cold latte.

"Mmm," I respond, smelling the intoxicating brew. "Thank you!"

She smiles, eyes glimmering like jewels under the kitchen lights.

"For you," she hands Ando a neatly wrapped sandwich. "It is still warm from the panini press."

My brother's face beams with anticipation.

"Thank you, Mommy!" he states as he licks his lips.

Quickly, he unwraps the sandwich and takes a huge bite. His face immediately crinkles into the most hilarious expression that I have ever seen. Softly, he moans as he starts to chew. I should have asked for a panino too.

"Good?" I query as I take a long gulp of my drink.

"Very," he grins, mouth still full of the aromatic sandwich.

"May I have a bite... please?" I dare beg.

He says nothing only stares at me.

"Fine," I huff. "I'll take that as a *no*."

Ando nods as he takes another bite.

Our mother clears her throat to get our attention.

"How was your evening?" Dad interrupts our lighthearted banter, his eyes narrowed like he already knows about our adventure. "Anything out of the ordinary happen while we were away?"

I take a sip before answering.

"Nope. It's been quiet. Right, Ando?"

Not knowing what to say, my brother looks at Dad, then at me, then back to Dad.

"Uh huh," he mumbles, and then takes another bite before he is cross-examined.

Our mother gets that same omniscient expression.

"Are you sure?" she grills as she removes her cardigan in the warm room.

We both nod.

"You really want to stick to that story?" she queries.

Then Mom taps her heeled foot as we all stand around the kitchen island, all except Ando, who is sitting on a dining stool.

"We watched tv," Ando advises after swallowing.

Shaking his head, Dad pulls out his smartphone and hits an app.

"What's that?" Ando questions as a picture loads on the small screen of the device.

Our father frowns as he looks at the screen then hands the smartphone to his wife who looks at it with an unamused glare.

"What are you looking at?" Ando and I both ask in unison.

"Footage," Mom and Dad also answer as one.

"Footage of what?" I begin, turning to my brother who sets his last bite of the panino on the paper it was wrapped in.

Our parents look at each other, then at us.

"You were home all evening?" Dad speaks first.

This time, Ando and I pause a little longer than we should have. Before we can figure out what to say next, our mother growls loudly.

"Did you two know that this villa has a security system?" Mom educates.

Great!

"Why did you leave the villa?" our father grumbles, reviewing the action on the screen.

"And why does Ando look like he's been drinking?" Dad continues.

Knowing it will be worse if I continue lying, I confess to everything.

"He was sleepwalking… I think," I inform, feeling sick to my stomach.

"You think?" Mom replies sarcastically and who could blame her.

Everything rushes past my lips. How we were watching Italian soap operas… Ando dashing out into the street… me unable to find my phone… the charming cottage in the cypress grove… even the short, plump being whom claims to be Melpomene the Muse.

Breathe!

"And that's what happened," I ramble feeling suddenly dizzy. "It all happened so fast."

Mom and Dad glance at each other, both frowning and speechless for a brief moment.

"Repeat what you just said," my stepdad requests. "Only slower… much, much slower."

So I do.

I explain everything that occurred from the moment Ando fell asleep on the sofa beside me up to the instant they started their formal interrogation. Every single detail is revealed until my brain feels completely and utterly empty.

"I see," is Dad's only response.

My mother simply presses her fingertips to her throbbing temples as if trying to subdue an oncoming migraine or perhaps easing one that has already arrived.

Whatever the case, she looks extremely tired and concerned.

Abruptly, my brother speaks.

"She gave me this," he informs as he reaches inside of his shirt to reveal a thin leather-strap necklace with a smooth rounded multicolored stone that acts as a charm. "Isn't it cool?"

"What is it for?" I interrogate, examining the necklace.

"Melody says it will protect me from any supernatural spells," he beams. "And it will keep the nightmares away."

We all stand speechless until David breaks our silence.

"How do we really know who this thing is?" Dad wonders aloud.

I agree but say nothing.

Mom speaks, at last.

"Get your coats," she orders. "We're going to make an unexpected visit."

Just as before, the home of *'the Muse'* appears before our eyes as all four of us stand speechless in the cypress grove outside of town. Only the sound of a hooting owl and something slithering along the leaf-littered ground makes any noise. In fact, it is so quiet that I can hear my stomach digesting.

Before anyone can comment on my loud digestive processes, David breaks the silence.

"Marina," he whispers, his eyes glued on the door of the neatly-kept cottage. "This can't be a good idea."

"It is," his wife responds as she tries to peer inside the large front window, but inside is too dark to make anything out. "Stop worrying so much."

"Suppose its Amphitrite in disguise or… or something *else*," Dad groans.

Ando holds my hand but stays silent.

"I don't think it's Amphitrite," I interject into my parent's tense banter.

"Why?" Mom asks, now on her tiptoes.

I think for a few seconds.

"When Amphitrite is near, I get *'signals'*," I confide, hoping to be of some help.

Slowly, Dad turns to me.

"What sort of signals?" he questions, staring at me queerly.

"The hairs on my arms stand on end and my chest tightens," I confess under my breath.

"Does the same sensation happen when you are with *'the Muse'*?" my stepfather adds.

"No, it doesn't," I state flatly, curious to why it does not. "Actually, now that I think of it, I feel safe and inspired when I am near her."

A genuine smile spreads across my brother's face then at last, he speaks.

"I'm not afraid of her," Ando admits without hesitation. "She's nice."

"Ando," I nudge his elbow. "Be quiet. She'll hear you."

He pouts then rudely sticks his tongue out at me.

"I trust her."

"Ando!" Dad snaps quietly. "Please… *Shh!*"

Obviously irritated, my brother folds his arms across his chest and becomes still once more. He looks at me then at Mom then at Dad. All the while, I can see the gears inside of his mind turning.

"Get outta my head, Lena," he mumbles, giving me an intense stare.

"I can't help it," I acknowledge unable to control my abilities.

"Quiet you two," Mom orders, her facial expression stern.

207

Suddenly, the cottage door swings open, and the attractive older woman steps out onto the front stoop. She is wearing a fluffy terry-cloth robe, her long, silky hair wound up in a loose bun, eyes shining under the pale moonlight, smile bright as the day.

"What took you so long?" she states with a large grin. "Come in! I have been waiting for you!"

CHAPTER SIXTEEN

Inside is just as lovely as before: quaint, clean, and cozy with a hint of mint and warm chocolate lingering in the air. The kitchen window is propped open and gives a welcoming view of the spectacular garden. Even our parents are impressed with the manicured rows of fruits, vegetables and flowers bathed in pale moonbeams.

"More tea, dear?" our host asks as she stands beside Dad with a steaming kettle.

He smiles then shakes his head.

"No thank you," he states warmly, cheeks rosy.

Gracefully, she returns the kettle to the warming tray on the coffee table then picks up the serving tray resting beside it.

"Perhaps another almond biscotto?" she tempts, holding the silver tray towards him, neatly stacked with the freshly baked delicacies.

David beams, eyes sparkling.

"I'm full... truly," he beams, patting his nonexistent belly.

Gently, she returns the tray and turns her attention to my mother.

"It has been a long time, Marina," the grandmotherly lady chuckles. "The last time I saw you was the night you scared the daylights out of Tiberius."

She laughs wholeheartedly, making us all giggle too. All except my mother who has not taken her eyes off of the mysterious stranger since we arrived. Something tells me we are in for an interesting conversation.

"So you're supposed to be Melpomene," Mom snarls, eyes narrowed, the talons on her right hand extended to two-inches in length. They are sharp, deadly and ready for battle.

Unaffected by the obvious show of predaciousness, the woman smiles pleasantly.

"Call me Melody," she instructs. "Melpomene is so... antiquated."

Melody winks in Ando's direction.

"Little Ando suggested the name for me and I definitely have grown fond of it," she speaks the words and they sound like wind chimes dancing on a gentle breeze.

"Okay, *Melody*," Mom winces. "Who are you and what do you want? We have had our fill of evil creatures trying to harm us. I have no tolerance left for these sick games."

"Marina," the being comforts. "I will not harm you or your loved ones. After all… " she pauses looking at each of us, "…they are my family too."

"I don't believe you," Mom challenges, slowly rising from the floral-print sofa.

Melody stays where she is, seemingly oblivious to Mom's show of aggression.

"Who the hell are you?" Mom probes again, but this time slower and with more emphasis.

The woman smooths the soft material of her robe before she speaks.

"You know who I am," Melody's voice is unwavering and confident.

My mother continues staring as she folds her arms across her chest boldly.

"My grandmother died before I was born," she hisses.

"That was a rumor," Melody insists, shaking her head.

"Prove that you are who you say you are," Mom dares with a smug look on her lovely face.

The other woman clears her throat, a family trait perhaps.

"What would you like to know?" Melody smiles as if she is going to take a test, a test that only she knows the answers to.

Mom's eyes narrow. Her fists clench. Her right foot begins to tap an agitated beat against the hardwood floor.

This is not good! Not good at all!

It reminds me of the shows on cable, specifically the science documentaries about sharks. All of the 'experts' want to chum the water with buckets of bloody fish guts then wonder why the sharks begin to attack anything that moves, including each other. This is what I think might happen. Mom, in her agitated state, might strike out and instead of biting Melody, might bite one of us instead. I do not think there is a Band-Aid big enough or a bottle of mercurochrome large enough to heal that wound. Might as well roll over and get ready to meet your maker.

Finally, she speaks.

"Tell me about Akheloios."

Surprisingly, Melody smiles even brighter than she did before.

"Your grandfather was an amazing man, correction, god," she coos with a glimmer in her spectacular eyes. "God of all bodies of fresh water, back then at least, before the rebellion on Mt. Olympus happened."

As we watch her intently, her irises change from dark brown to blue to green, finally stopping at a warm amber hue. It is a subtle change that you will miss if you blink. One minute they are one color, then *poof,* they are another.

"He was my soulmate," she reveals as her smile fades to a frown. "I never knew what love was until him—"

"Describe him," my mother interrupts, interested about hearing about the man who stole the heart of a muse... if she actually is a muse. "The aunts seldom speak of him."

"Tell us about him," Ando chimes.

She chuckles, the sound airy and light like puffs of newly spun cotton candy.

"Alright," Melody says in a haze. "Let me see. Where shall I begin?"

"From the beginning," Dad interjects with a broad grin.

"Very well," she purrs, gently touching his hand, a strange expression comes over him and he abruptly reaches into his front shirt pocket retrieving a petite notepad that he always carries in case an unsuspecting idea creeps over him. Rapidly, he scribbles like he is afraid the notion will escape before he can document it.

He is such a nerd.

"When did you meet him?" I question, eager to know more about my family's unconventional past.

Slowly, Melody takes a seat beside David.

"I was a mere lass when I first set eyes upon him," she giggles girlishly. "Only a few thousand years old; a young woman for all intents and purposes, naive to the ways of the world."

Melody's cheeks redden like a blushing bride.

"Where did you meet?" Mom drills, memorizing her answers.

"We met in Greece on the banks of the Achelous River," Melody answers without falter. My mother appears to ponder the response, and I can imagine her mentally checking it off of her unseen list. I wonder if Melody gives the wrong answer, will Mom rip her to shreds right here and now? I hope she gives her a head start. It would be a shame to ruin such an expensive rug.

What in the world? That was a rather callous and disturbing thought!

Pushing the morbid idea aside, I continue listening to Melody's replies.

"What was he doing there?" Dad's interest increases as he returns the small notepad to his front pocket.

"Was it love at first sight?" I swoon at the thought of Andrew the first time I saw him in the front office at school wearing his uniform, backpack flung carelessly over one muscular shoulder. It seems so long ago, but it was less than a year.

The muse snickers and blushes then heartily laughs as she recalls the events of their meeting.

"It was definitely *not* love at first sight," she informs good-naturedly.

My eyes widen with disbelief.

"Really?" I question with surprise.

Melody nods as she touches both palms to her heated cheeks. This action must have softened my mother's repose because she retracts her intimidating talons back to their original hiding place beneath her skin. This act I take as a good omen.

"It was more like exasperation at first sight," the Muse smirks. "Your great-grandfather was a stubborn man. Seldom admitted when he was wrong and was relentless in getting what he wanted."

With a glimmer in her eyes, she glances at my brother who is busy dipping his third biscotto into a teacup of rich, milky tea. He looks up when the rooms grows quiet, his expression one of pure embarrassment. It is classic Ando.

"Much like a certain young man I know."

Ando grins awkwardly but continues his ritual of dipping then sucking the drenched cookie until it dissolves in his mouth.

"Why did he exasperate you?" my brother tries sounding out the long word and gets it right on the first attempt.

The woman's gaze lingers on the piano in the corner, all the while, grinning.

"He was trying to compose a song, but could not get further than the first line," she recounts.

"He was a composer?" Mom questions, finding her voice again.

Melody laughs and this time accidentally touches David's hand. Almost immediately, my stepfather retrieves the notebook again and begins to jot more ideas down. We all look at him curiously, all except Melody, who simply nods approvingly.

"He was attempting to be a composer," Melody reveals. "As memory serves, he was doing a poor job of it."

"Did you inspire him?" Dad asks, looking up from his task, his attention temporarily distracted.

Melody chuckles, the sound like jingle bells used during the holidays.

"I certainly tried," she replies with a saucy wink.

Somehow, I feel tingly all over. Nothing like when my arm hairs stand at attention if danger is close, but like all of my cells are electrified. It only happens when I am here, with her; the strange, yet charismatic woman, a *Muse*, who makes everything seem more vivid... more in tune.

"I met him every day for an entire month before he was able to finish the song," Melody informs, tapping her right foot just like Mom... just like me.

Without warning, she sputters a full-on belly laugh.

"Weeks later, I realized he was pretending so we could spend as much time together as possible."

"Did he know you were a Muse?" Mom quizzes with suspicious eyes.

"No," the woman blurts. "Not at first."

"How did he find out?" Ando enthusiastically questions.

"All supernatural beings have a *'force'* inside of them, and more often than not, other supernatural creatures are drawn to that force," she tutors proficiently. "It is similar to a homing beacon for lack of a better term."

It is this comment that tugs at my interest.

"All supernatural creatures have this?" I ask, tensely.

"Yes," she confirms with a nod. "They most definitely do."

I do not know why, but a disturbing shiver, not from cold since outside is a comfortable seventy-eight degrees with a soft breeze wafting in from the sea, but from another more disconcerting thought. Maybe this is why strange things keep coming after me. Perhaps since my Siren genes have clawed their way to the surface invading my once normal life, I will be forever cursed to be pursued by evil, nasty, ancient *'things'*.

My stomach does a lurch that nearly brings up its entire contents.

Unsure if Mom or Ando has heard my quandary, I try to think of other things. Anything else, including, but not limited to, the National Anthem and the soundtrack of *The Rocky Horror Picture Show*. It seems to be working because no one has given me *'the look'*.

Every teen knows *'the look'*. It is universally translated to: *'If you say another word or roll your eyes at me again… be prepared!'* Unfortunately, I have been on the receiving end of *'the look'* on one too many occasions with both Mom and Dad, and most recently the aunts. For example, I stumble into *'the look'* when I forget my parents are in close proximity and I inadvertently say *'damn'*, or worse. On other occasions, I know I am going to get *'the look'* when I *'accidentally'* (on purpose) push my brother out of the way when he is moving too slowly. It is not my fault that I cannot help the clever trappings of doing something wrong in order to earn *'the look'*. Getting into trouble draws me in like a fish to a shiny lure.

Shaking the idea out of my brain, I return to the ongoing conversation of which I have missed much during my inner monologue. Realizing this, I focus all of my concentration on Mom's next question.

"So, eventually, you fell in love?" Mom glares at the Muse.

The woman nods.

"What did he look like?" I wonder out loud, curious to what a river-god looks like.

Melody gets another faraway gaze.

"He was rather tall, six feet four, as a matter-of-fact," the Muse recounts with a bright smile. "And quite a handsome specimen, if I do say so myself, with eyes as black as midnight and hair even darker, with a smooth olive complexion."

"He sounds dreamy," I sigh, loving Melody's description, my heart longing for Andrew.

"Sounds wonderful," my mother states sarcastically, bursting Melody's bubble. "Tell us something only you and the aunts would know... something important."

Clearing her throat, Melody answers.

"He had a scar on his right cheek that he got from a swordfight with Ares, the God of War."

"Oh no!" Ando and I both gasp.

"Why did Ares want to kill him?" Dad bellows in shock.

Melody only shrugs.

"A dispute over a woman probably," she states passively. "Your great-grandfather was a lover not a fighter."

"Was he badly hurt?" Mom inquires, still unsure of what to think about the woman in front of us.

"Do not despair," the Muse reassures. "His mark did not detract from his appearance. It actually healed to the exact contour of his cheek and if you did not know of its existence, you would never even notice it."

Relieved, I let out a held breath.

"Whew!" I sigh. "That's good."

Mom's right foot begins to tap a staccato once more.

"Tell me something else... anything that only the aunts would know," my mother states firmly. "I need something more important that can be verified."

Melody thinks for a brief moment like she is going through a file cabinet located in her mind. I can tell she is honestly searching for something... *anything*... that can prove her identity. Suddenly, I feel sorry for her.

"At one time, Poseidon was completely enamored with me," she pauses. "And in case you are wondering, no, I did not encourage him on that matter."

My mouth hangs open.

"Poseidon... Ruler of the Oceans?" I interrogate with unadulterated surprise. "Was in love with *you*?"

"I am not boasting, but I was quite a heartbreaker back in those days," Melody blushes.

Dad smiles mischievously.

"You still are," he blushes too, his expression making Mom slap his shoulder.

"Thank you," she coos like a dove as she strikes a playful pose. "When Poseidon found out about our love, he had a powerful oracle curse us. That curse is what has kept us apart for millennia."

Mom's face beams. At last, she appears to be convinced.

(Mostly).

The Muse gives a warm smile that if possible, could be compared to rumors of *Helen of Troy*, whose beauty was said to have launched a thousand ships. Well, in my opinion, Melody's loveliness could bring all of those ships back home again with a few extra in tow.

"Ask them about it," Melody encourages. "They were only two years old when it happened, but it was an event they could never forget. Especially since Sirens never forget."

"I didn't know that fact," I blurt, glad that another detail about our kind is revealed.

Melody nods with pride.

"They are the only ones, besides me, who know the truth," she states flatly, clearly disturbed by the memory.

Stiffly, Mom stands and begins to herd us like sheep.

"We have to be going," she insists, without making eye contact with our host.

"So soon?" Dad, Ando, and I all whine.

"Yes, right now," Mom orders firmly. "I have to verify this with Ligeia and Leukosia."

My probable relative's features sadden.

"I was hoping you would stay for breakfast," the Muse entices. "The sun will be up soon. I would love the company. I am ashamed to say that I have been alone for far too long."

Mom shakes her head, but still holds fast to her determination to communicate with the aunts about this urgent piece of information.

"I'm sorry, but we really must go... right now," my mother repeats, clearly frazzled from the news.

"Are you alright, Marina?" Melody asks, sincerely concerned over my mother's haste to verify her words.

"Yes!" my mother snaps.

We all stare at her as she glances around, making sure she is not leaving anything or anyone behind.

"The aunts will want to know about all of *'this'*," Mom waves her arms toward the Muse reminding me of those funny-looking, inflatable characters that you see a lot at car dealerships.

"I want to stay," Ando pouts, still clenching a half-eaten biscotto in his right hand.

"Kids, say goodbye," Mom instructs, ignoring her son's plea.

The sweet older woman turns in the direction of the small, yet functional kitchen.

"I have eggs, peppered bacon, and spicy sausages," Melody also seems to be ignoring Mom's rush to leave. "There is also fruit we can pick from the garden. I even have a large jug of cold goat milk from—"

"Thanks, but no thanks!" Mom exclaims in a hurry.

"But Marina—" Melody reaches toward her, but Mom avoids her hand.

"Don't touch me!" my mother barks, motioning at the lady's hands. "I've been studying you."

My mother's talons reemerge, longer and sharper.

"Your power is in your touch," Mom announces loudly.

"I cannot control it," the Muse admits. "I am a Muse. Just as you are a Siren. You must understand."

"I do understand… you're a witch… a mindbender," my mother accuses vehemently, startling us.

Melody gasps and my heart begins to ache for her… for me… for all of us.

"I am *not* a mindbender!" she exclaims, her voice full of disgust. "As a Muse, I have the power of empathy. I can sense people's emotions, but I certainly cannot bend them to my will."

The tension is growing within the walls of the small cottage, yet we are all stuck. It is as if we are being held in this place with supernatural super glue.

"What's a mindbender?" Ando inquires before I can.

"Not now, Fernando," Mom huffs with a roll of her eyes.

"Please… stay," the woman who may or may not be my long-lost great-grandmother pleads.

"If what you profess is true—" Mom maneuvers us toward the exit, "—we'll be in touch soon."

"And if it is not?" Melody queries already knowing the answer.

"If it is not, the next time I see you, I'll kill you without hesitation," Mom coldly educates without care.

Hearing those words, the Muse clasps her hands.

"Fair enough," she accepts Mom's consequence without further debate.

Tripping over our own feet, my mother gets us outside. I turn to say goodbye, but the cottage is no longer there. All that remains is the thickly-grown cypress grove and an onlooking bird of prey. Upset at my mother's behavior, my stomach lurches.

"Where is the cottage?" Dad pouts as he turns around in a circle similar to a dog chasing its own tail. "It was here a second ago."

"C'mon," Mom orders taking Ando's hand. "Let's get out of here. I need to talk to the aunts!"

CHAPTER SEVENTEEN

For the last several hours, my mother has been trying to contact the aunts, who, as usual, are not responding. I have also tried calling them with no luck. No one is sure what to do next.

"Maybe we should go back to Isla Flora," Dad declares as he sits on the grayish-blue sofa beside Ando's sleeping form; his body curled-up into a ball with his teddy bear, Alfredo, tucked under his chin.

"We can't!" Mom barks, causing me to jump, the calming effects of being around Melody the Muse, my probable great-grandmother and matriarch of our Siren line obviously wearing off. Unfortunately, with Melody not around to suppress my mother's hot temperament, David and I are unsheltered from Hurricane Marina.

Slightly afraid, Dad stares at her, a worried expression across his handsome features.

"Why not?" he asks after a moment of silence.

"Because… because," Mom tries to explain, but can only say: "Just because, alright?"

"No, Marina," Dad's voice becomes stern. "Our children are in danger here! Things are trying to harm them! This woman, Melody, claims to be your grandmother... correction, a Muse you believed died hundreds of years ago."

"It won't matter if we go home or not," Mom reveals with a teary-eyed glance.

"What do you mean by that?" I butt-in.

Silence.

"Explain," her husband interjects. *"Please!"*

For as long as I can remember, David's sentences become more abrupt and to the point the more agitated he is. Right now, he must be at the end of his rope. That is never a good sign since Mom's temper tends to flare when my stepfather is in this heightened mode. Ando and I have learned to make ourselves scarce during times like these. Unfortunately, we are in no position to run and hide, and besides that, our parents might need referees.

Mom finally concedes and says:

"One of the reasons why we had to come here this summer..."

"Yeah?" both Dad and I respond.

Mom pauses again, her eyes darting to the windows, but her gaze is locked on the horizon.

"There's more," she sighs sadly. "Much, much, more."

Mom looks at her husband before continuing.

"I told you about *The Calling*."

Dad nods, acknowledging that she has.

"But I didn't tell you or Selena," she mumbles, turning to me next, "why it's important for her to be here this particular year... her sixteenth year."

"Well, that certainly sounds ominous," I grumble under my breath, feeling like I am suffocating under many layers of fleece blankets.

My stepfather sits straighter, his brow furrowed.

"What is the importance of being in Capri for her sixteenth year?" he quizzes suspiciously, but my mother remains silent. Her hands are moving at her sides as if they have a mind of their own. All of this is just making my stomach hurt more.

"Out with it, Mom!" I interject, more than a little perturbed at her and this awful sounding news.

Finally, she sits on the loveseat, clasps her hands in her lap, takes a soothing breath and begins.

This cannot possibly be good.

"There is a reason why I lived on land for the first part of my life," she explains with a wry smile

"What is the reason, Marina?" David probes impatiently, his stare fixed on his fidgety wife.

"Siren DNA is very similar to human DNA for the first sixteen years of life," Mom seems to be choosing her words carefully. "During their early years, they only have lungs; their gills don't usually develop until sixteen. Also, their webbing lays dormant during that time as well and they can only consume cooked food—"

"Ando has gills," I remind, glancing at my sleeping sibling.

Mom smiles.

"Your brother has always been special," she reminds. "And, after all, he is the first and only male Siren. Who knows how his abilities will develop."

"So in other words," Dad interrupts. "For the first part of their life they are essentially human beings."

"Exactly," my mother answers with a frown.

"That's why when I was born you had to leave the sea," I add, following along as best as I can in my weary state.

"Yes," Mom acknowledges. "You were essentially a human infant and couldn't survive in the sea."

"And you were the same?" Dad interjects.

She nods, giving him another smile.

"I was," Mom replies, biting her bottom lip, another one of her *tells* that something is amiss. According to my observation, Sirens would make awful card players; they have absolutely no poker faces.

"That doesn't sound scary," I laugh, feeling my anxiety draining. Mom frowns and looks back outside at the setting sun; the horizon is filled with streaks of plums, golds, and cobalt, with just a splash of burgundy.

"There's something you're not telling us," Dad accuses as he studies his wife's mannerisms. Mom inhales deeply as she tries to figure out her next statement. David and I stare at her in silence, processing what was said.

"Without, '*Ta nerá tou Spilaíou tis Seirínas—*'"

"What the heck does that mean?" I blurt, wishing I was more fluent in Greek which is the language Mom reverts to when she is under high levels of stress.

"It means, '*The Waters of the Siren Grotto,*'" Mom clarifies.

"The Siren Grotto?" I gasp, remembering what Amphitrite said. "Amphitrite wanted me to tell her where the location of the Siren Grotto is!"

Mom's face reddens with rage.

"She knows about *Ta nerá tou*... sorry, the Siren Grotto?" Mom snarls through her question.

I nod swallowing hard.

"What's so important about the waters of the Siren Grotto?" Dad questions needing clarification.

Suddenly, my mother stands, her hands still clasped. She mumbles something in Siren that I do not understand as she now starts to pace the meticulously kept tiled floor.

A bead of perspiration appears over her brow as I watch her anxious movements and her worry-lined features.

"Mom," I whisper, breaking her silent rant. "I need you to tell me what is so important about my sixteenth year."

"Marina," Dad speaks, his accent soft and soothing like he is comforting a wounded animal. "We can't help if we don't know what we are dealing with."

"I can handle whatever it is," I say confidently, even though I feel my chest tightening.

Mom comes towards me but stops when she is arm's length away. She smiles, but unfortunately, it never reaches her eyes. Since there was nothing necessarily bad said before, I brace myself for what is to come next, and sure enough, the worst thing happens: Mom sighs twice in a row.

Oh no!

I am learning that horrible information is always delivered after one of my mother's patented double sighs. Hopefully, this is not a family trait.

"If a young Siren stays on land too long," she pauses, swallowing hard. "They *may* become completely human."

Huh? This is news to me!

"How exactly?" Dad probes; glancing at her and then me.

I can tell that his scientific curiosity is getting the better of him. Ever since I can remember, David has been fascinated with the unknown. Unlike me, he feels right at home in the middle of chaos. I suppose that is why he loves and accepts the 'unique' family that he has been given.

Needing to unburden herself, Mom is compelled to continue this revealing piece of information.

"Their gills are dissolved into the body, like they'd never existed at all. The same happens with their scales. There would be no need for heightened senses or the talent to manipulate bodies of water. Even the ability to communicate with sea life would not develop, and they would lose the gift of song."

"In other words," I whisper. "I would be normal?"

"In theory," my mother frowns. "There has never been a Siren to abdicate her calling."

"But there's a chance," I smirk, finding this fact comforting.

"That is correct," she whispers back.

"I could live with that," I admit, feeling an enormous weight being lifted from my chest. The idea of living the remainder of my life as a regular, no-frills human female delights me; thrilling me beyond belief and I find it difficult not to grin like a village idiot.

Mom gives another heavy sigh as she contemplates finishing her educational lecture. Knowing her well, I know that if she begins to twirl her hair in conjunction with pacing or tapping her right foot, well, let us say that the world that we know it is about to end. My eyes are glued to her. In fact, unbeknownst to me, I have been holding my breath and am totally surprised when my gills activate without my permission. It does not hurt or anything, it just catches me off-guard.

Both of my parents see this, but do not react.

Dad just mouths: *Put those away, please.*

I do; proud that I have more control over the errant organ.

Mom clears her throat to get my attention.

"On the other hand, if a Siren stays in the sea too long, it becomes more primal, more animalistic... crueler," she almost cringes at her own statement.

Her revelation makes me shudder as well. David on the other hand wears the most unusual expression. I cannot tell if he is mortified or elated. I decide that it is probably wiser not to analyze him for fear I might not like the answer.

"Even our skin and organs become tougher, more efficient, more impervious to external damage," Mom gives examples like a good teacher would as she takes a deep breath. "We become more like the stalagmite sediments that flow through our veins."

"That's what you meant by: *'the sea makes our heart cold'*," I reply. "It *literally* hardens us."

"The aunts are a perfect example of this," she carries on. "The longer they are with us physically, they show more human characteristics. They laugh more. They cry. They feel compassion, sympathy and love."

"They also get annoyed and pouty when you 'accidentally' eat all of the Doritos," I grumble, recalling their near fit when the bag was found empty. I tried to explain that you cannot just eat one of the addictive chips, but were they sympathetic to the snack food's hold over me?

No! They most certainly were not!

On the other hand, when Ando devoured almost an entire box of *Hostess Twinkies*, did the aunts practically disown him?

No! They most certainly did not!

The only reason I can think that they overlooked his crime was due to his age and cuteness factor. Not to mention that he has a special place in their hearts since he is the first and only male Siren. Hence another way my brother leads a charmed life.

Am I jealous? Not really. I just hope he realizes how easy he has it.

Mom studies me with an amused grin, silently telling me that my thoughts have invaded her mind and that I should have been more willing to share the last of the *Doritos* with the aunts. However, Ligeia and Leukosia crossed the line when they gave me the silent treatment for such a long period of time.

Thankfully, she does not address 'the brother' issue.

'Selena, please pay attention,' I hear Mom's voice in my head. *'This is important.'*

I nod my acknowledgement and focus once more.

"Did you hear what I just said?" Mom questions aloud with a wry little smile.

Blushing, I nod again; hoping *my* cuteness still lingers.

Mom giggles.

Whew! I still got it!

Almost instantly, my mother regains her composure.

"As I was saying—"

"But when they are alone in the sea they lose those traits," I finish her thought.

"That is correct," Mom acknowledges.

"You still haven't clarified about the significance of the Siren Grotto's water," Dad reminds. My mother instinctively reaches up and takes several strands of her curly tresses between her fingers and immediately begins to twirl.

Crap!

Then her right foot starts tapping away reminding me of a nervous rabbit.

Crap! Crap! Crap!

"In order to keep balanced, a Siren needs to recharge, so to speak, in the minerals and high concentration of volcanic ash that only exist in the grotto. It is why *The Calling* brings us back here, to where our line began, so that we can seamlessly move between both worlds."

Mom takes a much-needed breath.

"It would be dangerous to walk on land without human emotions. We'd hurt or possibly even kill someone... most likely on purpose. We would be a threat to everyone we'd meet. Love would become obsession. Anger would become rage. Dislike would become—"

"Hatred," I murmur, recalling my strong dislike of Amy Jacobs. To this, my mother slowly nods.

"Yes, hatred," she finally speaks bluntly. "If a young Siren doesn't return to these waters, you could lose every shred of your humanity... it could drive you so completely mad that you could even turn on everyone you care about, even us."

Dad gives a low whistle.

Completely overwhelmed with everything, my mind starts to race. My pulse quickens. My palms begin to sweat. It does not take long for dizziness to set in.

"Why does Amphitrite want to know the location of the Siren Grotto?" I nervously query.

Mom shrugs.

"Probably for the effects that its waters give," she narrows her eyes. "Most likely, it would make her nearly invincible."

My stepdad, however, is still mulling over Mom's description of the Siren Grotto.

"Fascinating," he remarks in his analytical mode.

Mom frowns as Dad continues.

"The minerals and other sediment in the water contained in the grotto keeps Ph-levels stable in your kind," he thinks out loud. "I'd love to get a sample of it."

He gets a dreamy look in his eyes as his mind magically transports him to the mysterious Siren Grotto where mythological Sirens were raised away from the prying eyes of mankind.

"You can't!" Mom informs rather aggressively, catching us off guard.

"Why not?" we both ask stunned at her unyielding tone.

Mom turns her back on us, but she forgets to guard her thoughts from me, and I inadvertently hear.

"Because the concentrations are so strong," I divulge, unable to stop. "It would kill anyone who doesn't have our genes."

She pauses again.

"It almost killed me," Mom admits on a shaky exhale.

"What?!" David exclaims, shocked at his wife's admission.

The words hover over me like a thick, stifling fog.

"What do you mean?" I whisper. "You almost d-died?"

Mom turns back around revealing her tear-stained cheeks and red-rimmed eyes.

"I was sick for almost a month," she fearfully tells. "I couldn't hold down food, a relentless fever took hold, and I had terrifying hallucinations that made me actually pray for death. If it weren't for my mother and the aunts giving me small doses of their venom every day, I would have died."

"Humans would definitely die," I groan like I am in pain.

She nods again.

"But you're not human," she reminds. "You are so much stronger."

No matter what she says, the doubt has taken root and begins to grow.

"I could *die*?" I stumble over the realization.

"Selena," she adds. "You are *pure* Siren."

Slowly, I shake my head.

"No," I whisper. "I come from your hybrid cells. I'm not like the aunts and I'm not like you… I'm something *else*."

The silence around us becomes palpable and I wish I could escape.

"Red Tide," she inadvertently blurts, wiping her tears with the back of one hand.

Dad and I look at her quizzically.

"Red Tide?" Dad repeats. "Why did you say that?"

"Did I?" she counters as if she had said it by accident.

"What is the significance of Red Tide, my love?"

"What is it exactly?" I read about it once in Earth Space Science, but do not remember the explanation. Putting on his scientist-hat (so to speak) Dad clears his throat before explaining:

"The term *'Red Tide'* is a common reference for an occurrence recognized as an algal bloom, which is caused by several species of dinoflagellates by which the bloom appears as either red or brown in color."

Mom and I both cock our heads in confusion as the very technical explanation flies over our heads, past the Earth's atmosphere and out into the vastness of outer space.

"English, please, David," Mom winces up her mouth as if she has bitten into a thick slice of lemon peel.

Dad rolls his eyes at us.

"In simplest terms, it is a discoloration of seawater made by a bloom of poisonous red dinoflagellates; the majority is marine plankton, but they are extremely common in freshwater habitats too."

"Oh!" I exclaim, finally understanding.

Mom nods at her very intelligent spouse.

"Sometimes the sediment from the Siren Grotto—which is often misdiagnosed as *Red Tide* by scientists—seeps into the oceans and is carried by the currents across the globe. It is so strong that it can kill fish and, in some instances, people also," she adds to the already ominous explanation.

"Crazy, but still... *fascinating*," Dad kisses her cheek as he compliments.

Mom shakes her head at her husband.

"David, stop saying that," she replies, gently slapping his shoulder. Even such a light tap makes him cringe with pain.

"Saying... what?" he laughs, trying to lift the mood.

"'*Fascinating*,'" she mocks with her best impersonation, which being a Siren, sounds exactly like him in every way.

"I'm sorry Marina," he chuckles. "But with Sirens there are always consequences. If I didn't view it as *fascinating*, I would have made *'a run for the border'* a long time ago."

Well... there you have it.

Becoming human...

Reverting to a cold-hearted fish...

Or possibly death.

Not great choices...

Lately, I have been dreaming about Andrew... *a lot!* Nothing disturbing, thank heavens, just about him in general. Mostly I dream about what he is doing in Isla Flora; if he is safe... if he is happy even though I am not there. For some reason, I always experience the dream from his perspective.

Strange!

Tonight, the dream is extremely romantic. We are on the beach at sunset, walking hand in hand, chatting about nothing of importance. It feels so real, so right. Just being a normal teenage girl. That is what I want, to be completely normal.

"Lena!" Ando's voice comes to me in my dream, a dream with lots of kissing with Andrew. "Lena! Wake up!"

My eyes try to focus in the almost pitch-black bedroom as my dream is ripped from my grasp bringing me back to reality.

"Are you awake?" he frowns from the foot of the bed, eyes wide.

"What are you doing in here?" I chastise, glancing at the nightstand clock. "It's not even six in the morning."

"I'm sorry," he apologizes, giving his patented puppy-dog eyes, the look he knows I cannot resist.

"Ugg!" I groan into my pillow as I roll onto my stomach from my left side. "Go back to bed or I'm going to tell Mom."

Ando huffs as he leaps over my legs and lands on the empty side of the queen-sized mattress.

"I can't go back to sleep," he complains, moving around so much that the bed feels like a small boat on a rough sea.

"Why not?" I ask, flopping around in order to find a more comfortable resting place.

There is a long pause.

"I had another dream," he admits at last.

Adjusting the top sheet over my head, I ask, "Did anyone die in it?"

Ando sighs.

"No."

Wanting to get back to my wonderful fantasy, I feel my patience waning as parts of the dream nudges my brain anew. Desperate to fall back asleep, I respond to my brother's dilemma; not caring if he gets upset of not.

"Then go back to your room and try to get some more rest," I order flatly, hoping he will do as he is told. "It's a big day tomorrow. We're going to the museum in Anacapri."

"Lena?" he whispers after a long minute passes.

"For goodness' sake, Ando!" I huff. "I'm tired. If I let you stay in here, will you please try to go back to sleep?"

There is a short pause before he answers.

"Ok... I'll try," he replies, sounding adorable.

"Good boy," I praise, turning onto my back with my eyes closed.

"Lena?"

"What do you want now?" I growl.

"Does the museum have dinosaurs?"

I open my eyes in order to glare at him.

"I don't think so," I huff, warning him that he is about to be scolded.

"Then what are we going to see there?"

I think for a moment, trying to remember the trifold brochure that our parents brought home a few days ago. The information it contained is a little foggy right now, but I concentrate, and it comes back to me. Clearing my throat from the raspy quality of sleep, I tell my brother about the exhibits.

"There's meant to be pottery, paintings, artifacts from a long time ago, and even some treasure that they found on several sunken ships," I rapidly ramble.

I feel the mattress move as Ando settles closer to me, without Alfredo, which surprises me.

"Where's your bear?" I ask as I yawn.

He giggles.

"The dream didn't wake him," he jokes, causing me to smile briefly. "He's still in bed. He was hogging the covers and snoring really loud."

I chuckle at the idea of a teddy bear snoring.

"Stop being cute," I warn with a grin. "Close your eyes."

"Lena?"

I yawn for the second time, wishing I could let slumber take over, but I answer my brother knowing that if I do not, he will simply bother me until I do.

"This is the last question you ask me, okay?"

"Okay," he agrees, snuggling against my side.

"Sirens are magical… right?" Ando questions, sincerely wanting to know the answer.

"Definitely," I answer, getting more tired.

"And muses are magical?" he adds.

"Absolutely," I nod.

"We come from gods and goddesses," he states proudly.

"According to everything I've researched and what the aunts and Mom have told us, we are magic made corporeal," I explain the best that I can with a groggy brain.

Once again, there is a long gap of silence before he continues.

"What does *corporeal* mean?" he asks, his tongue sounding heavily slurred with sleep.

Softly, I chuckle.

"It means in physical form, you know? Something you can touch… something you can feel," I explain slowly.

"Oh!" he whispers as he pulls the covers up to his chin and tucks it around his body like a mummy lying in a sarcophagus. "Lena?"

I growl, poking him in the side with my finger until he snorts and bats my hand away.

"Do I have to lock you in the closet?" I tease, now enjoying our time together.

He giggles.

"No," his voice is low, sleep creeping into it.

I laugh at his good-naturedness and curiosity.

"Please, go to sleep," I beg.

Finally, we both settle down, now thoroughly exhausted. Dawn is quickly approaching; I can hear it in the air and smell it even with the windows closed.

"Goodnight, Ando," I murmur as I close my eyes.

"Goodnight, Lena," he whispers with a yawn. "Sweet dreams."

CHAPTER EIGHTEEN

The next morning starts out like any other. Outside my window, the birds are singing songs of welcome. Down below the rocky cliffs, the surf churns a perfect musical accompaniment. The soft floral-kissed winds rustle the branches, adding yet another layer to the natural ballad. It could not be any better than this.

It is at that moment that I catch the tantalizing aroma of breakfast. My stomach complains loudly that it is time to break the fast. Placing my left hand over the grumbling organ, I try silently reasoning with it, but it only makes it worse. Next, I verbally chastise it, but it gets louder and more defiant.

"Fine, you win," I mumble to myself. "I'm getting up now."

Still sleepy, I roll out of bed, and make my way to the bathroom I share with my brother, who is no longer sleeping with me, but most likely has made his way in the direction of the delicious scent. He always wakes hungry and stays that way until he closes his eyes at night. I can only imagine what he will be like when he hits puberty. Our parents will most likely have to get second jobs in order to feed him.

The thought makes me laugh.

With the growing scent of food permeating the entire hallway, I make haste to the bathroom. Swiftly, I wash my face; brush my teeth and hair then powerwalk toward the source of the yumminess. It takes only a minute to reach the kitchen which is located on the opposite side of the large private villa.

As I enter the kitchen, the first person I see is Mom who is standing watchfully over a large frying pan currently on the stove. The room smells of brewing coffee which normally I enjoy, but today it is giving me a headache. Mom looks up from her task and smiles.

"Mmm," I hum, stepping into the area where the rest of the family has already congregated. "What smells so good?"

Ando greets me first.

"Mom is making pancakes," he hums a little tune of excitement.

"Chocolate chip pancakes to be exact," our mother adds, grabbing a handful of the dark morsels. "Would you like me to make a smiley-face on yours?"

I wince at the thought.

"Mom, I'm almost seventeen," I remind unnecessarily.

She sighs sadly.

"I know, but—"

"If it's my choice, I'll just have pancakes without the face," I interrupt, shaking my head.

Good-naturedly, Mom pouts.

"Still with chocolate chips?" she beams hopefully.

I giggle and nod.

"Of course," I answer with gusto.

"After breakfast, we need to get ready for the trip to Anacapri," Dad reminds, pouring himself a cup of coffee. He does not even bother to add sugar or milk like he usually would. "I've spoken with the curator, Ms. Santori, who is expecting us early."

"Do I have to go?" I query without thinking, still feeling groggy.

Mom and Dad glance at one another with curious expressions.

"I thought you were looking forward to going?" Mom questions with her hand still holding the spatula in mid-flip.

"Yeah," my stepfather interjects. "You were so excited yesterday. What happened?"

I shrug my shoulders as I move toward the refrigerator. My desire for something to drink suddenly overwhelms me, and I imagine that I am a camel who needs to store liquid for a long journey through the desert.

"I don't know," I respond, glancing at my little brother. "I didn't get enough sleep for some odd reason."

Ando looks down at his comic book, filled with guilt.

"You can nap in the car," Dad informs. "But we are all going."

"I'm not a child," I remind, the hairs on my arms standing on end. "I don't understand why it's so important for me to go."

"Because it will be a fun outing for the whole family," Mom injects as she pours another quarter cup measurement of pancake batter onto the hot griddle pan. "And we need a break from all of the craziness going on."

"Why can't I stay here?" I argue.

"Stop arguing with your mother," Dad orders firmly as he sets the table with the everyday dishes.

A sudden sharp pain lances through my temple and I growl then glance at the window, wanting, no, *needing* to be in the sea and away from people. Looking down, I feel another pain, but this time it is coming from beneath my fingernails. I can picture red hot pokers hidden under my epidermis. Somehow, I manage to will it away.

"Are you alright?" Mom questions as she studies my behavior.

"No! I'm not alright!" I snap without warning, causing my family members to jump.

David attempts to approach me, but I step back, widening the gap between us. I stare at him, warning not to come any closer. As I stand there waiting, my skin begins to itch. Just a slight irritation at first then it starts to increase.

"Lena!" my brother shouts. "Your arms!"

Worried, I glance at my arms. Sporadic clusters of scales decorate my limbs. Not very many, but they are brighter and harder than they have ever been in the past.

"What's happening?" I whisper to no one in particular as I plop down on the nearest chair.

From the corner of my right eye, I see Mom wetting a dishtowel in the sink then she grabs the salt shaker and empties half of the container onto the material. Quickly, she rushes over with the damp cloth and places it on one patch of scales. Immediately, they return to their unseen resting place.

"Is that better?" she asks, voice dripping with concern.

"Much better," I reveal, filled with relief.

"What's on that cloth?" David interrogates, wide eyed.

"A little salted water," Mom reveals, giving a tense smile. "Her body is craving the sea, specifically seawater."

"What does this do?" he touches the edge of the towel.

Mom grins.

"It is a quick fix that gets the salt onto the affected areas," she educates like a professional with a doctorate in Siren.

"That feels great," I inform on an exhale.

"Here," Mom says, handing me the small towel embellished with decorative vegetable pictures. "Put it on all of the other spots. They will be gone before you know it."

Appreciatively, I nod and obediently do as I am told.

"I'm so sorry," I whisper to the room in general. "I don't know what came over me."

The guilt over becoming so angry for absolutely no reason batters me and I cannot make eye contact with any of them; especially my stepfather who is currently looking at me with such sympathetic worry. In his dark eyes, I see only his fatherly love for me.

"Please, let me stay home," I beg, not wanting to be around people.

My stepdad opens his mouth to say something, but Mom cuts him off before he can get the words past his lips.

"I'm not leaving you alone, Selena," my mother resolutely announces.

"Why?" I squeak as tears begin to well.

Mom remains silent as she resumes making the golden spheres of goodness.

"I can get some more sleep and I'm sure I'll be in a better mood when you get back from the museum," I say, faking happiness.

Mom glares at me.

"I said… you're going with the family to the museum," she answers gruffly.

"Just tell me why?" I plead unhappily.

"Because you're teetering on the edge of becoming a full-fledge-Siren and if I'm not around to keep you under control, I am afraid you'll do something horrible… something you will not be able to come back from!" she shouts. "Then it won't matter if you complete *the Calling* or not!"

"I can control myself!" I insist, raising my voice as I stand and make my way to the refrigerator.

Silently, I begin debating my reasons for wanting to stay at the villa, but David comes to my mother's defense.

"Enough," Dad's voice gets a tad louder. "This is not a debate, Selena. You're going with us."

Once again, I snap.

"You're not the boss of me!" I shout. "You just like pretending to be my father, but you're not!"

Suddenly filled with rage, I slam the fridge door closed almost breaking it away from the hinges. Fuming with rage, I stomp back to my chair and practically throw my body onto it. Surprisingly, it does not break. The family looks at me like I have lost my mind. I think I might have too.

Mom quickly turns off the burner and steps between David and me. Her face is completely blank and I cannot read her mind, but the chill that suddenly goes down my spine brings me back to my regular self.

"I-I'm sorry," I stammer, feeling like I am an exhibit at a freak show. "I d-don't know what came over me."

Mom and Dad are still staring at me, but Ando does not seem affected. Before I can apologize again, he speaks up.

"It's my fault," Ando confesses to a crime he had nothing to do with. "I woke her up because I had a dream, b-but..."

I stare at him dumbfounded that he would take the blame. He did wake me, but the rest is my fault. I am the one yelling at David and creating a scene. Quite often, I feel sorry that my family has to put up with my crazy, violent mood swings. Sometimes, I wish I could live alone on an island and not have to deal with any of this drama.

"It's not his fault," I state meekly, rebuking his false claim. "I felt happy then all of a sudden... I was so angry."

"How do you feel now?" Dad asks, his coffee cup held between both palms as if they are cold, but the kitchen thermometer shows it is a comfortable seventy-eight degrees.

"I'm better," I admit in a soft voice.

"Are you sure?" Ando questions in a similarly softly spoken tone.

"I honestly feel fine," I say, nodding.

Mom, on the other hand, has not spoken, not one word; she only looks at me with an omniscient gaze.

"I'm really sorry," I state clearly, truthfully. "I promise it won't happen again."

Dad frowns like he does not believe me and so does Mom. My brother gives me another small smile, but he quickly blocks his thoughts. I try to hear what he is thinking, but I keep hitting an invisible barrier as if he has hit the mute button to his brain.

How can he do that?

I have been practicing concealing my thoughts. Not because I am planning to do something unscrupulous. Everyone needs privacy. It is difficult to have that as a Siren.

Suddenly, I start to feel inadequate which does not help my current mood.

"It will not happen again," I remind everyone as my mother rests a plate stacked with several steamy golden pancakes topped with a pat of butter and a generous pouring of thick, sweet, maple syrup in front of the seat I currently occupy. Sitting on the plate next to it are two thick slices of peppered bacon.

My tummy growls in admiration, but I cannot eat yet.

"There will not be another outburst today," I promise sincerely.

Dad nods, this time he seems convinced, but he still gives me a warning.

"See that it doesn't young lady," he states, resting a reassuring hand on my shoulder. "See that it doesn't."

We eat breakfast in silence. No one dares even breathe hard for fear that something else might trigger one of my wild outbursts. Needless to say, I wallow in guilt at spouting all of those awful things to Dad during the meal. He could barely look at me after that. Mom only glanced in my direction once with that same all-knowing façade. It was quite unnerving. Ando was the only one not to hold my actions against me. Thank goodness for my understanding sibling. I do not know what I would do without him.

"Okay, you two," Mom announces, loading the dishwasher. "No more dillydallying. Get ready. Dad wants to leave soon."

"You got it, Mommy!" Ando replies as he leaves the table and hands our mother his used dish.

After finishing my meal, I take a quick shower and slip into a pair of jean shorts, an emerald-green, scoop-neck t-shirt with white ankle socks and white sneakers. On a whim, I braid my hair into two and apply a thin layer of coconut flavored lip gloss.

Simple... no-fuss required.

Of course guilt still weighs heavily on me, to the point that I cannot bear the sight of my reflection in the bedroom mirror. Honestly, I cannot fathom why I got so upset, so hurtful... so *Siren*. These outbursts are going to get me either grounded for life or worse. Hopefully, there are no supernatural prisons for mythological creatures that break the law. If they do exist, I am certain they would be unimaginably horrific.

"Selena!" Mom yells from the living room. "Are you ready yet?"

Rolling my eyes for no reason, I yell back.

"I'll be right there! One moment!"

"You're gonna make us late!" Ando's voice joins in from the hallway outside of my closed door.

Dad's deep voice follows.

"We are scheduled for the ten-thirty tour," he reminds in his fatherly way as I hear his heavy footsteps also pass by.

"I said, I'll be there soon! Geez! Keep your pants on!" I add the last part under my breath, not wanting to be in even more trouble than I already am.

Taking more time than necessary, I undo my braids and consolidate them into one.

"Much better," I apprise with a tense grin at my reflection.

I am just about to leave the room when my cellphone unexpectedly rings. Startled by the sound, I pick up on the fourth ring.

"Hey woman!" Nicole's voice comes through choppy, but still audible.

"Hey back!" I giggle, bursting with elation.

"How's Capri?" her tone is light and airy, which automatically uplifts my down-in-the-dumps spirit.

I chuckle before answering.

"It's incredible!" I admit with a smile so wide that it hurts my face. "But I wish I was back on Isla Flora. I miss you guys!"

I really do!

Nicole laughs, making me feel more grounded. More… Me.

"How is everyone?" I query, hoping she will give me an update on the gang before I have to leave for the stupid museum outing with my family.

"They're great!" she informs cheerfully. "Jenny is still in Ireland visiting cousins. Mike is away at football camp this week."

"How's Andrew?" I ask, sheepishly.

There is a brief pause.

"As a matter of fact, he's standing right next to me," she roguishly reveals, her comment makes my pulse race.

Keep it together!

Don't act like a fool!

Stay calm! Be cool!

"He is?" I try to sound nonchalant but fail miserably.

"He was too chicken to call you himself," Nicole blurts impishly, and I can only picture how red Andrew's cheeks must be turning.

"Why?" I grin, already knowing the answer. It is the same reason my face is beet red too.

Nicole snorts loudly.

"He thought you might have met a local hottie and forgotten all about him," she confesses, trying to put both of us on the spot just because she can.

Then I hear Andrew's voice in the background but cannot decipher what he is saying. The next thing I know, Nicole shouts as he grabs the phone from her. I hear him murmur '*Ouch!*' then there is a brief silence and I wonder if I have lost the signal.

At last, I hear the voice that I have been missing for the past several weeks.

"Hi stranger," Andrew snickers. "How's my favorite Siren?"

I chuckle and blush at the same time.

"I'm fine," I beam, smiling ear to ear like a geek. "How's my favorite teen heartthrob?"

I can actually hear him blushing too.

"I am keeping busy at my mom's office until my dad and I meet up for a few weeks," he states with a positive attitude.

"I see," I chuckle playfully. "What does she have you doing?"

"I archive old articles and keep the office tidy," he reveals matter-of-factly.

"Are you getting paid?" I question, hoping for his sake that he is.

"Yeah, but only minimum wage," he explains.

"Minimum wage is still better than nothing," I remind, wishing that I had a summer job as well.

I could use some spending money. My parents do not believe in giving allowance for completing chores. If you live under their roof, it is your *'job'* to keep it spotless without complaint or payment. Once I tried changing their minds by making a pro/con list, but they only scoffed and made me fold the laundry anyway. That was the last time I mentioned it, fearful they might make me paint the house or some other tedious task.

Another pause comes through the receiver.

"I miss you," he declares as he lowers his voice so only I can hear.

"I miss you too," I beam, disregarding how sappy I must sound.

"When are you coming home?" the teen probes as if he is a detective.

"In a few weeks, hopefully," I reply, elated that he is thinking about me as much as I have been thinking of him.

"Any chance you might come home sooner?" he probes confidently.

I wish!

"I don't think that will happen," I inform, hearing Dad's voice at the door, telling me to hurry.

"Are you having a fun summer?" Andrew questions. "Met anyone... new?"

I grin at the fact that he thinks he has competition for my affection.

"Well," I say cheerfully, "I did meet someone here."

There is a disturbing silence before Andrew says, "Oh! I see."

"Yeah," I respond, trying to keep a straight face. "He's a sweetheart."

"Is that so?" Andrew mumbles flatly, clearly irritated.

"Polite... understanding... caring," I continue teasing, feeling the desire to burst into hysterical laughter at Andrew's tone.

"I'm glad you found someone to keep you occupied," he utters uneasily.

"Do you want to know his name?" I ask, trying not to laugh.

"Not really," he huffs again, obviously at the end of his rope.

"C'mon," I poke playfully. "Don't be like that."

"Fine," he sulks. "What's this dude's name?"

"His name is Fishy," I inform then slap my hand over my mouth so I contain my mirth.

"What kind of name is *'Fishy?'*" he counters, clearly stumped and annoyed.

Unable to control myself any longer, I feel the laughter rush past my lips in a rapid burst.

"The kind of name that you give to a cuttlefish," I bray, followed with several uncontrollable snorts.

He laughs, easing the tension.

"You're playing with me," he pouts again.

"Yes," I admit with another hearty chuckle.

"There's no one else?" he asks for reassurance.

"Not a one," I add, shaking my head.

"Ok," he snorts too. "Make sure it stays that way."

"Do you forgive me?" I question, knowing he will not hold my prank against me. It is not in his nature to be vindictive.

"Maybe," he states impishly to get my goat.

My eyebrows hitch as I now pout.

"Maybe?" I snap. "Why maybe?"

"Bring me a souvenir and I'll think about it," he jokes, keeping me on my toes.

I smile.

"I can do that," I giggle.

"I really do miss you, Selena," he states nervously, but with all sincerity.

At his revelation, I feel my heartbeat increase.

"I really do miss you too," I timidly confess, but this time I do not blush.

There is a loud knock on the door that startles me and I almost trip over the area rug beneath my feet.

"Selena!" David shouts. "Tell Andrew you'll call him back later!"

My mouth opens wide.

"How did you know that I am on the phone with Andrew?" I shout so he can hear me.

"Your mother and brother can hear your thoughts and by the look on their faces, they're about to be sick," Dad chortles at my expense, knowing that piece of information will definitely get me off of the phone.

"I've got to go," I relay. "We're going to a museum."

"Have fun," Andrew responds happily. "Talk soon."

"Of course," I giggle again. "Stay safe."

With a much happier heart, I hang up.

That will be enough to keep me focused. Soon summer vacation will be over, along with *The Calling* and I will be back on Isla Flora where I belong. There I will not have to worry about dangerous beings stalking me. Soon I will be going home.

After hearing Andrew and Nicole, I truly feel at peace.

He misses me!

CHAPTER NINETEEN

The drive to the opposite side of the island is uneventful, yet enjoyable. My parents chat as Dad drives, while Ando and I play thumb-war in the back seat. I let him win a few times so he would not feel sad.

Bored now, Ando taps my knee to get my attention.

"Lena?" he says with a sad face.

"Yeah?" I reply, tearing my thoughts away from the previous night's events.

"Do you think we'll see Melody again?" he queries wistfully, his eyes bright.

I nod reassuringly since I want to see her again also.

When I am near Melody, it is the only time that I feel like my normal self. Most of the time, I feel as if I am trapped in someone else's body, and I cannot get out. I pretend to be happy and many times I am happy, but more often than not I just feel lost. Like a fish out of water.

Pun intended!

"I'm sure we will," I playfully mess-up his hair as he attempts to knock my hand away.

As we continue driving along *Via Giuseppe Orlandi*, Anacapri's main street lined with those now familiar whitewashed homes and a variety of specialty local shops, we arrive at a building so architecturally exceptional amongst its plain-faced island neighbors. Majestically it sits with its deep-red façade. And although it is curiously adorned with marble fragments, it is still pleasing to the eye.

"We're here!" Ando shouts as the large villa-like museum comes into view.

Mom giggles as she unbuckles her seatbelt.

"It's different, isn't it?" she expresses with a smirk. "The first time I saw it, I thought the architect must have lost his senses, but over time it grew on me."

"Wow!" I whisper to myself. "It's *definitely* different."

"This reminds me of something out of Ripley's Believe It Or Not," Dad beams, his tone filled with awe.

"Mommy, you've been here before?" my brother asks, putting back on his sneakers.

Mom looks over the building before answering.

"The last time I visited Anacapri the museum was closed due to renovations," she explains. "It had gotten damaged by several terrible storms, but it looks terrific now."

"Were *'we'* the cause of the terrible storms?" I smirk, wondering how often a Siren is to blame for *'natural disasters.'*

Mom crinkles up her nose good-humoredly.

"Not that time," she winks saucily making us laugh.

"It is magnificent!" I announce, letting my eyes caress the red-colored exterior.

Everyone nods in agreement.

"I feel like I've been here before," I casually state, not understanding why it seems so familiar.

Mom looks at me blankly but says nothing.

"Maybe you remember it from the brochure," Dad offers up a plausible explanation.

"You're probably right," I agree, unable to shake that peculiar feeling of *déjà vu*.

"You're probably picking up on my memory of this place," she announces with confidence.

I smile.

"Good," I add, taking a breath.

"Let's go inside!" Ando grabs Mom's hand then Dad's while I flounder behind. "Hurry, Lena!"

I giggle at how excited he is.

"I'm right behind you," I respond, shaking off my apprehension.

Then quite artfully, Ando changes the subject to his favorite pastime: eating.

"Did you know that there's a snack shop here?" he eagerly mentions. "They have pastries, sandwiches, pasta salads and different kinds of drinks."

"How can you be hungry already?" I tease, still stuffed from breakfast. "We just ate not too long ago."

Ando stares blankly at me.

"You had five pancakes," I remind with a smirk.

He blushes but keeps his happy expression.

"Do you have a tapeworm?" I joke again, but this time I duck just in time to avoid the flying museum brochure that my brother throws at my head. It is a good thing that my reflexes are improving otherwise I would have been clipped. I laugh as it whizzes by my head which only makes my brother more frustrated.

"Stop it you booty-head!" he insults with a glaring stare that makes me want to laugh even more.

"Dog-face!" I sling back mischievously.

"Daddy!" he exclaims defiantly. "Lena called me a dog-face!"

Dad snickers as his son's ulterior motive comes into realization.

"Both of you behave," David chuckles.

Then he turns to Ando.

"You can't possibly be hungry already," my stepfather chastises with a hearty belly laugh.

"We just ate breakfast less than an hour ago," Mom agrees with a grin.

"Can we get something after the tour?" my brother negotiates like a seasoned professional.

"We'll see," David steers the conversation away from food as we step inside the building.

"Welcome, *Senoras y Senores*, to *Casa Rossa*!" the attractive female tour guide greets the assembly of twenty or so museum patrons. "*Buenos dia!* Good day!

"My name is Ariella, and I will be your guide for the duration of the museum tour. Feel free to ask me anything… dealing with the exhibits… of course."

Ando raises his hand.

"Yes, young man," Ariella smiles at my brother. "Question so soon?"

He nods.

"What kinds of stuff do they sell at the snack shop?"

The woman chuckles but looks amused.

"Oh, lots of delicious pastries, paninis, chocolate—"

"Do they have Nutella sandwiches?" he interrupts.

Totally embarrassed, I roll my eyes and hide behind my museum map.

"Ando," I nudge his arm with my elbow. "Quit asking about food."

"I'm hungry," he whispers, not deterred in the least.

Ariella thinks then responds.

"They do not have Nutella sandwiches."

"Aww man," he sighs disappointed at her revelation.

"However," she continues. "They have mini cakes that have Nutella in between the layers."

At that piece of information, his face beams.

"Thank you!" he glows and is now ready to begin the tour.

Ariella smiles brightly, blonde highlights in her auburn locks gleaming under the museum's special lighting. She seems pleasant, but something about her rubs me the wrong way. Shaking it off, I listen intently to her opening monologue.

"*Casa Rossa* was built between eighteen-eighty-six and eighteen-ninety-nine by famed American, *Colonel John Clay MacKowen*. The building was constructed beside an *Aragonese* tower dating all the way back to the end of the fourteen-hundreds. It represents the perfect example of a typical eclectic, residence-museum which was fashionable toward the end of the 19th century..."

The tour is actually extremely educational and interesting. Engulfed in the presentation, we follow our guide as she leads us through the different rooms filled with many fascinating objects. I am glad that my parents made me accompany them.

"This landscape titled *'Gulf of Naples with a View of Capri'* was painted by *Oswald Achenbach* in eighteen-ninety-four."

"It's lovely," Mom whispers to Dad who then nods in agreement, their hands intertwine as they stand examining the painting of the museum when it was a home.

"The next statue we come to was donated to the museum a couple of decades ago by an anonymous patron. According to our curator, it was originally discovered hidden in the most holiest of places in the year fifteen-nineteen, but disappeared shortly after," the young woman informs.

This particular statue catches our attention and for good reason. It resembles my mother: long, spiral curls, almond-shaped eyes, pouty lips, round face with high sculpted cheekbones and that mysterious, all-knowing smile.

Uncanny!

"Ariella?" I boldly raise my voice so she can hear me over the instrumental music seeping into the open space from hidden speakers around the vaulted ceilings.

"Question?"

Clearing my throat, I ask, "What is this sculpture called?"

She smiles, full of white teeth.

"It is named: *La Sirena*."

"Siren," I repeat in English.

"*Si*," she answers in Italian.

"Who created this one?" I probe, unable to take my eyes off of it.

"It was created by an unknown artist and found in a vault at The Vatican."

Oh! My! Goodness!

"It's so *lifelike*!" I announce louder than I intend. "It is incredible!"

Ariella laughs at my outburst.

"To tell you the truth, it's my least favorite piece," the woman informs the crowd. "I find it *cliché*."

Feeling provoked like a dog being poked with a stick, the vein at my right temple begins to pound. My palms begin to sweat and against my better judgement, I flick her off when she turns to move to another exhibit. Hoping to clear the murderous images floating around my head, I turn to my parents who are busy hugging and giggling.

Ignoring the embarrassing sight, I decide to take a closer look at the sculpture. It is a beautiful woman with long curly hair that goes past her waist, wearing only a crown of sea flowers and a priceless necklace made of gold and multicolored jewels around her neck.

Upon the realization, I gasp my shock.

"Holy crap!" I mutter at the strange resemblance. "Mom? Is that you?"

My mother turns a soft shade of pink confirming my suspicions. Unsuccessfully, she tries to pull Dad away, but he refuses to move. His eyes are now open to their fullest point.

"Marina," he whispers. "Is that really you?"

In an instant, Mom becomes flushed and flustered.

"Don't you want to see the next piece?" she asks with a reddened glow.

Ignoring her request, my stepfather takes another look then excitedly interrupts, interjecting:

"Holy moly! That is you!"

"Mom," I blush. "Is *this* the statue you posed for?"

She nods.

"Y-you're... naked!" Dad blushes too, and squeezes Mom's hand tighter.

"*Shhh!*" she chastises, eyes turning from bright aquamarine to a dark sapphire. "Someone will hear you."

"Where are your clothes?" Dad grills his wife.

"He put a tail on me," she snickers. "Even after I explained the difference between Sirens and Mermaids. Stubborn, temperamental fool."

"Wow!" my stepfather whistles, making me uncomfortable. "I guess you've always been quite a honey."

"*Quiet!*" Mom counters even louder.

"Did you and Leonardo Da Vinci have a... *thing*?"

Insulted, Mom smacks him several times on the shoulder... *hard*.

"Ouch!" he wails making the other people in our group turn in our direction.

"We were friends," she educates firmly. "Just friends. Back then, posing nude for an artist was no big deal. It was actually quite an honor."

"I see," says Dad with a snicker, earning him another hard thump. "My wife is such a hot tamale."

"Mom, did you donate the statue to the museum?" I interrogate the guilty Siren.

Her cheeks heat even more as she nods again.

"You stole it?" David exclaims in shock. "From the Vatican?"

We all stare at her. It is all so unbelievable.

"I didn't steal it!" she announces with indignant annoyance. "It was a gift… it was my property anyways."

With that said she folds her arms across her chest and huffs.

"I was visiting Rome that year, to take care of some personal business when I ran into a chatty friar who blurted about this hidden vault that had been recently found in the catacombs underneath the Vatican."

We continue to stare, mouths still gaping.

"With the help of the very willing young friar, who was more than happy to point me in the right direction, I 'reacquired' it," she righteously adds with a mischievous smirk.

"Marina!" Dad scolds with a suppressed chuckle. "That's so wicked."

Ando laughs.

"Why did you donate it?" I question, knowing that there is space for it in the villa's main garden.

My mother's eyes sadden.

"Every time I looked at it, I was reminded of another friend I had lost to time," she sighs, and the sound is full of longing and regret. "So, about twenty years ago, I left it on the doorstep of my favorite local museum."

She winks, shrugging off her temporary sadness.

"I was pretty hot, wasn't I?" she jokes, playfully posing.

All of us chuckle, all except Ando whose face scrunches with disappointment.

"What is the matter with you?" I prod.

"It is called Siren," he translates the sign.

"Yes," I state, gazing at a part of my mother's past.

"Huh," he mumbles, brow scrunched up.

"Is there something wrong?"

"It's got a tail," he cocks his head to the side like a curious beagle. "But it's supposed to be of a *Siren*."

"Yeah," I huff, not understanding his dilemma.

"Sirens don't have tails," he educates. "That's a mermaid."

"I know."

Sadly, he shakes his head and slowly walks away.

"Sirens with tails… " he grumbles. "How stupid is that."

The tour ends on an up-note in the museum gift shop. Ariella takes the time to chat with the group about upcoming exhibits and special events while encouraging patrons to support the museum by giving donations and purchasing souvenirs.

"And once again," our tour guide says cheerfully. "Please feel free to browse our lovely items before you leave. *Gratci!*"

I do not know what possesses me, but I follow her into the employee breakroom and pull her aside to ask her a question.

"Why don't you like the sculpture of the Siren?" I quiz boldly.

Dazed, she responds.

"I'm not sure. It is lovely, but really... Sirens?" the woman counters. "It looks so trashy."

Trashy?

"They are certainly *not* trashy," I reciprocate, feeling my pulse quicken.

Ariella looks nervous.

"*Scusami*... excuse me... I did not mean to offend you, but I am entitled to have my own opinion, *Signorina*."

"Have you ever studied the Siren lore?" I ask, pulling out my cellphone in order to access the search engine.

"Umm," Ariella hums uneasily. "I have another tour group in fifteen minutes, and I am late for my break."

"I just want to explain about these amazing creatures—" I begin but get interrupted.

"*Por favor*... I do not have the time to research now."

"It will only take a few minutes," I explain, pulling up *Google*.

As I continue my rant about mythological architypes and their effects on modern day trends, Ariella's face becomes stern.

"Listen to me! I am trying to be nice, but you are not taking the hint. I do not care... one bit... about nasty, trashy, ugly Sirens!"

Shocked by her uncomplimentary description of my kind, my eyes widen. My fists clench. My abdominal muscles tense. All I want to do is rip her bottle-dyed head off of her way too skinny body.

And that's what I decide to do.

Blinded by rage— a rage so overwhelming that I suddenly only see in black and white— I step toward her and grab her. Instantly, I feel my fingers tightening around the warm flesh of her tanned throat. Beneath my palm I feel her pulse beating furiously and then at a much more unhurried pace. Her lovely face drains of life-giving liquid as I squeeze just a bit harder. She struggles, lashing at my face and upper body. I feel her legs kicking against me and realize that I am holding her body a few inches off of the ground. Again, she flails and flails until her punches reduce to merely soft thumps, much like that of a toddler's.

Everything seems to be moving in slow motion. The way her face contorts. The way her hair falls loosely around her shoulders as she fights against the inevitable. The way—

"That's enough!" Mom's voice brings me back from the precipice in which I teeter. *"Selena!* Let her go, dammit!"

Before my mind can focus, Dad pries my hand away from Ariella's neck. The young woman's body slumps into his trembling arms; unmoving, and without breath.

"Lena!" Ando looks at me in horror. "You killed her!"

In an instant, I am back to my rightful senses.

Wordlessly, I gape at her, then glance at my horrified brother. My parents stare at me like I am a stranger, then I catch my reflection in the museum's employee microwave in the small breakroom. If I did not know that it was my own reflection, I would not have recognized the monster staring back. Dumbfounded, I shake my head hoping to understand how I got into the secluded space.

"Dear God!" I whisper, mortified at what I have done.

Mom pushes me aside and lays her hand, palm open, over Ariella's heart. In a frenzy of emotions, I hear her muffled prayer whispered through trembling lips.

Obviously rattled, my mother closes her eyes and concentrates.

Nothing.

Mom swears in Greek as she tries the ritual again…

And again…

Then one more time.

In the same dreadful silence we all wait, holding our collective breaths… waiting for Destiny to reveal our fates.

Please breathe.

A few seconds pass and to my relief the woman's chest begins to rise and fall, but only slightly. She does not look alright; there is also the evidence of dark finger-shaped bruises decorating her neck.

David checks the carotid artery in her neck, below the jawline.

"Her pulse is weak!" Dad informs with a worried sigh. "Should we call for an ambulance? Inform security… no… definitely no security."

In a rush, Mom waves us away as she kneels beside the unconscious woman.

"Stand guard by the door!" she orders gruffly.

"What are you going to do, Mom?" I dare ask.

She looks at me, tears welled in her eyes.

"Just… just keep an eye out."

Quietly, I do as I am asked and stand watch.

Before our eyes, Mom *turns*. She holds her breath as she summons her scales. With shaking hands, she rips one off of her body and rubs the viscous liquid contained in it on the marks that have formed on Ariella's neck. Then she does something that I would never have thought of, she puts it in the young woman's mouth and makes her swallow it. Slowly, but surely, Ariella begins to stir, her color returning; however, her eyes remain close.

"Is she okay?" I probe in a hushed tone, wanting to vomit.

"She will be," Mom clarifies with a small smile.

"I'm so sorry," I plead to everyone in general. "I am so, so sorry."

As we wait, Mom returns to her human form, but does not make eye contact with me.

"Get out of here," the Siren states calmly. "I'll meet you at the car."

"But—" I begin, but the sentence never forms.

"I. Said. *Go!*"

CHAPTER TWENTY

The ride home is uncomfortable, to say the least. Ando gazes out of his side window, pretending not to see me. Mom and Dad stare straight ahead, doing the exact same. Consumed by guilt, I sit remembering every single moment that I spent at the museum with Ariella.

"Is she alright?" I whisper.

"She will be fine," Mom informs robotically.

"I don't know what happened," I admit, holding back a flood of tears.

Mom sighs.

"The venom in my scale will cure any sort of internal damage you may have caused and the marks on her neck disappeared almost immediately."

Anxiously, I clear my throat.

"Will she remember what I did to her?"

"No," Mom reassures. "I wiped her memory and replaced it with a happier, less violent one."

"Oh!" I whimper, allowing one tear to fall.

"The Calling must be done soon," Dad reminds with a frown. "We can't have her around people. Who knows what might happen. God forbid she kills someone."

Been there... done that.

Mom nods in agreement.

I want to protest, but I cannot. It is true. I have no control over my actions. I realize that now. No matter what I say, the primal spirit inside of me is clamoring to be released. She is stronger than me, of that I am certain. Sadly, I will only be able to contain her for a short time, and then anything can happen.

"I don't know what came over me," I admit again. Inside of me, a build-up of acid sloshes around my abdomen, begging to be let out. "One moment, I was trying to get her to see reason... then the next... *Ugg!*"

"You'll need to be confined to the villa," my mother relays in a determined tone.

Again, my sour stomach begins to churn in revolt. My limbs suddenly and inexplicably start to ache... ache all the way into the marrow of my bones. Even the whites of my eyes burn like someone has thrown acid on them.

Filled with panic, I pound against the rear window and jerk at the door handle trying to escape as I try to get to the sea. My entire goal in life right now is to get into the water.

"*Stop the car!*" I shout, ready to break the door from the hinges.

Mom turns in her seat to face me, her complexion sallow.

"What's wrong?!" Dad yells, his face lined with concern and fear.

But his words do not reach my brain, I smell the sea. The tangy brininess of it. The pungent kiss of sea life.

"Let me out!" I begin to sob as Ando tries to hug me, but I push away his small hands and tug on the door some more.

"Lena?!" he sobs. "Stop it! Calm down!"

"Please!" I wail like a wounded animal. "Have mercy!"

As the vehicle turns the bend, I see it, the place that calls to me. The harbor with all of its bobbing ships is right there within my reach.

Attempting to stop me, Mom tries to reach for me, but I quickly avoid her grip.

"No!" she shouts. "Don't you dare jump out of a moving vehicle!"

"Selena, stop acting like this!" Dad orders while trying to steer the vehicle with one hand as he reaches behind to grab me with the other.

I can't think straight!

"Let... me... *Out!*" I screech, the sound hurting my own ears.

To my surprise, I hear the locks release and with one last maneuver, the door opens and I leap to freedom. Hastily, I dart across the remaining road and jump feet first into the cooling saltiness of the Tyrrhenian Sea. Immediately, my lungs retract and gills activate allowing me to gulp down several deep breaths. Instantly, my skin cools and my stomach calms. Unhurriedly, I swim toward the open ocean, needing to find some kind of peace. Some sort of normality.

'I'll be home after I calm down,' I use my telepathy to inform my mother and Ando of my agenda.

'Alright, but stay away from humans,' Mom commands firmly.

'I promise,' I state, fully intending to keep my word.

'Selena?'

'Yes?'

There is a long pause as I wait for her next words.

'You know that I love you... right?'

I have never heard the sound of desperation in my mother's 'voice'. Actually, that is not completely accurate. When David left us and took Ando with him, my mother gave up. She would not eat, would not sleep. All she could do was cry; cry and think of what she could have done differently. I hear that same desperation in her voice now and I hurt knowing that I am the cause of it.

A barrage of tears streams out, mixing with the salty sea, disappearing into the void.

'I know,' I sniffle back an unwanted sob.

'Ariella will be just fine,' Mom comforts with her parental tone that always makes me feel safe. *'I promise.'*

'I just need to clear my head,' I reply through my thoughts, feeling a tinge of pain as a strand of seaweed brushes against my overly-sensitive skin.

'Mom?'

'Yeah?' she answers softly inside of my head.

'I really am sorry about everything.*'*

'I understand, my love,' she maternally soothes. *'After all, I was a teenage Siren once too.'*

Then my mind goes silent and all I can hear are the currents rushing around me and the muffled hum of boat engines scattered throughout the harbor. Immediately, my senses increase as a school of tiny silver fish swim past my legs, their fins tickling as they rush by. A few feet away, my eyes lock onto a trap full of crabs, crabs that are climbing over each other desperate to escape. Without thinking, I race over to them, break open the lock on the trapdoor and free them, but before they can all escape, I grab the largest one and bite him in two and ravenously consume his remains; shell and all.

With a full stomach, I can finally process my situation. I am not myself. I have an emptiness inside that cannot be filled with anything conventional. I am not human. I never have been, never will be. I can only pretend that I am. I can don the garbs and talk the talk, but I am anything but human.

I am Siren.

When I get home, I will deal with the wrath of my parents, but for now... now I will let myself be one with the void. Like I was meant to do. Way back when the Sirens first came into this world.

I will just: *Be.*

I spend the next few hours swimming around the outskirts of the Marina Piccola harbor exploring the underwater crevices and hidden clefts in the limestone cliffs. Twice I got lost in tunnels that spread like tree roots under the island then unexpectedly they would suddenly end with me inside, leaving me disappointed at not finding a cavern as exquisite as the Blue Grotto at the end of my tiresome search. On another attempt, I squeezed into a deceptively narrow passage and almost got permanently stuck. Thankfully, I managed to suck in my tummy enough to escape. Other than that, I have been having an amazing time.

"We are glad that you are having a good time exploring," I hear the softly spoken words, not in my head, but right behind me as I exit another tunnel with a dead-end. Startled, I jerk around only to find the aunts glaring disapprovingly at me. Their faces are taunt and tense, leaving no mistake in my mind that I am in big trouble... monumental trouble.

"Tia Ligeia! Tia Leukosia!" I gasp, clicking and clacking nervously, not expecting to see them since they have been scarce for a while. "What are you doing here?"

Unbeknownst to them, playing dumb is my new strategy for staying one step ahead of any parental units, including severely pissed-off ancient Sirens looking for a confrontation. As I speak/think those words their faces grimace in perfect synchronicity. Witnessing it is more than disturbing. It is mind-blowing.

"The breaking news around the watercooler..." Leukosia begins with a reference that she heard on television when Ando convinced them to venture on land to check out our vacation villa. Her news reporter tone makes me snicker, and she gives me another upsetting stare.

"Sorry," I say in Siren, holding back another giggle. "Please continue with the oncoming lecture."

This time Tia Ligeia gives me a look that would terrify a giant squid and that is not an easy feat.

"Go ahead," I implore politely. "I didn't mean to be disrespectful."

Regally, she bows her acceptance of my apology.

"We know what happened at the museum in Anacapri," they reveal sternly, their tone forcing the hairs on my arms to stand at attention like soldiers in an army.

"What did I do?" I use my newly created tactic, hoping it will at least stump them for a minute or two.

They both stare at me, making me squirm like a worm on a fisherman's hook.

"Is this about the tour guide?" I pout, folding my arms across my chest defiantly.

"That is the logical conclusion," Ligeia states flatly.

"Mom told you," I concede, being ratted-out.

They shake their heads.

"Then how did you know?" I grill with surprise.

'When a Siren makes a kill —' they speak in perfect harmony inside of my mind.

'But I didn't kill her!' I snap, reminding them that I have not crossed that line. *Wait!* Technically she was dead. At least for a couple of minutes, which is not that long in the grand scheme of things.

"May we finish our train of thought before you interrupt?" they clack and click in a harsh tone. That combined with them giving me the evil eye, resonates even more profoundly to how far I have actually fallen from their good graces.

"When a Siren makes a kill, whether it is done with maliciousness or simply for self-preservation, there is a ripple that is created," they teach in a Socratic manner.

"A ripple?" I probe for clarification. "Like a ripple in water?"

They nod.

"That is correct," Leukosia confirms as she treads water in front of me.

"How can that be?" I begin in a huff. "The incident happened on dry land."

"Do you think your location matters?" they both interrogate sharply.

I shake my head.

"As a Siren you are able to draw power from the Earth, which includes all naturally created bodies of water," they educate somewhat smugly.

I still am not getting it!

"Please explain," I implore, tired of being lectured.

"We are of the sea," Leukosia continues. "Everything we feel gets amplified by the sea. Just as our emotions can cause storms or pleasant weather, so can our physical acts upon the other creatures that share this earth with us."

Next, Ligeia adds.

"When we eat too many of one species of clams we deplete the supply for everyone on the planet, just as when we take a life... especially a human life, an innocent life... the repercussions can be felt like spasms throughout every ocean, every river, every naturally formed body of water."

I stare blankly.

"Selena, everything is interconnected," they scoff. "Whether you are on land or in water, *we* will know whenever you violate the natural order of things," they scoff.

My eyes widen at the realization that I will never truly have a private moment again. These women, my family, will always be with me. Right now, I am not sure that is what I want.

"We felt your ripple over hundreds of miles of ocean," the blonde Siren states, more than a little miffed.

"We felt your rage heat the water currents," Ligeia continues her sister's thought, and then extends her hand and redirects the motion of the current.

"We felt the seabeds quake," Leukosia speaks again, gently touching the limestone of the tunnel's walls.

"Murdering a human because she irritates you is *not* the same as killing a crab because you are hungry," Ligeia blurts, her tone harsh.

Like quicksilver, they both grab me, forcing me to connect with the sea.

"Do you understand now?" they say in unison in a string of whistles and chirps.

Uneasily, I nod my comprehension.

"Speak child!" their voices boom, causing the sea to become choppy.

"Yes!" I reconfirm, terrified at what they might do. "I get it! I get it!"

Thank heavens their fury recedes and they return to their usual curmudgeonly selves. My red-headed aunt frowns with folded arms, while her sister simply glares at me. Even a passing shrimp feels the tension and pretends he does not see us.

A few seconds pass as they size me up.

"It seems that a certain young Siren has been creating waves with the local sea life," Leukosia finishes her comment at last.

"What else did I do?" I huff, feigning innocence.

"We were patrolling the island's east side and ran into a pod of dolphins who claim that a young Siren stole several large tunas right from underneath their beaks," Leukosia stealthily reveals.

"Their description matches you to a tee," Ligeia's tone softens.

My mouth gapes as I devise a believable excuse.

"Hey!" I clack indignantly. "I called *'dibs'* on them!"

They look at each other, and then at me.

"What is *'dibs'*?" they repeat awkwardly.

"You know... *'dibs',*" I say again hoping they will miraculously understand.

They click and clack rapidly between each other, so fast that I cannot translate anything, let alone come up with a game plan to hold off their wrath. By sheer luck I am able to decipher the words: incorrigible, masterful, and trickster.

That's not a good sign!

"Selena," they reply together. "Restate the definition of this word called *'dibs'* and no more chicanery."

Needless to say, the look they give me warns that no *'cuteness'* will work on them, so beware.

Foiled again!

"Sometimes people will call out the word *'dibs'* when they lay claim to something they really want," I explain without attitude. "It just means it belongs to you."

Again, they look at one another and clickity-clack as I watch patiently, holding my breath.

Finally, Tia Leukosia speaks.

"When on land, do as the people do," she states blankly. "When in the sea, do as the fish do."

"Huh?" I mouth and they understand.

"Sea animals do not comprehend the significance of *'dibs'* when dealing with catching their next meal," Ligeia reinforces without humor, the look on her face clearly disapproving of my childish behavior.

Now I feel awful!

"The next time I see that pod, I will apologize," I blush with embarrassment.

"You will also bring an offering with you," Ligeia adds.

"An offering?" I repeat with confusion.

"Yes," Leukosia nods with a tiny smile. "You will give them abalone… one for each of the pod members."

'Abalone,' I whisper loudly in my head. *'What in the world is abalone?'*

They discuss the subject between one another before answering.

"Abalone is an edible sea snail that has a shallow, ear-shaped outer shell," they speak in unison.

"Oh!" I exclaim, releasing my breath.

"Their shell is lined with what humans call *mother-of-pearl*," they knowledgably add to the description. "Apparently, people label it as quite a desirable product. I guess there is no accounting for taste."

They both shrug their shoulders like Ando taught them.

That brother of mine!

"Is there anything else?" I question sheepishly, wishing I had gone back to the villa.

They converse once more then turn to me.

'Yes,' both say in my mind. *'We understand that you need some clarification concerning the matter of our mother and father.'*

Surprisingly, the voice that answers next does not belong to me.

'Well, it's about time!' Mom scolds the aunts telepathically as if they were Ando or me. *'I've been trying to get in contact with you for hours. Didn't you hear me?'*

'We were indisposed,' they reveal vaguely then refrain from elaboration.

'We've been dealing with a being… a Muse who claims to be my grandmother, Melpomene,' my mother expounds rudely.

The aunts begin to chat in a language that not even my mother seems to understand. It is a series of the regular clicks, clacks, whistles, and squeals combined with what appears to be nonsensical words that would confound the greatest linguistic prodigy of our time.

After a few seconds, Mom blurts in my head.

'What are they doing? They just went silent.'

'They're talking, but I can't understand what they are saying,' I relay the scene since Mom cannot see what I do.

'Please explain,' my mother pleads, her tone clipped. As best as I can, I explain. When I finish, I hover in place above the rocky seafloor waiting for her response. When no reply comes, I break the silence.

'What language are they speaking?' I mentally probe my mom.

'It is the 'original tongue', ' she replies as if I should already know.

'What's that?' I counter, more confused than ever.

'Long story short, it is the formal Siren language,' my mother explains as best as she can. *'The version they speak to us is more simplified.'*

'Can you understand the original tongue?' I wonder in my mind as the sisters continue ignoring us.

'No, I can't,' Mom responds with frustration. *'They never taught me.'*

'Why not?' I blurt nonverbally. *'Aren't you one of* The Three?*'*

'I am not of the original Sirens, remember?' she reminds as we continue to wait for the aunts to acknowledge our 'existence'.

At last, they turn to me.

"Describe this creature," they command simultaneously in regular Siren.

"Melody is lovely—" I begin but get cutoff.

"Who is Melody?!" they bark angrily.

"Melody is the name that Ando gave her," I explain with heated cheeks.

"Oh!" they say as they smile.

"He thought she needed a more modern name," I continue.

"Go on," they request firmly.

"She is beautiful, not stunning like you all and Mom, but she has a captivating appearance that is timeless," I tell with complete admiration.

The Sirens urge me to continue.

'Her eyes change in color as her moods change and can hypnotize you without your knowledge,' Mom announces like a child seeing a butterfly for the first time.

"Tell us more," they beg, enthralled by our description of the Muse.

"She has unique hair," I disclose, unable to stop smirking.

"In what way?" they blurt, moving into my personal space.

"Her hair is ebony with streaks of highlights that range from gold to scarlet to deep purple," I describe in awe. "And when the light catches it, all of the colors bend and retract the spectrum until you don't know where one color starts, and the other begins."

"When you are near her, how do you feel?" Ligeia interrogates, with hope gleaming in her eyes.

I think for a second.

"Melody makes me feel inspired, at peace, and safe," I respond with a rush of words.

"And when you leave her presence?" Leukosia inquires.

"You feel lost and a bit… depressed," I reveal tearfully, wishing I will see Melody again.

The sisters look at each other then back at me.

"How does she smell?" they both ask at the same time.

Needless to say, their question surprises both Mom and me.

"Say again?" I blurt, not understanding.

"Does she have a certain scent?" they repeat, but my brain is having difficulty putting one and one together to make two. Instead, my mind adds it together and comes up with three.

Ugg! I'm starting to get a migraine!

Both Mom and I think hard. What did Melody smell of? Then it comes to both of us.

'Chocolate combined with a hint of baking bread!' Mom and I both shout excitedly in the aunt's minds, making them cringe.

Then it happens. Something that I have never seen in my brief existence as a Siren, Ligeia and Leukosia: They Smile! *At the same time!*

"She *is* Melpomene the Muse, Daughter of the Air and Light, Exalted Child of Inspiration, Wife of Akheloios the River God and Mother of *The Three*," they both purr with unfettered joy. "She is our mother!"

Wild with excitement, the sisters frolic over the seabed like lambs prancing through a field of wildflowers.

'Are you sure?' Mom probes ruefully.

"We are certain she is," they smile once again; the very sight of it makes me misty. "It is Melpomene."

I feel my tears begin to fall, but unlike my aunts, they remain in liquid form. Perhaps that metamorphosis happens with time and age. That hypothesis makes sense. I guess I will have to wait and see.

"Is there something she said to you to verify her identity?" they query together.

I smile.

"Yes, she did," I grin.

"What did she say?" they almost shout.

'Melody wanted us to ask about your father, Akheloios,' Mom jumps in after letting me guide the conversation.

"She wanted you to tell us about an incident that happened when you were children," I specify without giving any real clues, especially since I have no idea what the *incident* was.

They both sadden to the point that for the first time ever, I see a single tear form at the corners of their eyes. The liquid is opalescent with a milky consistency that stays in a perfect sphere even underwater. Slowly, it rolls down their cheeks and as it falls onto the sandy sea bottom, it congeals then hardens into an orb similar in appearance to a pearl.

"Your tears turn into pearls!" I click-clack-whistle-bray in shock.

"They do?" the sisters blurt, stunned at the revelation.

"Yes!" I manage to shout in my state of shock.

'There's no time for that now!' Mom pleads in pure anguish, needing desperately to have closure on this

important matter. *'Please tell us about what happened to your father!'*

"Very well," they respond as one. "Where shall we begin?"

Mom impatiently bypasses me.

'Begin at the beginning,' she entreats, sounding like the sisters.

"It was a day, much like today in many ways," they start in perfect synchronicity. "The sea was calm and the creatures that lived there were healthy and in good form. Mother was inside the house cooking steamed cassava porridge sweetened with coconut milk, while father was out back pulling weeds from the garden."

Their eyes glaze over as if transported to the exact time and place of the distant memory.

'How old were you?' Mom asks, enthusiastically.

"We were two Earth cycles old," they answer cheerfully and without hesitation.

I mentally feel my mother's breath hitch as it is sucked in like a penny into a vacuum hose and her mind begins to swirl.

'Please continue,' she projects, even more glued to their story.

"Father asked us to check on how much longer until our meal would be finished, so we ran inside to check," they agree with a barely-there nod.

"And then... " I encourage, aching to hear what happened next.

"We did not see what unfolded, but we all heard a loud crash, like a lightning bolt striking the ground then reverberating with such violence and force that it shook the entire island," the sisters use hand gestures to add life to their performance.

'What happened to Akheloios?' Mom shouts in our heads almost deafening all of us. The aunts grip at their ears in pain.

"We do not know," they sigh their rage, and the water surrounding them heats and the fish swimming around us suddenly disappear.

'You had to see something!' Mom snaps, her emotions on a rollercoaster ride of hills and valleys.

"Our mother led the way outside and tried to hide his slain body with her own," the Sirens reveal with pained expressions. "But when she caught sight of father, she let out a wail so powerful that it caused the majority of greenery on our property to incinerate, as though a quickly moving wildfire swept across the land destroying everything in its path."

'Who killed him?' Mom probes after a long uncomfortable silence.

"The only clue that was left was a golden spear etched in ancient writing," they reveal with vehemence.

"What did the etching say?" I question with wide eyes.

"God Killer."

CHAPTER TWENTY-ONE

It does not take long for me to make the swim along the rocky coastline of Capri back to the *Belvedere of Tragara*; the lofty panoramic promenade of whitewashed villas overlooking the small harbor. Since it is only a little past sundown, and the island center is still a buzz with people enjoying the unnaturally cool summer night, I call David from a payphone and he wastes no time coming to pick me up.

"I'm so glad that you called," Dad greets as I climb into the Range Rover. "We were worried about you."

I give him an absentminded smile.

"I'm sorry, Dad," I mumble, forcing myself to make eye contact. "I had no control over my actions, otherwise I wouldn't have acted so—"

"I get it," he replies, turning to face forward in order to maneuver through the semi-congested streets of the *Piazzetta*.

"Are you feeling better?" he questions almost timidly as if I am a wild animal that he has stumbled upon instead of his own daughter that he has helped raise for over a decade. Seeing the fear in his eyes breaks my heart and I promise myself to be more resolute in controlling my inner Siren.

"Please, Dad," I plead, feeling the tears forming, but holding them back. "Please, don't be afraid of me."

He manages a small grin that does not reach his expressive eyes.

Great! Soon my entire family will be frightened of me unless I can control my violent tendencies.

Up ahead, our vacation home comes into view. As we drive through the ornate iron gates, the property's landscaped gardens are framed by the vehicle's windshield. All along the driveway, an impressive array of native trees stand guarding the path, while blossoming flowerbeds enhance the manicured lawn and the decorative rectangular reflection pond that can only be partially seen from our current location. At the moment, there is a cool, salt-perfumed breeze blowing in from the sea. I never get tired of viewing the single-level whitewashed structure that completes the ground's regal appearance.

"Buona notte!" an unfamiliar male voice calls to us from the backyard.

"Who is that?" I nod in the direction of the man while getting out of the now parked SUV.

"That's Signore Romano," Dad smiles as he waves to the elderly gentleman who is dressed in coveralls dusted with dirt and spotted with dried paint.

"Why is he here?" I grill, my defenses high.

"He is the new groundskeeper," my stepdad informs with a grin. "He's extremely friendly."

For a few seconds, I study the man who has gone back to his work of pulling weeds and raking escaped mulch back into the flowerbeds. I guess he seems harmless enough, but you never can tell these days. Good guys and bad guys are difficult, if not impossible, to distinguish in my opinion.

"Don't look so concerned," Dad requests cheerfully. "He is harmless."

"I suppose so," I add under my breath.

As we open the front door, the aroma of pot roast permeates the entire house. My stomach lurches as I slap a hand over my mouth and concentrate on holding back a tidal wave of stomach acid.

"*Ugg!*" I gasp as beads of perspiration appear across my brow.

"What's the matter?" I hear Ando's voice from the living room.

"The smell is making me nauseous," I admit, not liking the spotlight that seems to be following me wherever I go.

He sniffs the air.

"It doesn't smell bad to me," he reveals with a smile. "It smells really tasty!"

I only smile, but replace my hand over my mouth.

"Hey!" Mom appears in the hallway dressed in a pair of shorts and a t-shirt, her hair up in a high ponytail causing her to resemble... *Me!*

"Hi, Mom," I mumble, once again finding it problematic making eye contact.

"Are you hungry?" she asks, glancing toward the kitchen.

"Not right now," I reply, wishing I was in the bathroom instead of being quizzed by my family.

"Go get cleaned up," she advises sympathetically. "You don't want to smell like a fish when we see your great-grandmother."

The idea of visiting Melody again instantly cures my nausea.

"Really!" I exclaim with unbridled enthusiasm. "We are going to see Melody?"

Mom nods with a huge smile.

"But you have to take a shower first," she giggles, holding her nose.

The night is void of color. High above, a thick blanket of rainclouds has blocked any evidence of stars or of the moon. Even the wondrous vertical slabs of gray-stone cliffs and the similarly-shaded coastline topped with greenery, appear less vibrant than usual, and the rough sea is the same caliginous hue. The air which is normally fragrant with the aroma of citrus, salt and olives, is still; scentless and lacking in charm.

Even David senses that something is off.

"Why is it so dark?" he questions Mom, who is glancing around the dimly lit path leading to the woods that the cottage usually inhabits.

"I'm not sure," Mom answers in a hushed tone, making us wearier.

Ando, the bravest of our group, takes Dad's hand and holds it securely.

"There's no breeze," my brother whispers, looking over his shoulder. "But it's chilly."

I nod in agreement and almost reach for Mom's hand but decide against it. I am a Siren. Sirens are not afraid of anything (or so I would like everyone to believe).

'Sirens can feel fear,' I hear Leukosia's voice inside of my mind.

'Tia Leukosia?' I blurt with surprise. *'Is that you?'*

'Who else would it be?' she states plainly and without humor.

'Where are you?' I question, looking around at every shadow.

'We are close,' another voice startles me.

'Tia Ligeia?' I ask, stopping in midstride.

"What's the matter?" Mom frowns, stopping also. "Why are you just standing around?"

"Can you hear them?" I ask, my eyes darting nervously from side to side.

"Of course," she replies, walking once more. "We all can."

Both Dad and Ando nod in agreement making me more aware of my growing paranoia.

"C'mon, Lena!" my brother encourages. "I don't like it out here."

"Me either," I pout, looking at the dark road in front of us, wondering why we did not drive. It would have been much safer, and we could simply run over anything that may attack us.

"Hurry you two!" Dad orders, quickening his pace. "We're almost there."

Mom is several yards in front and her pace is increasing. Afraid of being left behind, I quicken my steps to match hers, but having shorter legs than her makes it almost impossible to keep up. I end up jogging to keep pace. David, on the other hand, has no issues keeping up with her. Without hesitation, he scoops Ando into his arms and continues the journey without breaking a sweat; unlike me, who is now covered with it.

As we pass a large leafy bush, a blue lizard jumps from one of the branches and lands at my feet, which makes me yelp like a scared puppy.

"*Get a grip!*" I whisper to myself.

A few minutes later, we are traipsing through the dense woods. On an overhanging branch, movement catches my attention. Thankfully, it is only an owl. The same owl from before hoots at us then flies to a closer tree.

Why is that bird always here?

Slowly, he turns his head in my direction as if he understands what I am thinking. His large, round, soulful eyes lock onto mine and we stare at one another for a brief moment. Filled with curiosity, he flies to a closer branch, I assume to get a better view of us. He is a stunning creature covered in feathers of gold, black, beige, and hints of copper.

"Melody," Mom calls into the darkness. "Are you still here? It's us!"

Almost immediately, the cottage fades in. The sight of it is a thing of beauty: simple, yet quaint. To our relief, the door is already open and, in the doorway, stands the aunts with Melody between them. Their resemblance is uncanny.

"You're here!" Ando claps joyfully.

"We are," the aunts answer simultaneously.

"When did you get here?" Mom smiles, taking Dad's hand in hers and squeezing it hard enough to make him wince.

"Not long after we left Selena," they relay verbally.

"How did you find this place?" Dad probes with a grin. "It's not exactly on the map."

They both smile again, and like before, the sight of it wigs me out.

"Mother showed us the way," they reply with childlike grins.

We all stand in the woods too elated to move, until Melody intervenes.

"Come inside," the Muse beckons gleefully with all smiles. "We have a great deal of catching up to do."

My great-grandmother is flitting to and fro, from the living room where we sit, to the kitchen where she is preparing an outlandish feast. The aroma of whatever is being prepared trumps the pot roast that my mother was cooking at our vacation home. For some reason, the scent wafting out of the kitchen is not making me gag.

"What are you cooking, Great-Grandmother Melody?" Ando questions as he follows her from room to room, helping her with miscellaneous tasks.

She giggles.

"Please, just call me Melody," she implores, patting the top of his head gently and in a very maternal fashion. "Great-Grandmother Melody is too much to say without becoming tongue-tied."

This time, Ando giggles.

"Alright, Melody," he blushes. "When I think of a better name to call you, I'll let you know."

She laughs while attending to the multiple pots on the stove.

"Sounds good to me," she winks playfully. "Selena?"

Melody calls to me over the pleasant chattering happening between my parents and the aunts in the living room. It is strange, around Melody they are extremely *Human*, not only in appearance, but in mannerisms. They are charming and charismatic with an enthusiasm that is infectious. They are even using hand gestures like Mom, Ando and I do when they speak. Even more baffling, their guards are down and they are actually laughing.

I can't believe they look so carefree... and they are wearing clothes!

Floral ankle-length sundresses with sandals.

"Selena!" I hear my brother calling for me this time.

"I'll be right there!" I shout back.

Swiftly, I hurry into the kitchen to see what the matter is.

Melody looks up from tending to something that looks like spinach bubbling away on the back burner.

"Selena, could you please cut some parsley, rosemary, and thyme from the garden?" Melody requests sweetly.

"Sure," I smile, excited to examine the garden up close.

"Watch out for Belen," she warns with a chuckle and a sideways glance.

Immediately, I stop in my tracks.

"Belen?" I squeak, eyes wide. "Who is Belen and why do I need to *'watch out'* for him?"

"I didn't know you have a dog, Melody," Ando states with a grin since he has always wanted a pet.

Melody chuckles mischievously.

"He is not a dog."

Ando winces up his face.

"What is he?" he probes, looking around.

"You'll see," she grins.

"Good luck, Lena," my brother salutes me as I peek outside.

"Thanks," I respond with a hint of sarcasm.

"There is a covered bucket with treats inside of it that you can give him," Melody informs, wiping her perspiring brow with the back of her hand and then her hand onto her white apron. "Do not give him more than two. He can be greedy."

Cautiously, I open the backdoor leading outside to the yard and scan the area for something resembling a pet but see nothing.

"Umm," I hum to myself. "Is he safe?"

"Mostly," my great-grandmother scoffs. "It depends on whether or not he likes you."

Determined to complete my task, I take a step outside… then take another… then finally a third that gets me to the top of the steps of which there are only five, a nice odd number. My mother once told me that odd numbers are considered lucky by Sirens. The last step squeaks as it feels my weight, so I quickly bypass it by jumping over it. I land like a tipsy armadillo onto the ground and almost topple over, but manage to find my balance before gravity takes hold of me and slams me into the dirt.

"You okay, Lena?" Ando shouts as he looks at me from the kitchen window.

"I'm fine," I assert, waving back.

"Do you see Belen?" he questions curiously.

Taking my time, I look around the well-ordered backyard. There is a shed near the back of the property that looks like a miniature version of the cottage itself. The garden is not fenced at all, but there are small woodland creatures like a couple of rabbits and a field mouse wandering among the rows of neatly planted plants and flowers. One bold rabbit digs up a carrot and with help from its mate, drags it away, but as soon as they disappear into the night, the hole fills back with soil and another carrot-top appears to take its place.

What the hell!

Suddenly, movement to my right catches my attention, and I turn to see what it is. To my delight, a brightly colored hummingbird feasts upon the nectar of a large, bee balm blossom growing nearby, completely oblivious to my close proximity. Everything about him is mesmerizing, especially his rapidly fluttering wings of lime green, pumpkin, plum, lapis and gold feathers elegantly sleek and aerodynamic; moving faster than my eyes can focus.

"He's amazing!" I state emphatically. "What's his name? Wait, does he have a name?"

Melody sighs.

"I'm sure he does," she sulks. "But he refuses to tell me what it is."

I cannot help but laugh.

"Try not to get off-track, Selena," Melody prompts from the now open window.

"Your garden is magical," I state in shock as I break off pieces of the different herb bushes and they all regrow the cut stems right before my eyes. "Amazing!"

"I wanna see Melody's magical garden!" Ando rushes outside.

"Pick one of those flowers," I request, pointing to a lovely climbing rose bush that decorates the outer walls of the cottage.

Ando, following my instructions on how to avoid the sharp thorns along the vine, carefully plucks a large fuchsia colored rose from the plant. Instantaneously, another similar flower replaces it.

"Wow!" Ando states in astonishment. "How is it able to do that?"

"Magic," Melody reconfirms from the window. "Bring me the herbs, please. Everyone is starving, young ones."

"Wait!" Ando hollers. "We haven't met Belen!"

"Maybe that's a good thing," I chuckle, looking around for some sort of demonic beast.

Needing us to pick up the pace, Melody makes a clucking sound with her tongue and a few seconds later, the leaves of a nearby birch tree begin to rustle.

"Something is in that tree," Ando whispers, holding my hand.

"Stay close to me," I order, pushing him behind me in case whatever it is attacks.

Determined for Belen to show himself, Melody clicks and clacks this time, but unlike Siren language neither Ando nor I are able to translate it. As we continue to view the woods, the branches on another tree, closer to the backyard suddenly shuffle calling our attention to it. All the hairs on my arms stand on end as my heart pounds loud enough that Ando gives my hand a little squeeze to calm my nerves. Then she coos like a dove and chirps a short melody. That is when he flies out of the cover of the leaves and lands on Melody's outstretched arm. It is the same gorgeous owl from earlier, the one who was studying us before the cottage appeared.

"That's Belen?" I gasp, full of wonder.

The Horned owl clucks and chirps in response.

Melody nods with a grin.

"Children this is Sir Belen, Belen for short," Melody smiles proudly. "Belen… this is Fernando, better known as Ando."

Ando stretches his arm out and waits patiently. Without hesitation, the owl flies to him and lands gently. Playfully, it spreads its wings and by flapping vigorously creates a whirlwind of air that moves Ando's hair like he is inside of a wind tunnel. My brother squeals with delight as the owl nuzzles his cheek with its face. It is a sight of pure fantasy. I smile to myself as I wait for my turn.

"What does the name *Belen* mean?" Ando asks, full of curiosity.

Melody thinks for a long moment before answering.

"Belen is the Greek word for *'arrow'*," she reveals.

"Why did you name him that?" my brother questions as he gently strokes the owls soft feathers.

"When he strikes his prey, it is as deadly and precise as an arrow," she smiles proudly.

"It's my turn, Ando," I remind, excited to be formally introduced to the bird.

Melody nods in agreement.

"Belen, the young lady is Selena," Melody introduces with a nod of her head; however, this time, Belen refuses to leave Ando's arm. Instead, he looks at me then back at Melody then retreats back into the nearest tree. My heart sinks fast. I was not expecting that response.

Silly bird!

"I am sorry, Selena," my great-grandmother apologizes for her pet's ill manners. "He is extremely temperamental, but I am sure he will warm up to you in time."

From the safety of the tree, Belen squawks at me and moves his head in a back-and-forth motion that shows his dislike of me.

"Hush Belen!" the Muse scolds.

Still in an agitated state, Belen ignores her.

"Fugerunt!" Melody exclaims in a different language and Belen flies away.

"What did you say to him?" Ando grills, his expression sad.

"I told him to go fly around," she giggles, taking the herbs from my hand. "Do not worry about Belen. He will be back after he finds a tasty morsel for dinner."

Satisfied with that answer, Ando takes Melody's hand and leads her back into the house. A little miffed that the owl did not care for me, I stand outside enjoying the cool night air.

"Come and get it!" the head of our family calls everyone to the dinner table.

Temporarily, I forget about Sir Belen and jog up the stairs to eat with my family.

My entire family.

That fact alone makes me smile.

As I reenter the cottage, the sight of my entire clan, minus Parthenope and Akheloios sitting around Melody's small dining table all squished together elbow to elbow, makes my heart skip a beat. Slowly, I walk toward them; the fragrant aroma of delicious delicacies tantalizes my taste buds.

"Everything smells delightful, Melody," I compliment. "What did you cook?"

Ando is right. We need a more great-grandmotherly term for Melody. Calling her by her given name, Melpomene, is not any better. I take the last empty seat at the table which is actually the bench from the Upright piano in the living room.

Melody blushes.

"I made a little bit of everything, since we have a variety of beings breaking bread tonight," she grins.

Scattered neatly on the table are an assortment of serving dishes filled with cooked meats and vegetables, bowls of salad and pasta, along with baskets of freshly baked brown bread. On a separate platter, there are a multitude of cheeses such as Gouda, Brie, Muenster, fresh balls of mozzarella, white cheddar, and goat cheese embellished with the fresh herbs I gathered from Melody's garden earlier.

"What's in that dish?" Ando asks, pointing to a blue covered casserole dish.

The aunts smile.

"Dessert!" they answer together.

"The girls made it," Melody interjects excitedly.

The rest of the table, including myself, goes completely silent. All I can hear is David swallowing hard, Mom gulping air, and Ando's heavy breathing.

"Th-the aunts mu-made this?" Mom stammers uncharacteristically.

Ando's eyes light up at the mention of dessert.

"What kind of dessert did you make?"

"Cherry cobbler," they grin.

"No way!" David shouts exuberantly, earning him a glare from *'The Girls'*. I never thought I would hear anyone refer to them in such a *sweet* way.

Harpies, maybe.

Piranhas, possibly, but I never, *ever* would refer to ancient bad-asses as *'The Girls'*.

"We can hear you," Ligeia and Leukosia glare at me.

I really must learn to block my thoughts.

"We should eat," their mother encourages. "Before the food gets cold."

Patiently, everyone waits for their turn as the various serving dishes get passed around the table allowing everyone to take their fill. Ando, of course, loads up on mostly meat and bread until Dad orders him to have some vegetables. David helps himself to a little of everything, so does Mom. The aunts avoid the meats, and concentrate on the breads and cheeses. Melody fills her plate with vegetables and bread while I take a heaping portion of the rare salmon.

"Is that all you want, Selena?" Melody questions: taking a little butter to smear on her roll.

"Yes," I smile, taking a bite.

Oh! My! Gravy!

"This is fantastic!" I moan my delight as Melody laughs.

"I am glad that you are enjoying it," she replies, taking a bite of her bread.

"Why don't I feel sick anymore?" I ponder out loud, right before taking another forkful of the succulent fish.

Melody smiles knowingly.

"Being near me calms you," she educates. "When you are stress-free, your digestive system returns to normal and your appetite returns."

"Makes sense," Dad comments after swallowing a mouthful of roasted beets.

"How is the cheese?" Melody queries her daughters.

"Perfect!" they reply in unison, making us all smile as they both reach for more mozzarella and a couple of slices of pumpernickel bread.

Mom opens her mouth to comment, but the words never get the chance to pass her lips. Outside, we hear a brash screech, followed by a loud crack of lightning and a menacing roll of thunder, right before the sky opens and a deluge of salt-tinged rain begins to fall. Violently, the storm bashes the thatched roof and pounds the glass windowpanes with a force so powerful that I worry they might shatter.

Everyone instantly stops eating; our eyes glued to the ceiling as sounds resembling footsteps can be heard overhead, causing the rafters to squeak from the weight of whatever is up there. Soon even the footsteps are drowned out by the relentless thunderstorm.

Another bloodcurdling screech pierces our ears.

"Belen!" Melody gasps. "Get the children down to the root cellar!"

Everyone hesitates for a moment too long.

"Now!" the Muse commands, showing her status as the head of the family. "There is an entrance under the area rug in the living room!"

"What's happening?" David blurts as he stands and grabs Ando's upper arm, keeping him close.

Before Melody can answer his question, there is another loud crash as the ceiling collapses, but this time it comes from the kitchen. *The Three* jump up with their scales in place and talons drawn, ready for battle. The sight of them in this warrior-like state is enough to chill the bones of any army. Whatever is on the roof had better be prepared to throw down because these women sure are.

Stunned, David stands gawking while Ando seems lost in the fray.

"Why are you just standing there?" Mom shouts, pointing to the rug beneath the coffee table. *"Go!"*

Without further hesitation, David and Ando rush to the other room. From where I still stand ready to fight, I see them move the coffee table, kick the rug out of the way and just as Melody said, there is a door that my stepfather pulls up that leads into the dark root cellar.

"Selena!" *The Three* bellow in our Siren language, the sound reverberates within the walls of the edifice. "Go to the cellar!"

"I want to help!" I shout over the pummeling rain.

"We will not have you in danger!" Mom, Ligeia and Leukosia proclaim in one combined voice.

"Yes, little guppy," I hear that terror inducing voice that haunts my dreams come from the direction of the kitchen. "I guarantee things are going to get dangerous!"

"Amphitrite!" I gasp, taking a step backward and bumping into my chair, which flips me backward. With a loud hurtful thud, I land on the floor on my back in a rumpled heap of haphazardly piled limbs.

"It has been a while, young one," Amphitrite smiles in her usual carefree manner as she comes into view in the kitchen doorway, her ego still firmly intact. Needless to say, she is an intimidating sight standing there, her statuesque form almost filling the passage completely. Her body is drenched, but just as before her hair remains dry and untouched.

"Pardon my appearance," the goddess apologizes as though she has been invited to some grand *soirée*. "Let me freshen up."

Just as before when she tricked me into believing that she was Ligeia, her long strawberry-blonde tresses start to shimmer and restructure until they transform into another stunning ankle-length toga, this time in the exact shade of the cloudy night sky; on her feet is a pair of crimson sandals that have knife-like miniature blades protruding from the toes. The color of the gown enhances her milky jade eyes, and her alabaster skin once again reminds me of luminous seafoam highlighting the crest of waves when the seas are at their most violent.

"You have not changed one-bit, little guppy," Amphitrite's remark makes my palms itch and my heart race. I try to speak, but before I can finish my thought, the vengeful goddess wags a boney finger at me. Her irises are glowing like cat eyes in the darkness.

Fearlessly, Melody bypasses *The Three* and stands toe to toe with the supernatural being. Amphitrite studies her curiously but does not seem to recognize who she is.

"Who are you?" the goddess questions, taking a step forward.

"No one of consequence," Melody replies without emotion.

"Do you know who I am, lesser being?" the *'woman'* stands straighter.

The Muse stands just as straight, arms folded across her chest, eyes narrowed as she sizes up her enemy.

"You are Amphitrite, Daughter of Nereus and Doris, Concubine of Poseidon," Melody lists the goddess' lineage like a well-educated professor of anthropology. The idea that her background could be read off like a takeout menu seems to have unnerved the other woman.

"I am no one's *concubine!*" Amphitrite snarls, losing her cool exterior.

"Poseidon left you for someone else, did he not?" Melody continues to prod.

My mouth gapes as Amphitrite's temper flares and she lunges for my great-grandmother's neck.

'Get everyone out of here!' I hear Melody's voice inside of my head, and from the look of Mom and the aunts they heard it too.

As we stare at the two entities, neither one backing down, Melody grips the goddesses' wrist and holds it almost effortlessly at bay. The Muse's eyes now shift to a wicked shade of onyx with flecks of gold. Amphitrite's eyes widen at the realization that this much smaller 'woman' is able to best her.

"This cannot be!" the strawberry-blonde haired being yells. With a hard shove, Melody pushes her back causing the creature to stumble momentarily then quickly rights herself. "What are you?"

"Muse," Melody reveals with a slight upturn of her naturally pouty lips. "The first Muse, actually."

The goddess lunges again, talons at full length, and manages to scrape Melody's arm, but instead of bleeding the skin immediately mends, leaving no trace that it was ever injured.

Holy cow! My great-grandmother is a serious badass too!

"Take the family and go!" Melody shouts at no one in particular.

"We can't leave you here alone!" I shout back as I leap to her aid, but to my surprise, Melody has erected an invisible shield around her and her foe's body, which I bounce off of when I bump into it.

Crap! Are muses more powerful than Sirens? I'm about to find out!

Ignoring me for the moment, Melody closes her eyes and all around us the cottage begins to flicker, flash then fade. In the nearby tree, Belen squawks and flaps his gigantic wings, then rises up and darts just like an arrow into the disappearing cottage. He lands on the goddesses' head with drawn talons, the sound of her shriek curls my toes.

"Get out, Belen!" Melody commands with a wave of her slender hand, sending an imperceptible force to push the furious bird away.

"What's going on?" I yell at my mother who has already retrieved David and Ando from the root cellar and is almost to the front door. Leukosia, following her lead, grabs me by the wrist and hurries me to the nearest exit, which due to our location is the backdoor. Before I can protest, she pushes me outside and holds me in place so I cannot reenter the vanishing cottage. Ligeia is still indoors and all I can see is her form being pushed toward the front door by an unseen force as Melody holds Amphitrite in place, giving her daughter a chance to escape.

Unable to tear my gaze away, I am mesmerized by Melody's strength and mental ability, but most of all her self-sacrificing nature. There is a sudden ferocious crack, followed by the acidic scent of burnt metal and blinding smoke. Without warning, another indiscernible sonic wave explodes outward; its force throws us all several feet up and away. Thankfully, the leafy carpet softens our landing. From our scattered positions, all we can do is stare as the cottage fades into the mist, the only sign that it was ever there are several clumps of material from the roof.

Up above on a tree branch perches Belen, who gives a sad *'hoot'* and flies into the surrounding woods, leaving us speechlessly staring after him.

CHAPTER TWENTY-TWO

The entire family, including the aunts, spend the next two hours searching the woods where Melody's home normally resides. Unfortunately, we find neither Melody nor Belen; both have disappeared like the mist that usually hides their homestead. All we can do now is sit in the living room of the villa planning our next move.

"Where could they have gone?" Mom interrogates the aunts, who are both staring out of the glass doors leading to the terrace. The ominous layer of storm clouds that earlier covered the sky has already drifted out to sea, carrying that disturbing eeriness with it. A refreshing gust of wind has blown away the stifling odor of earlier and the soothing fragrance of crisp citrus and tangy olives replaces it. Another favorable sign is the return of the animals. Even the mosquitoes are a welcomed 'bite'.

"What was the last thing you saw, Selena?" Mom turns her attention on me; the last person to see Melody and Amphitrite locked in a stalemate.

"Was our mother unhurt?" Leukosia and Ligeia prod with wistful filled eyes. "What was her condition?"

Unsure of how to respond, I shake my head.

"Neither one was hurt," I confirm thoughtfully after all gazes remain on me.

"Are you certain?" David asks next, his expression dark with concern.

I nod, wishing I had seen more, that I knew more. I am just as lost as they are. Even more so since I have dealt with the diabolical goddess on more than one occasion and have come up wanting.

"Maybe we should go back and take another look?" Ando states as he reaches for his sneakers and starts to put them on.

"The aunts and I are going back to the woods," Mom informs parentally. "The rest of you are staying here."

"But Mom—"

"No *'but Mom'* young man," our mother stops him in midsentence. "This isn't a game."

"Please, I want to help find Melody," he pouts. "She trusted me first."

Mom shakes her head as she gives him a quick kiss to the forehead.

"Stay here with Daddy and Lena," she orders with a look that would halt a tidal wave in its track. Angrily, he nods then without a word, stomps down the hallway to his room where he firmly closes the door behind him. Knowing her son, Mom turns to my stepfather.

"Could you please activate the security system after we leave so he doesn't escape?" she half-smiles.

"I'm right there with you," David agrees as he kisses his wife on the cheek.

"Good luck, Mom," I implore, giving her a tight hug then turn to do the same to the aunts, but they avoid my grasp. I guess Melody's humanity has worn off and they are back to their normal Sireny selves.

"Thanks, sweetheart," my mother responds, with a grateful grin. "Watch over Ando and Dad."

"I will," I promise.

"We have to go before sunrise, Marina," Leukosia reminds, as she and Ligeia walk toward the front door and retrieve the keys to the Range Rover.

"What happens at sunrise?" Dad grills his wife.

"Sirens can only track their prey for a few hours before they lose their scent," Mom confesses guiltily. "Once that happens—"

"Then they become the prey?" Dad repeats with a surprised expression.

"Poor choice of words," Mom confirms uneasily.

"Marina, we must go!" Ligeia exclaims impatiently.

"I know… I know," Mom sighs heavily, the burden of all of this weighing heavily on her shoulders. "I'll call with an update as soon as I can."

"You better," he challenges, unafraid of the powerful beings in front of him getting ready to go on a hunt for the matriarch of our family and her possible abductor.

Mom stops long enough to give him a passionate kiss.

"What's that for?" he asks, face reddening in public.

"Just in case," she whispers.

"Don't say that," he warns. "It's not funny."

"I'm sorry, my love," she sighs, giving him one last kiss. "Be safe."

"You too," Dad implores.

With goodbyes said, *The Three* leave to find Melody and hopefully bring her back alive.

The sudden rap on my door startles me more than the spine-tingling horror story I am currently reading. I stumbled across the *Frostbitten* blog online and read the author's short stories and was totally impressed. I do not usually read scary books, but this writer has a real knack for *'giving hope then taking it away'*. Now, I am hooked.

"Who's there?" I blurt, wondering if a prowler would knock before entering.

"It's me, Lena," Ando answers in a hushed tone.

"I thought you were already asleep," I scold, trying not to snicker.

"Can I come in?" he asks, and I see the shadow of his little feet shuffling outside of the door.

"Go sleep with Dad," I gently encourage, not wanting to share my bed tonight.

"He's waiting up for Mom," my brother informs sadly.

"You should keep him company," I encourage with a sneaky grin.

"Please, Lena," he pouts and I can imagine the face he is making.

"Come in," I finally give in.

"Thanks, Lena," he smiles sleepily as he opens the door.

Before I can change my mind, he jumps onto the empty side of the mattress and burrows under the comforter.

"Where's Alfredo?" I question, missing the sight of his furry companion.

"I left him," Ando yawns. "What are you doing?"

"Just reading," I reply, but before I can elaborate, I hear his soft snores.

Poor us!

In a perfect world, we would not have any worries, let alone have to deal with a lunatic sea goddess who wants the location of our familial home and is willing to kill to get it. Normally, this is not something that a six-year-old boy should be dealing with. It is also not something his almost seventeen-year-old sister should be dealing with either.

I am just about to return to my short story when another knock stops me.

"Selena?"

It is my stepfather. His voice is tense and worrisome which causes my senses to shift to high-gear. David is the rock of our family. This is not some invented flattery. There is no denying that when the rest of us are unsure of what to do or how to handle a situation, my stepdad can always figure out a plan on how to fix it. To hear him with a slight waver to his voice makes me want to throw up my arms in surrender and board the next flight back to Isla Flora.

Unfortunately, we cannot do that because the evil will only follow us there.

"Are you awake?" he asks quietly.

"Yes," I whisper, hoping to not wake Ando.

"Is your brother with you?"

"Yes," I add, but do not elaborate when he starts to stir.

Quickly, I grab my robe and push my feet into my slippers as I tiptoe toward the door. Standing in the hallway looking desperate is my stepfather. I already know why he is upset.

"Has Mom come back home yet?" I query, tying the fabric belt of the robe.

He shakes his head as he runs a frustrated hand though his hair.

"Do you want me to try contacting her telepathically?"

"Could you please?" he huffs without hesitation.

Understanding his frustration, I nod and immediately close my eyes in order to help me concentrate on getting a signal. It is not a reliable signal like the one on a cellular device. This connection is hard to make and easy to lose and sadly there is no satellite to blame when a signal cannot be formed. I hope for David's sake that I am able to do it without any problems tonight.

"Are you getting anything?" he utters in less than a minute of me trying. "Anything at all?"

"Shh!" I hush, concentrating with all of my might. "Not yet. Give me a reasonable amount of time."

"Alright," he huffs again as he starts to pace up and down the narrow hallway, his broad shoulders barely able to maneuver in the tight area without grazing the walls on either side.

'Mom?' I think as loud as I can. *'Can you hear me?'*

No answer.

'Tia Ligeia? Tia Leukosia?' I mentally call to the aunts as well, hoping that they may answer.

The airwaves are clear, but silent.

"Any luck?" Dad questions, his eyelids heavy with sleep.

Disappointed in myself, I shake my head.

"I'll try again," I attempt to smile for his sake, but cannot control the muscle in order to complete the simple task.

Dad and I continue the ritual, me concentrating on contacting Mom and him pacing nervously as he waits. We do this for almost an hour before I give up.

"I'm so sorry," I apologize as a migraine slams into my brain. "I can't get a hold of her or the aunts."

"It's okay," he manages a smile for me, but it does not reach his eyes. "I'm sure she'll be home when she can."

I nod, but my imagination runs away from me and I cannot help but wonder if two first generation Sirens, one second generation Siren, and an ageless Muse can defeat an undefeatable sea goddess. I am sure there is nothing in Yaya Parthenope's biography that tells of something as epic as this. Suddenly, the urge to consult Grandpa Theodore's journal becomes overwhelming and my first priority.

"Well," I proclaim, giving my stepdad a quick kiss to his cheek. "I think I'll turn in now."

"Alright," he frowns and turns to retreat to the living room to continue waiting for Mom. "Do you want me to transfer your brother back to his own bed?"

I grin.

"Nope," I mumble. "I kinda like the company, especially since—"

"Since everything is going to hell in a handbasket?" David finishes my sentence.

"Exactly," I nod.

Dad allows himself to chuckle, easing our tension just a bit.

"Goodnight, sweetheart," he says as he walks away.

"Goodnight, Dad," I respond, watching him turn the corner.

As soon as he is out of sight, I rush into my bedroom where Ando is fast asleep in the same position that I left him in. I envy him being able to relax his mind enough to go to sleep. My brain is so completely wired that I could not sleep even if I wanted to. Instead, I decide to read the journal and maybe, just maybe, it will shed some light on our predicament.

As quietly as possible, I open the closet door and find my large suitcase. Slowly, I unzip it, careful not to wake Ando and retrieve the old leather-bound journal that once belonged to my grandfather. Not my grandfather, Marcus

Antonius, the Roman sea captain, but my Greek grandfather, Theodore Thermopolis, the architect/mythology expert. Sadly, if I think about my complicated lineage too much, it will only make my migraine worse.

Not wanting to turn on the light, I sit on the floor cross-legged and switch to my Siren-vision. All of a sudden, the journal is illuminated as if I am wearing night vision goggles. I see everything crisp and clear. One of the perks of being otherworldly, I guess.

On a mission, I thumb-through the worn pages looking for anything remotely associated with sea goddesses, Poseidon, Ares, Amphitrite... anything at all that may help us fight the powerful being that wants to find the Siren Grotto.

"There has to be something," I whisper to myself, my palms sweating profusely as I turn the pages. "Yaya Parthenope must have mentioned Amphitrite."

It seems like an eternity before a short passage catches my attention. Eagerly, I read it:

There is no escaping the sea-witch, Amphitrite...

I have tried to reason with her, tried to express my neutrality towards her and her vile husband, Poseidon. My heart belongs to

Marcus and that is where it shall remain. Yet she does not believe. It is Poseidon that pursues me, not I him. It is because of her jealousy and vengeful nature that I am forced to leave my child and her father... on land... without me and in order to keep my sisters safe, I will leave them too and venture out on my own.

Needing more information, I rush to my laptop and power it up. Hastily, I search for any sites about Amphitrite. It is not long before several websites pop up. Encyclopedia Britannica says:

> Amphitrite, in Greek mythology, the goddess of the sea, wife of the god Poseidon, and one of the 50 (or 100) daughters (the Nereids) of Nereus and Doris (the daughter of Oceanus). Poseidon chose Amphitrite from among her sisters as the Nereids performed a dance on the isle of Naxos. Refusing his offer of marriage, she fled to Atlas, from whom she was retrieved by a dolphin sent by Poseidon. Amphitrite then returned, becoming Poseidon's wife; he rewarded the dolphin by making it a constellation...

Confused, I sit in the same position for several minutes, contemplating what I have just read. All of this trouble started eons ago because Poseidon, God of the Sea, could not keep it in his pants. Why should our family suffer for his lack of fidelity, lack of loyalty? We should not have to, but apparently, we do. Amphitrite blames our kind for her husband's wandering eye and even though my grandmother, Parthenope, rejected his advances, her familial line is persecuted, nonetheless.

Again, I turn to the laptop and continue searching for more facts. To my dismay, all I find are pieces of incomplete sightings of mermaids mistaken for Sirens or references to Ovid's ancient writings. Some of those accounts are actually true; I learned this from my mother and the aunts. However, most of these accounts are fiction that we let people believe so they will never truly believe in our existence. Instead, we let them trust that mythology is only a simplistic way of understanding the world around us, but the truth is that supernatural beings exist among human beings.

For their sake, this fact must never come to light.

Tap! Tap! Tap!

From my restless sleep I cannot tell if the knocking is in my dream or coming from somewhere else. The scene around me is quiet and serene. What I hear in the distance is annoyingly loud.

Knock! Knock! Knock!

Dear Father!

"Will I ever sleep again?" I groan, hearing the relentless pounding once more.

"Lena!" I recognize my brother's voice and bolt upright, Ando is sitting up too, his eyes bright and terrified.

"Huh?" I say still cloaked in a groggy haze. "What?"

"Lena!" he exclaims, pointing to the window. "I heard tapping... from outside!"

"Why didn't you check?" I ask, rubbing the sleep out of my eyes.

Ando glares at me, speechless that I would even suggest such a thing. My brother is no fool. Actually, he is quite the opposite. At least one of us is.

Cautiously, I slink off of the bed toward the closed window where the sound is coming from. Slowly, I make a gap in the curtains and peek out into the lingering darkness. Cautiously, I stare out of the closed window. My heart is thumping like a drum inside of my chest. My breathing is labored, and my palms are dripping with sweat. Unable to see, I switch on my night vision and examine the backyard.

Tap! Tap! Tap!

"Screech-Squawk-Screech!"

"Belen!" Ando shouts in my ear almost deafening me.

"Belen?" I proclaim as I unlock and open the window causing the alarm to sound.

The high-pitched squealing of the mechanical security device echoes throughout the entire house. Ando is covering his ears. Belen is flapping his wings in annoyance. I, on the other hand, rush out of the room towards my parents' bedroom. As I turn the corner to get to the living room, I find Dad already disarming the pesky device.

"What happened?" Dad yells. "Why did you open your bedroom window?"

"It's Belen!" Ando shouts as he and the feisty owl race down the hallway. "He was tapping on the window!"

"Who is Belen?" Dad asks as the bird lands on the back of the sofa.

The owl chatters and hoots his thoughts.

"Belen is Melody's friend," Ando informs with a large grin.

"Really?" Dad smiles and touches the bird's left wing and Belen lets him. "He's magnificent. Nice to meet you, Belen."

Seeing how friendly the owl is, I reach toward him with my right hand, and as soon as I am within touching distance the darn bird pecks me! Thank heavens it did not break the skin. More than aggravated, I stare at him, and he has the nerve to stare back.

"Why don't you like me you silly bird?" I scowl, rubbing the area which is now red.

Belen actually turns his head away from me and gently begins rubbing his fluffy feathered cheek on Ando's forehead, making him laugh.

"Stop it, Belen!" Ando says, giggling like a hyena. "That tickles!"

"Thanks a lot, bird," I grumble and then stick my tongue out at him.

"Why are you here, Belen?" Dad asks, but of course does not expect an answer.

What happens next blows us all away.

"Mom's hurt!" Ando gasps. "He wants us to follow him!"

"How do you know that?" I inquire, my mind racing to comprehend.

Ando shrugs.

"I don't know," he huffs and rolls his eyes. "I just do! I can hear his thoughts."

"Do you trust this bird?" Dad grills us.

"I guess so," I grumble, glaring at Ando and then at Belen.

"I do!" Ando raises his voice. "He's Melody's friend!"

"That's good enough for me," Dad admits. "Get dressed! Your mother needs us!"

In less than five minutes we are in our rental vehicle following Melody's pet as he flies in the direction of the highest plateau on Capri. Effortlessly, he glides letting pockets of air help him on his journey. When we reach our destination, he lands weightlessly on a thick birch branch and waits as we scamper out of the vehicle.

Out of the car, the air is humid and sticky. I instantly start to perspire, and I wish that I could call in a storm to cool us down.

"Don't do that!" Ando verbally slaps me. "Belen says it will make tracking Mom harder."

"Is that what the bird says?" Dad questions with a frown.

Ando nods and click-clack-chirps to his new confidant and to our surprise, Belen answers back.

"You can truly understand what he is saying?" I question, feeling jealous.

"I can," Ando responds, looking just as confused.

"Sirens aren't supposed to be able to speak to land creatures, only ones from the sea," I recap the lesson that

Leukosia gave me months ago when we were still on Isla Flora. "How can you talk to him?"

"I don't know, Lena," Ando answers sassily. "We'll find out *after* we find Mom."

Without further hesitation, Belen springs off of the branch and flies into the air. For several minutes, he circles the area until he spots something.

"Let's go!" Ando beckons, leading the way. "He's found her!"

Sprinting in the direction that Belen is soaring, we stumble upon a cave hidden among the gray cliffs.

"She's in there?" our parent asks and Belen nods in response.

So cool!

"Marina!" David shouts, leading the way into the dimly lit space. "Honey! Are you in here?"

Nothing.

"Mom!" I call out next. "Please say something!"

"Mommy!" Ando sniffles as he takes Dad's hand. "Can you hear us?"

Still there is nothing.

Immediately, David takes out his cellphone and switches it to 'flashlight' mode. The space fills with glorious artificial light.

Thank heavens for technology!

🦉

The cave is much cooler than outside. All around us, the rocky, uneven walls are damp with moisture and clumps of moss cling to the surface. A few blue lizards are gathered near the ceiling, and a small black snake slithers across our path, but does not bother us.

"Stay together," Dad orders, and Ando and I follow without question.

"Marina!" Dad shouts again, the vein at his temple pounding with agitation and concern.

"David?" Mom's soft voice comes from the back of the space.

"Mom!" I answer, rushing past my stepfather toward the sound. "We're here!"

"We're coming for you, Mommy!" Ando adds with a grin.

"I am back here!" she shouts, helping us through the now meandering tunnel that seems to be longer than expected.

"Honey, where are you?" David bellows.

"I am here!" Mom responds in desperation. "Do not leave me here!"

"Just hold on!" he hollers.

As we walk, the cave has become totally dark. Black like tar dark and my night vision turns on by itself.

"Dad!" I squeal as my all too sensitive Siren-vision is blinded by the cellphone. "It's too bright!"

Quickly, he switches it off.

Ahh! Much better!

"Umm," he begins. "Now, I can't see."

If our situation was not so dire, this would be hilarious.

"We'll guide you, Daddy," my brother thoughtfully intervenes. "Lena, can you see her?"

Glancing around, I spot our mother curled in a ball on the dirt covered ground. Her long black hair hangs in wet clumps around her face hiding her delicate features. Cold, her arms are wrapped around her body trying to trap what little warmth is left in the cave.

"Marina!" David shouts, reaching her first. "We're taking you home."

Slowly... carefully... David turns her onto her back.

It's not Mom!

It is the old woman from the restaurant... the one with the fish!

"Holy crap!" I yell, grabbing David and Ando and yanking them behind me.

"Who are you?" I growl, showing my teeth, trying to look more menacing than I actually am.

The woman smiles showing her ragged, shark-like teeth. Terrified, I try calling my scales, but nothing happens. I try calling my mother and the aunts, but that does not work either. All I can do is hope this creature is not more powerful than I am.

"No one of importance," she hisses, sounding just as a snake would.

"Answer me!" I glare angrily, hoping to instill some fear in her.

"You may call me Pythia," she responds.

We all stand watching her, waiting for her next move. This thing can sound and look like my mother, but she is not a Siren. Examining her solid appearance, I make the conclusion that she is not Amphitrite.

"Precious Selena," the old woman purrs, the sound is hollow and emotionless.

Furious, Dad pushes me aside as he confronts the woman.

"David the Brave," she cackles, the sound like nails on a chalkboard.

Ando puffs out his chest, but remains where he is.

"Ando, dear sweet boy," she cackles, turning in his direction.

"Where's my wife?" David interrogates, both hands clenched into fists, ready to fight.

"She is not here," the woman replies, slowly standing.

"Where... is... my... wife?" he repeats gruffly, taking a step forward.

"Good question," she huffs. "I was tracking her, but Sirens are slippery creatures. She has eluded me."

Thank goodness!

"How did you trick Belen?" Ando asks, just as confused as the rest of us.

"In the end, he is only a bird," she chuckles. "Any way, that is not Belen."

"What?" the three of us gasp in shock.

The being shakes her dark mane, and as she does so, the hairs lighten back to a weathered gray. Before our eyes, her body shrinks and hunches and plumps until she looks the same as she did at the restaurant when she delivered a dead fish to our table in front of everyone eating in the café.

Whistling loudly, she calls for the Belen imposter. In the blink of an eye, the bird flies into the cave and lands on his master's shoulder. With one snap of her finger, the bird sheds his owl appearance and transforms into a large black raven with beady little ebony eyes.

"This is Umbra," she introduces her counterpart.

The vicious raven caws and bobs his head in an agitated motion.

Wow! Do all birds hate me?

"What did you do to Belen?" Ando sneers.

"Nothing," she grins. "He is probably with your great-grandmother or perhaps your mother and the sisters have found him."

"You're a witch!" I snarl, walking to her.

She shakes her head.

"I am not a mere witch," she says losing her cheesy smile. "I am something more powerful than you can possibly comprehend."

As I run toward her, eager to show her my newly-found Siren strength, she raises her hands and chants in a language that resembles Latin. All of the oxygen in the cave is sucked away and immediately David, Ando, and I begin to suffocate. Somehow, David manages to grab us both by the hands and runs toward the entrance, but when we are almost near the exit, we hear a thunderous clap of the cavern imploding and the rocks at the entrance break off and fill the entrance, blocking our way.

Gasping like fish out of water, we choke and wheeze until our bodies give up. From my peripheral vision, I see David drop first, then Ando, while I try with my all to push the rocks out of the way. It is not long before my vision blurs and my body hits the ground with a loud thud. All there is is sweet oblivion and the sound of the lizards scurrying near my head.

It is hot now. Too hot. The sun's rays beat down on my skin, warming it like a favorite blanket would.

"Selena!" I hear my mother's voice. "Open your eyes!"

Slowly, I wake.

"Mom?"

"Are you alright?" my mother asks, her hands brushing the hair out of my eyes and away from my heated forehead.

"Is it really you?" I whimper, unable to muster the strength it would take to defend myself if it is not.

She nods.

"It's really me," she gushes, kissing my cheek.

"Prove it," I gasp another much-needed breath.

"Do you want to be grounded now or later?" she jokes.

"It's you," I grin, feeling better.

Suddenly, I remember Dad and Ando.

"Where are the guys?" I ask, sitting up.

"They're fine," she says pointing a few feet away where the aunts are watching over David and Ando while they slowly sip coconut water from the husks. Mom offers me some too, which I gladly accept. With one long gulp, I consume it all.

"What happened?" my mother probes.

I quickly explain about the tapping at the window and Belen, or who we thought was Belen, leading us to this cave. Haphazardly, I give an explanation about the witch or whatever she was as Mom and the aunts listen intently. When I finally finish, my mother speaks.

"The same woman from the restaurant?" she frowns.

"Yup!" I reply, breaking open the coconut husk and scooping out the squishy jelly inside, devouring all of it ravenously.

"And the fake Belen told you I was hurt?" she adds.

"Uh huh," I respond as I continue to chew the sweet and tender coconut flesh. "He told Ando."

"Your brother can communicate with land animals?" my mother asks with surprise.

I nod again, my lungs returning to normal.

"Where is Melody? Did you find her? Is she okay?" I blurt my thoughts without care of how desperate I may sound.

Mom lays a comforting hand on my shoulder.

"We haven't found Melody or Belen," Mom informs bleakly. "But from what I saw last night, Melody can hold her own."

"That's true," I agree, licking my lips of the sweet liquid.

From where I sit at the mouth of the cave, I see where Mom and the aunts removed the rocks that were blocking our exit. It looks like they lit a stick of dynamite, but in one of the larger stones there is an indent that looks like a fist. It is impressive to know that the women in my family can truly move mountains. One day, I hope to do the same.

"We should get home before sunrise," Mom states anxiously. "The aunts need to return to the sea."

"What about Melody?" I question once more, looking disappointed that we could not find her.

"Right now my main concern is for my family," Mom gently pinches my cheek. "We've had enough supernatural antics for one night."

Gently, she takes my hand and pulls me to my feet. She encircles my shoulders and leads me in the direction of the parked Range Rover. Ligeia carries Ando while Leukosia assists David. Tonight, we have more battle scars than usual, but at least everyone is alive and able to fight another day.

I hope.

I say a brief prayer that we will find my great-grandmother and her loyal pet.

I say another prayer that we never meet the old woman again.

CHAPTER TWENTY-THREE

Sleep comes to me in spurts. Ten minutes here, twenty minutes there. I almost get an entire hour, but a nightmare starring Amphitrite dressed as Michael Meyers from the movie *Halloween* and Pythia sporting a *Leatherface* mask from *The Texas Chainsaw Massacre* haunts my unconscious.

As I run from the two serial killers hunting me through the mall on Isla Flora, I hide behind a statue of Poseidon in the fountain located on the main floor. As I wait for my hunters to leave, the statue starts a conversation with me about how Melody broke his heart then Parthenope did the same.

"Like mother like daughter," the Sea God huffs with a wave of his hand as he stares down his pointed nose at me in my crouched position.

Before I can reply, Michael Myers finds me, but thankfully I am startled awake before he can plunge his enormous butcher's knife into my skull. I wake screaming. In my state of panic, I try to move but I cannot due to the sweat-drenched covers wrapped around my body like a mummified corpse. I am not afraid to admit that I would pay a million pieces of gold to get a full night's sleep. Sadly, I do not know how much more of this I can tolerate before completely losing my mind.

As usual, I grab my robe and make my way to the kitchen. For a brief moment, I deliberate whether or not to make myself more presentable, but I realize that I do not care. If my hair is standing up like Medusa's snakes then so be it. Since we had such a horrible night, no one should fault me for looking as badly as I feel.

As I enter the kitchen, Mom greets me.

"Good morning, sleepy head," she says, trying to sound happy, but coming up short.

"What's good about it?" I reply snippily, not caring at the moment.

With red-rimmed eyes, she gives me a stern stare then continues cutting an assortment of fresh vegetables.

"What's wrong with you?" she enquires, cocking her head to the side like a bird.

"Well... if I don't answer *The Calling* soon, I'll cease being a Siren apparently," I reply reaching for the jug of orange juice. "Or I'll turn into a land-walking, no-conscience-having, possibly murderous fish-girl."

Mom reaches for a glass bowl currently half-filled with chopped celery, onions and diced potatoes. From the smell coming from the Dutch-oven on the stovetop, she has already started simmering the chicken stock. This is a good sign that we will be having her famous chicken pot pies for dinner tonight.

"Don't you think you're being a tad melodramatic?" she actually laughs.

Something inside of me starts to bubble.

"It's not funny!" I snap, putting the clear container back into the refrigerator without filling my glass.

My mother continues to watch me but remains quiet as she sizes me up.

"I didn't ask for this life," I remind for the umpteenth time. "I just want to be a semi-normal teenager who only has to worry about my hair not frizzing, which dress to wear to a school dance or if I have a boyfriend or not."

"Don't you think I wanted the same thing when I was your age?" Mom questions firmly, waving the knife around arbitrarily.

"How would I know what you wanted when you were my age?" I retort, almost on the brink of tears.

Then my mind drifts to Andrew and what he would think about all of this. Surprisingly, he still wants to date me even though I am a freakish creature, go figure. But now *this*. This is more than anyone should have to deal with.

"This is so unfair," I mutter as I sit at the dinette wishing this was all a bad dream.

For the moment, Mom stops chopping a large carrot and wipes her hands once more on the red apron around her waist. She joins me, her face filled with love and tranquility. I do not know how she can always find the silver lining to any problem.

"Don't worry until there's something to worry about," she says giving me a grin and a wink.

"I don't believe that's possible," I admit, letting her hug me.

"Anything is possible," my mother replies and embraces me tighter.

By midafternoon, my mood has not changed. In fact, it is worse. I have come to the decision that I truly loathe being a Siren. My brother, on the other hand, loves it. Right now, he sits on the balcony railing like he is immortal, building underwater scenes with his Legos. I, on the other hand, lean against the railing wishing I was a regular girl, back home hanging out with my friends and holding hands with Andrew as we stroll through the mall window-shopping.

Shocking me, Ando jumps up to a standing position on top of the white, stucco railing and pretends he is a tightrope walker in the circus.

"Be careful!" I reprimand, grabbing him by the waist so he does not tumble down into the sea. I know he would probably love the thrill of it, but someone might see him and think the worst, then we would have to deal with the local authorities probing about why a six-year-old fell off of a cliff into the sea and survived. And not just survived but wanted to do it again.

"I'm not afraid," he says as he flexes his muscles pretending to be *The Incredible Hulk*. "I can't wait to try cliff diving like you and Mommy."

Ando jumps a foot into the air and lands in a graceful pose.

"You're such a boy," I tease with a chuckle.

My brother grins at the offhanded compliment then his gaze locks on something.

"Do you see it?" Ando squeals, pointing to the same dark shape on the horizon that we had seen so many weeks ago.

I squint, barring my eyes from the bright sunlight with the back of my hand. Instantly, my stomach turns into a pile of knots while my cheeks redden, and my palms sweat.

Why now?

"I see it too," I answer on a nervous exhale, wishing it away, but it stays firmly in place, mocking me.

"What are you looking at?" Dad questions as he comes to stand beside us on the patio as we look out at the distant horizon. "Is that *thing* back?"

"Yes," Ando and I reply at once.

Dad groans his disappointment.

"It always freaks me out when you do that robotic answering together thing," he rebukes without malice.

"Sorry," we do it again, but not on purpose.

Ando smiles mischievously.

"It's a Siren thing," he says as if it is a normal occurrence.

"It certainly is," Mom agrees as she comes to stand to the left of her husband. Adoringly, she smiles at him and takes his much larger paw in her mitt. She always calls David's hands paws. When I was younger, I asked her why she did that and her response was: 'They're large and strong, but gentle at the same time.'

They really are.

"Can you see it, Mommy?" Ando questions, turning back to the shape that keeps flickering and fading in and out.

"I can," Mom reveals with an off-putting expression.

"Why is it back?" I ask, not hiding my agitation.

"Because you haven't fulfilled your destiny," she reminds. "I think it's your time."

Hearing these words, something inside of me clicks and I know what must be done.

"Mom?" I query, my heartbeat accelerating.

"Yes, honey?" she replies with hope in her voice.

"You're right," I take a deep breath. "It's time."

That evening, after the last rays of sunshine depart the Earth, Ando, Mom, and I leave the villa via the long jump down the side of the very high cliff facing the *Marina Piccola*. The sea is relatively placid and the soft hint of night-blooming Jasmine perfumes the air. The last songs of the gulls echo against the exterior surface of the silver-gray cliffs, and combine with the drumming of the crashing waves against the coastline. The sound fills our ears as we plummet into the Tyrrhenian Sea. A fairly inconspicuous, barely audible splash is the only clue that we were ever there.

"Are you sure this is a good idea?" I clack to Mom as she swims to my left, my brother to my right.

"We need to do this," she clicks back reassuringly.

"Isn't Ando too young?" I state, looking at my brother who is busy scanning the surrounding area.

Mom gives him a bright smile.

"It won't hurt," she says with a confident tone, but her eyes dart away telling me silently that it will hurt, a lot.

Ando swims a little farther ahead as he plays tag with a Maltese Skate that betrays its hiding place against the bumpy seabed in order to have a little fun with my exuberant brother. It amuses me to watch how carefree they are considering my mind is mulling over every possible thing that can go wrong during *The Calling*.

"I don't think Ando should come with us," I click-clack-whistle my objection causing both Mom and Ando to glare at me.

"Why do you say that?" Mom asks with a confused stare.

Sensing the growing tension, the Maltese Skate returns to his spot on the sea floor; his skin is the perfect camouflage against the stony surface.

"He's only a quarter Siren, plus he's the only male Siren… *ever*," I remind. "How do we know the water in the Siren Grotto won't harm him, possibly kill him?"

Ando sticks his tongue out at me.

"I'm a Siren!" he chastises sternly with sharp clicks and clacks. "It doesn't matter that I'm only a small bit. I'm still strong."

Mom nods, giving him a wink.

"I totally agree," she states with a confident smirk.

I shake my head at both of them. Their naivety concerns me. How can they be so certain?

"You're taking a lot on faith," I tease.

"Sometimes faith is all that's needed," our mother gives me a wink then concentrates on our current path.

Half an hour later, I dare ask, "Mom?"

"Yes, my love," she answers with a broad smile, obviously enjoying the evening swim to… to… somewhere only Mom knows.

"Can you tell us more about the gods?" I ask in a tumble of Siren words.

Our mother remains quiet then suddenly points to the outcropping of multihued coral and sea plants.

"Did you know that we can blend into any underwater habitat?" she reveals, changing the subject.

Ando's face beams.

"Show us!" he clamors with a litany of clicks, clacks and high-pitched whistles. "Show us!"

Obligingly, our mother calls to her scales; the sight of her already blends into the surrounding depths. Silently, she glides through the weightless space toward the miniature coral reef. Without a word, she settles cross-legged on the sandy bottom and stays as still as a statue. Only her hair gently sways as the current caresses her impeccable shape.

'Can you see me?' our mother thinks, and we hear her clearly.

We know she is there. We just saw her among the seaweed and the other marine life, but for the life of me I cannot distinguish where she begins and the sea ends.

"We give up, Mom," I smirk, knowing that we will never find her.

Suddenly, she retracts her glossy scales and comes back into view.

"Cool, right?" she chortles girlishly.

Ando starts doing backflips.

"Teach me!" he orders, his movement makes my dizzy.

Mom laughs at him.

"Stop moving around like a lunatic dolphin and we can give it a shot," she informs.

"Alright," he agrees and comes back to an upright position.

"Mom!" I call out in a firm click, needing to get her to answer my previous question.

Ignoring me, she helps Ando focus on calling his scales, which has never appeared before, and is the same now. For all we know, he does not have that ability. Just because he has some powers does not mean he has all of them.

'Lena!' he shouts at my brain. *'I do have scales! They just aren't ready to come out yet!'*

"If you say so," I harass playfully in Siren.

"Mom!" he whines.

"Selena, leave your brother alone," our mother comes to his aid, as usual.

Getting impatient, I blurt, "Tell me more about Amphitrite?"

She turns to me with a grimace.

"I will continue to bother you until you tell me," I add, folding my arms across my chest.

Something in the way she looks at me this time, tells me that it is time for me to know.

"A long time ago… " she begins.

"… in a galaxy far, far away… " I joke making myself snort at the *Star Wars* reference.

She glares at me, and I hold my hands up in surrender.

"I'm sorry," I snort, enjoying our playful exchange. "Please continue."

"As I was saying," she sticks out her tongue. "Back in ancient times, when gods and goddesses ruled the Earth, there was a royal hierarchy."

I nod.

"Zeus was the leader, right?" Ando shows off his mental prowess.

"He was the father of the gods," she responds.

"He lived on Mt. Olympus," I interject.

She beams proudly.

"Very good, Selena!" my mother compliments, making me blush.

"But there were other gods who ruled over the underworld and the oceans, right?" Ando clacks loudly.

"That's correct," Mom praises in Siren-speak.

My brother grins because he remembers the mythology lessons from the aunts.

"Please continue, Mom," I remind, trying to keep her focused.

"Sorry," she says clearing her throat. "Where was I? Ah! The hierarchy." I nod as she carries on, "There were three brothers. Zeus was the youngest of the three. His brother, Poseidon was given dominion over all of the world's oceans, rivers, lakes... basically anything water related."

"And the third?" my brother asks as he spots a cluster of ginger-colored seahorses and calls them over to where we are having our conversation. Happily, they surround us allowing us to touch their rough skin.

Mom gives them a warm-hearted smile then continues.

"The third brother was, Hades, god of the Underworld."

Ando's cheeks redden.

"The Underworld is where souls go after they die," he mumbles.

Mom simply nods and continues her story.

"Poseidon, being the ruler of all of the watery realms, needed a wife, but not just any wife. She had to be of the sea."

My brows furrows as I ask, "What does '*of the sea mean*'?"

"It means created from the sea as in the molecules and essence of the ocean."

Understanding finally dawns on me as Mom's explanation sinks in.

"Amphitrite is like us! She is made with the same materials as Sirens!" I gasp. "No wonder she's so strong."

"That is correct," Mom acknowledges with a frown.

My mind races at the thought.

"She must be extraordinary to be the goddess of all waters," I ponder all of its meaning out loud. "Why does she hate Sirens so much?"

My mother's facial features turn worrisome as she circles around my main question.

"Their marriage was arranged," she educates. "It was not one based on love or admiration or respect. It was one of necessity made to bring two powerful houses together in order to obtain more power."

My mother's brow furrows.

"Any children created by their union—" she begins then stops abruptly.

Her gaze fixed on something in the distance.

"Would be even more powerful than Poseidon or Amphitrite," Mom finally continues, swallowing the lump that suddenly appears in her throat.

"With that extra strength, they could overthrow the other gods and goddesses including Zeus and Hera, his wife, and Hades and his spouse, Persephone," I reveal wisely, making my mother nod in agreement. "But why would that have anything to do with us Sirens?"

Mom takes a deep breath, and her gills move in accord with her breathing. It is a fascinating sight watching the external portion at work. I smile realizing that I sound like my stepfather.

"Poseidon always loved music," our mother relays. "According to the aunts, one day as he swam though the ocean's depths exploring his soon to be kingdom, he came across a stunning creature with the voice of an angel and fell instantly in love with her kind nature and selfless personality. He promised her the riches of the seas, but she was already in love with another."

My eyes widen as my mind puts one and one together.

I sigh before responding.

"The lovely singer was Melpomene the Muse, our great-grandmother and the one she loved was Akheloios, our great-grandfather."

Mom nods sadly. The knowledge of her heritage and the problems associated with being a part of our clan seems to weigh heavily on her. She tries to shake off her depression, but does not seem able to do so. All I can do is give her an encouraging smile. That helps a tiny bit.

"In the end, Poseidon married Amphitrite, but in his heart he only loved Melpomene," she adds smugly.

"Keep going," Ando perks up as the story becomes juicier in content.

Our mother takes another deep breath and continues.

"Amphitrite, knowing that he would never love her as he loved the Muse, grew more jealous and enraged and eventually tried to kill Melpomene during her most vulnerable moment—"

"While she was giving birth?!" I shout in clacks and high-pitched squeals.

Mom nods, her features tense.

"Yes," she finally replies. "The sea goddess tried to destroy the object of Poseidon's affections in order to have him for herself. Unbeknownst to her, Melody had no designs on the narcissistic Poseidon."

Closing my eyes briefly, I can almost imagine the hubbub that my great-grandmother caused in her heyday. I have felt the charm that exudes so naturally from her. I doubt anyone can withstand her prowess.

Even with Mom's explanation of past slights between the mythological creatures of times long past, I still have many questions; questions that need serious answers.

Apparently, so does my brother.

"Why did Zeus help Melpomene?" Ando jumps into the conversation as the sea horses say goodbye, continuing to their original destination.

Mom smiles as she explains.

"Zeus, also completely enamored with your great-grandmother's amazing beauty and gift of song, protected her from his brother's wife by shielding her with his supernatural force field as well as creating a safe haven for her to raise her children."

"Zeus created the Siren Grotto?" Ando chirps excitedly.

"Yes, he did," Mom smiles brightly as she replies. "Because he loved her too."

My head is spinning out of control.

"Did any of the deities of that time realize how powerful Melody's daughters would become?" I ask, overwhelmed by all of this new information.

Our mother contemplates my question for a few seconds.

"I seriously doubt that," she admits casually.

"Why do you think that?" I ask, more interested in our past than usual.

"As arrogant as the gods were, they believed no one would ever surpass their skills," Mom chuckles at the thought. "In their minds, how dangerous could the offspring of a Muse and a river god actually be?"

I nod at her seemingly accurate assessment of our beginnings.

How could anyone have known indeed.

Ten minutes later, as we follow Mom toward the direction of the horizon, another question comes to mind about *The Calling* ceremony. It all seems so rushed, so unplanned like Mom just woke and decided on a whim that tonight was the night.

"What is the significance of tonight?" I ask, enjoying the slight chill of the sea as it rubs against my skin.

Mom glances up toward the glassy surface above and sighs. Moonbeams pierce the surface scattering its light in delicate prisms. The pattern is almost alive with movement.

"Tonight is the Summer Solstice," she admits whimsically, lost in her own thoughts.

"What's the Summer Solstice?" Ando questions in a small, cute voice.

Mom grins.

"It is the day that marks the beginning of summer," she educates. "It is also the longest day of the year."

"That's good," I respond, not understanding the reason that it is special.

"Did you know that Greece is one of only a few places in the world that are in two different hemispheres?" she questions, sounding like Dad.

I shake my head.

"Yup!" she grins. "Greece is located in both the Northern and Eastern hemispheres."

"So… ?" I urge for her to fill in more details.

"So," she huffs. "Our kind was created on one of the most powerful days of the year in one of the most sacred places on Earth. That is why we are blessed with so much: beauty, intelligence, song, and the power to tap into the strength of Gaia. It is said that we may be even stronger than all of the gods combined."

"I'm sure we're not stronger than the gods?" I reply doubtfully. "Really?"

The look she gives me tells that she wishes I would just believe.

She continues, adding:

"It was on this day… hundreds of years ago… that I completed my own *Calling*," Mom says whimsically. "It is the most powerful time for our kind. It was also on the Summer Solstice eons ago that Melpomene the Muse gave birth to the Sirens. Right here… " she waves her arms like a tour guide, "… in these very waters."

"Wow!" Ando exclaims.

"It is sort of surreal," our mother confesses as she takes one of my hands and one of my brother's.

"It is," I agree, giving her hand a gentle squeeze.

Ando chuckles as he does the same.

"It is a family adventure," he snorts, making bubbles appear all around his head.

Mom and I laugh at him laughing. My brother. There's no one else like him.

Unexpectedly, Mom stops, and cocks her head to the left.

"Can you hear it?" she queries.

Ando and I stop too, both of us listening for whatever our mother now hears.

"I don't hear anything," I reply, feeling uneasy.

Ando closes his eyes and concentrates as well, but from the befuddled look, it is clear that he does not hear anything out of the norm.

"It's like a low hum," Mom explains. "Are you sure you don't hear it?"

My brother and I both shake our head.

"Sorry," Ando apologizes for us. "Maybe—"

'Quiet!' Mom blurts in our heads. *'There's something else.'*

My hairs do that standing on end thing again as my little brother maneuvers his body between our mother and me. I can feel his form shaking as mine does the same. Mom is the only one who appears to be as steady as oneof the ancient boulders on the *Marina Piccola* seabed.

"Something else?" I gulp. "Is it something dangerous?"

"I'm not certain," she replies, moving in front.

'Should we turn back?' I whisper internally.

Ando nods.

'I think we should go back to the villa with Daddy,' he thinks telepathically. *'He's probably worried about us being out here without the aunts. We should call them.'*

'I agree,' I concede, the uneasy feeling transforming into one of foreboding and dread. *'Let's wait on* The Calling *until the aunts are with us. After all, when the three of you are together, you're a force to be reckoned with.'*

That is the truth.

Watching Mom, Ligeia, and Leukosia in action a few days ago makes me extremely proud and terrified at the same time. They were one in mind, one in power, and one in purpose. They broke an invisible wall and almost destroyed the Blue Grotto in seconds, not even the almighty sea could do that with all of millennia of beating against it.

Nervously, I clear my throat.

"This doesn't feel right, Mom."

"Hello, Marina," another voice, smooth and confident, clears its throat behind us, causing us to all turn. My stomach drops into my feet and both Mom and Ando stare in silence. "You should really listen to your daughter."

Amphitrite greets with one of her impeccable smiles, reminding me of a Great White Shark about to devour its prey. The sea goddess swims toward us then stops a few feet away. Her jade eyes are glowing like cat's eyes in the most unnerving way. Just as before, her hair billows all around her form with a life of its own. It would not surprise me if the darn things reach out and grab us.

I knew this was a bad idea.

The being smiles and I realize that my thoughts have betrayed me.

"This was a monumentally bad idea," Amphitrite confirms.

Chapter Twenty-Four

The pit in my stomach has grown into a large sinkhole that is rapidly filling with terror and bile. If my extremities were not trembling so badly, I would have already fled the scene. Unfortunately, fear and pride glues me to this spot. Attempting to seem less terrified than I actually am, I decide to fake being courageous.

"Get away from us!" I snarl at our nemesis.

"Yeah!" Ando clickity-clacks, joining the taunting. "You're a big doodie head and you don't scare us!"

"Children," Amphitrite states with a grimace. "You cannot live with them, but you *can* eat them."

Amused at her own joke, she makes a biting motion at Ando then bursts into crazed laughter. Her comment makes me wonder if children were actually sacrificed back in the day and then eaten to appease some cannibalistic deity. If we make it out of this mess, I will have to research that subject.

Amphitrite's browbeating certainly does not sit well with our mother, whose eyes flash with rage.

"You will not threaten my children!" Mom growls, baring her teeth like a shark getting ready to take a cursory bite before going in for the kill.

"Come, come, Marina," the goddess responds, waving her off like she would a gnat. "I do not have time for idle threats."

"What do you want?" Mom pushes for an answer as she swims backwards using her body to shield us. "If you come any closer, I will kill you!"

Unaffected by our mother's words, Amphitrite moves a few feet closer. Her jade-green eyes locked on our mother as she sizes-up her opponent. As usual, Mom's face is hard like marble, and difficult to read. If she is afraid, no one can tell.

Amphitrite speaks next.

"You know what I want."

"I'll never tell you where the Siren Grotto is!" Mom defies through exposed teeth.

"Little Marina thinks she is Siren enough to defeat me," the other woman giggles, but the sound is hollow and superficial.

"Leave!" Mom orders as she cautiously backs away.

"Not until I have my answer," the Sea Goddess replies unruffled as if we are nothing worthy of heightened emotions.

'Why is the location of the grotto so important to you?' I yell telepathically at her, wishing to know why we are in mortal danger because of it.

"That is for me to know and you to… " the graceful creature purrs as she uses one finger to make the dots.

I ask my question again, wanting to know why this being is willing to commit murder in order to have access to the grotto.

"Why is the Siren Grotto so important to you?" I dare drill in Siren.

Stopping in her tracks, Amphitrite takes a deep breath.

"The properties contained in the waters there have the ability to extend life," she utters dryly and without blinking.

"But you're a goddess," I blurt without thinking. "Aren't you already immortal?"

There is another pregnant pause as she steadies herself.

"My power comes from the seas, oceans and rivers," she counters. "They are dying and eventually so will I."

"Will the same thing happen to us?" Ando finally speaks up.

The goddess shakes her head.

"From what I know, the sediments in the grotto's water will keep your kind young and strong for an eternity," she practically spits the words.

Amphitrite looks at me then my brother. Kindred to a ghostly specter, her features shift and then reform as her expressions change. Her eyes, once milky jade in color, now flash between turquoise and burnt umber. More terrified than ever, we begin to slowly back away.

"Are you afraid, little guppies?" her voice now mimics my own.

"No!" Ando barks viciously, making me proud to be his big sister.

"We're not scared of you!" I add, trying to appear fearless, hoping she falls for my performance.

"Shh!" Amphitrite responds, holding up her right index finger. "I could destroy you without breaking a talon."

As we watch, the nail grows into a four-inch, black talon, the point razor sharp. I gulp as she turns to me once more. Her cheeks redden for some reason.

"Young one," she coos. "Tell me what you know."

Defiantly, I glare, getting more than a bit upset that she keeps showing up demanding to know things I have no clue about. Panic begins to fill every cell in my body as I feel her rummaging around in my private thoughts. It actually physically hurts.

"I've told you before, *witch*, I don't know anything!" I roar, hoping to shock her. "And even if I did, I would never tell you!"

"Very brave for a little girl," Amphitrite sincerely compliments.

"Go away or I'll summon all of the Sirens," Mom warns, calling on her scales.

Amphitrite snickers as though all of this is a game.

"By the time they arrive, you and your half-breed offspring will be fish-fodder," her words are spoken softly, but terrorizing just the same. "You are only one. You are no match for me."

"I *will* call my aunts," Mom reminds, but her voice trembles a bit.

The creature hesitates for a moment, weighing her options and thankfully, seems actually concerned about dealing with Ligeia and Leukosia teamed up with our mother. *Wait!* We are three! Ando, Mom and I are three! The aunts once told me: *To summon the power of the sea all that is needed is three.*

"Grasp hands!" I command with a no-nonsense edge to my steady voice as I grab the volcanic glass charm around my neck.

To my delight, Mom and Ando immediately comply.

"Foolish guppies," the woman insults as she hovers ever closer, her hair as still as a board, unaffected by the motion of the sea. "You are nothing, you are krill."

Just as before, when the creature tricked me into meeting her in the harbor and almost killed me, she raises both of her arms and flings Mom, Ando, and me several yards away. Mom lands on a stalagmite formation jutting a foot or two out of the seabed while Ando, thankfully, lands in a patch of soft seaweed. I, on the other hand, bump my head on a piece of branch-like coral. Instantly, I smell the familiar coppery fragrance in the water, the image of sharks bombard my brain as I scramble to my feet.

"Stay down!" Amphitrite barks like a general, her face contorted with rage.

Against their will, my legs buckle sending me back to my hands and knees. Concentrating on what needs to be done, I force my body to an upright position and briefly look up to see that my brother and mother are trying unsuccessfully to do the same.

Focusing my strength through the piece of black glass, I think of what to say. Suddenly, it comes to me. It comes to me similarly to when I am close to... *Melody!* It has to be divine inspiration! Maybe I am channeling her power. There is no time to analyze now. I will just accept it as fate or faith, whichever one works.

Clearing my mind of everything else, I begin.

"I invoke thee, spirits of the watery depths," I chant, hoping for a miracle.

The ancient being comes closer, her expression curious, her hair like a strawberry-blonde lion's mane billowing behind her.

"What are you doing?" she asks innocently.

Ignoring her, I continue.

"I command all of its creatures great and small," I adlib, not quite certain of where the words are coming from.

Again, she pushes me back and this time my body hits the sea floor, the force of impact creating a crack where my body lands. All I can see are stars.

"I command you to come to me!" I click and clack, willing my wishes to be followed, by what I do not know.

'Silly child,' the goddess smiles, her thoughts echoing inside of my foggy brain. *'You are no match for me.'*

Just as before, I begin to feel a vortex forming around my feet and realize that Amphitrite is conjuring one of her deadly whirlpools. Weightlessly, my legs lift off of the ground as my form starts to spin where I stand. Unable to steady myself, my stomach lurches and I pray that dinner stays down. All I can do is close my eyes and will the water to calm, but of course nothing happens.

"Foolish guppy!" the goddess laughs. "You think you are of *The Three*, but you are beneath them. You were birthed from the loins of a half-breed... *An abomination!* You are nothing!"

Trying desperately to ignore her insults, I try again.

"Be still! I command you... Be still!" I click and clack, getting dizzier by the millisecond.

Focus, Selena! Focus!

"I command you... *Be Still!*"

This time, to my amazement, the currents slow and become motionless like water in a fish tank without a filtering system. Even the natural sound of the sea as it churns decreases and almost stops completely. Surprisingly, the whirlpool disappears just as quickly as it formed.

Huh!

Amphitrite's jade eyes narrow to thin slits.

"*Anoixe!*" she clamors furiously with both arms outstretched towards the seabed. "Open!"

Immediately, the stony ground beneath our feet begins to tremor, softly at first then it erupts into a full-blown quake. The movement is so vigorous that small pieces of sediment can be seen floating in the water surrounding us. Even the sea is becoming warmer.

"*Close!*" I yell, fueled by rage. "I command you by the will of *The Three* to close!"

Just as quickly as it started the seabed quiets and returns to its former placid state. Where we stand the ground is still, but the earth begins to pulsate under the pale creature's sandaled feet.

Amphitrite's eyes widen in disbelief as she loses her footing and stumbles. I can only imagine the astonishment she must feel that someone like me, someone that she considers beneath her, has managed to destabilize her. I cannot help but smile at our reversal of fortunes.

"Be still!" she orders the ground, but it keeps its beat.

Once... twice... on the third massive earthquake she stays on the ground prostrated at my feet.

Righting herself, she closes her eyes and begins to chant.

"Chtapódi... chtapódi... " Amphitrite says monotonously.

Chtapódi? What the heck does that mean?

From nowhere, I feel a tightening around my chest as eight gigantic tentacles wrap around my torso. I look around noticing that Ando and Mom are also trapped in the deadly grip. Ando's face is turning purple. Mom's eyes look like they are about to pop out of her head, and my bones are bending like they are about to snap.

Octopus!

"What the—!" I scream, but all I hear are the bubbles rushing out of my open mouth.

The strong creature's tentacles contract and release briefly, allowing me to take a much-needed breath.

'Release us!' I gasp and focus my efforts on loosening the giant octopus's hold. *'Listen to me, mighty Polypus! I will not ask again!'*

Still his grip tightens, leaving me with no other recourse.

Taking shallow breaths, I grasp the piece of glass tightly between my two closed palms, just like I would if I was praying and think about Melody. One-word flashes in my brain, but it is in Greek and I cannot pronounce it. Then as if my mind switches from English to Greek, it becomes clear.

"Flame," I wheeze with great difficulty. *"Flóga!"*

Like a pot on a stove, the temperature around me becomes hotter and hotter and my body actually begins to sweat underwater. Energy is being released through my pores in such a way that it resembles the red glow of heating coils. The startled octopus recoils, releasing us and quickly then swims away as it shoots its inky defense into the area, disappearing into the murky depths.

Without hesitation, my thoughts are back on my adversary as I make the ground convulse again.

"Stop this!" she commands, surprised at my ability as she falls helplessly at my feet once more. But I cannot stop it. I do not know how to stop, and even if I could stop, I do not want to. This new power fills every fiber of my soul, oozing out of my pores like perspiration. My head is dizzy, and I love it!

"Let the Earth shake!" I keep chanting, allowing the intoxicating strength to flow through my veins.

From far away, I hear my mother's voice calling to me.

"Selena!"

Ignoring her, I refocus my attention on the being before me. Without effort, I instruct my body to levitate, just a foot above the seafloor as I move my mother and brother a few feet away. Like in a dream, I hear them gasp as their bodies are gently relocated, out of harm's way.

Feeling the entire ocean fueling my efforts, I add: "Let the strength of *The Three* flowing through my veins become corporeal!"

"Selena, stop!" Ando shouts, but I cannot stop; I am no longer doing this. Something else is stirring inside of me.

Is this what it feels like to be a goddess?

"*Veni foras!*" I shout and realize it is not in my head anymore, but in the water around us.

I can speak underwater?

Damn!

I can speak underwater!

And not the clickity-clackity language of the Sirens, but real words!

Am I supposed to be able to do this?

"You impudent child!"

I shout again.

"*Veni foras!* I command you... *Come Forth!*"

Around me, the sea begins to move in slow motion like someone has hit a button on a remote control. Mom and Ando are calling to me, but their words are too sluggish to understand. Even Amphitrite is moving at a tortoise's pace; only I am moving normally. However, even in her current state of limited mobility, she is still able to cut my face with just a thought and I feel the warm liquid flowing from my cheek.

"*I cannot be beat!*" the goddess intimidates, waving her hands as she uproots several coral plants out of the ground, hurdling them at my head, one after the other. The spiny branches scrape at my skin until the sea surrounding me turns a soft shade of pink.

"Come Forth... *Veni foras!*" I shout again, ignoring the sting of the salty liquid.

Then it happens.

Out of my peripheral vision, I see the remaining coral branches stretch toward Amphitrite and encircle her arms, legs and torso, holding her securely in place. Coming to our rescue is a school of Pelagia noctiluca jellyfish. The aggressive glowing jellyfish surround her, stinging her with their painful tentacles. Moray eels arrive next, and not just a couple, more like a hundred; all of their teeth showing and their electric currents displacing the depths around them.

"*No!*" the goddess screams as she tries to escape the rapidly approaching hoard. "I order you to stop!"

It is not surprising that the animals ignore her command.

"*Thávo!*" I utter, filled with triumph. "*Bury this witch!*"

As we watch the sand below, Amphitrite's feet begin to shift and whirl creating a gigantic hole. As I scrutinize, the creature is sucked into it along with the hoard of eels, jellyfish and coral, leaving only a barren clearing roughly twenty feet in diameter. When time returns to normal, I stand staring at the spot where the all-powerful goddess once stood as my mother and brother gape at me in horror.

The bathroom that Ando and I share is unusually cold. Goosebumps decorate my skin as I sit at the granite vanity table letting my mother tend to my wounds. The tension is thick and unrelenting. Several times Ando and Dad have peeked in on us but are unwilling to enter.

"*Ouch!*" I yelp. "That stings!"

Mom frowns but does not make eye contact.

"It's antiseptic," she murmurs, adding another dab to my cuts. "It's supposed to sting."

Nervously, I ask, "Are you upset with me?"

Now, that is a loaded question.

I keep replaying the events of the confrontation with the sea goddess over and over in my mind, but I still do not understand why my mother and brother are so perturbed with me. After all, I did save us from an untimely death at the hands of a psychotic Greek Goddess. In my opinion, they should be throwing me a party or at least baking me some cookies. Instead, I am getting the silent treatment.

"Should I be upset with you?" my mother probes apprehensively.

"No!" I snap. "You shouldn't be upset with me. You should be grateful."

My mother glances at me then stands and walks out of the room. Noiselessly, she heads down the hallway and disappears into the kitchen. I do not know what possesses me to follow, but I do.

"Mom!" I call after her retreating form. "I didn't mean for it to come out like that!"

As I enter the kitchen, my mother is already cleaning. Clenched in her hand is a sponge and she is diligently wiping off the already immaculate kitchen countertops. Obsessive compulsive cleaning is another one of my mother's coping mechanisms. I truly hope that this is not a hereditary trait that will manifest when I am her age.

"Mom, please talk to me," I beg, sitting on the closest barstool.

Before she can respond, I hear feet shuffling outside of the kitchen door and notice two pairs of shadows under the crack of the door. It is my busybody brother and stepfather of course. What is it with the men in my family being nosier than the women?

"I didn't mean to do whatever I did," I halfheartedly apologize. "It just... happened."

"You channeled your great-grandmother," she mutters with an unbelieving glare.

"I think so," I reply, mulling it over. "Who else could it be?"

"That's what worries me," Mom blurts. "We don't know who or what you could have tapped into. There are powerful beings that roam the Earth."

I didn't think about that. I just assumed it was Melody.

"Please don't be angry with me," I plead once more.

At that moment, Ando pokes his head into the room, but quickly retreats. Mom and I wait for his next appearance. The third time my brother checks on us; he actually decides to come inside of the kitchen. I smile to myself when I see that he is holding a sandwich and drink. Silently, he studies us, or rather, studies me. His thoughts are blocked from me and I know that that is not a good sign.

"Why would I be upset with you?" she answers with a question, which is what she does when she is upset.

"I'm mad at you," Ando speaks, at last. He had been quiet since our confrontation with Amphitrite, which was two hours ago.

"Why?" I growl, feeling extremely defensive.

He remains silent as he takes another bite of the tuna salad sandwich followed by a long drink of bottled iced tea that he has been carrying around the villa with him.

"If you both have something to say," I pause, trying to control my emotions, which right now are off the charts. "Just say it."

Mom looks up, her expression is calm on the surface, but she keeps biting her bottom lip; my mother's nonverbal speak for there are no words to express how disturbed she truly is.

"Mom?" I prod again, hating the growing tension between us. "Are you angry?"

"Yes," she answers, still not looking at me directly.

"Please, talk to me," I shudder even though the room is warm, stifling actually.

"What is there to say?" she answers with another question.

"What did I do that was so wrong?" I ask, rubbing my arm where a purplish bruise is now forming. The spot is tender to the touch. "I saved us… didn't I?"

"You did a great job," my mother whispers and tries to fake a smile.

Ando's brows hitch to his dark hairline.

"You were scary, Lena," he bluntly divulges, verbally delivering a devastating blow to my psyche.

"How was I scary?" I question, genuinely confused.

"You were speaking… *underwater!*" he informs with wide eyes.

"So?" I respond oversensitively.

"So? So, Sirens can't do that!" he huffs, taking another sip of his drink. "The aunts said so!"

"Maybe the aunts don't know everything," I dismiss with a snarky smirk.

With more than a little aggravation, I scratch at the lump that has developed at the back of my head, right where it slammed against the coral when Amphitrite threw us. The bump is now the size of an extra-large walnut. Thankfully, it is not bleeding anymore, and Mom has already cleaned it and applied medicine.

"How did you do it?" Ando continues with the interrogation.

"I'm not sure how I did it," I say honestly.

"And you were speaking another language," my brother reminds.

"Was I?" I ask with all seriousness, not remembering.

Ando nods.

"When did you learn to speak Latin so fluently?" Mom confronts with a weird expression. "I've heard you practicing, and your skills are rudimentary at best, and that's on a good day."

"I must have heard David and just picked it up. No biggie," I add with a grin.

Mom stares at me.

"What's the matter now?" I whine, feeling anxious.

"Did you just call your father by his first name?" Mom queries uneasily.

"I don't know," I respond, still touching the back of my head.

"Lena?"

"What is it?" I answer gruffly.

"What about the other stuff?" Ando questions with a nervous look.

"What other stuff?" I say with a sigh.

"You know," he states, playing with a crumb of bread he dropped on the table.

"Wa-well… " Ando stutters. "What about making the earth open and calling those jellyfish and eels? How did you do that?"

I give him my patented Mr. Spock eyebrows.

"We can call sea animals," I respond, feeling my blood pressure surging inside of me.

"I know," he says as he jumps off of the dining chair and takes his napkin to the garbage can. "But I didn't hear you call for them. We were all linked, remember? You didn't use Siren language either."

Mom just watches me with a weary look.

"You're being silly," is the only thing I can say. "I saved us."

Even I cannot believe what I am saying.

"Mom was terrified. If I didn't do what needed to be done, we'd all be—" I reply smugly.

"Dead," Mom finishes my sentence.

I smile, waving my hands at them.

"Exactly," I mumble.

Lunch is simple, grilled ham and cheese sandwiches with canned tomato soup to dunk them in. This is usually one of my favorite meals. Not only is it nostalgic and easy to prepare, but it is seriously tasty. However, with all of the negative things happening recently, I can hardly stand the sight of it.

"You're not eating," Dad states the obvious. "Aren't you hungry?"

Ignoring his question, I stare outside, wishing I was in the sea instead of here.

"Selena?" Mom chimes in. "Your father asked you a question."

"Huh?" I manage a one-word response and even that is difficult.

The sea is calling me. It is mournful and sad, just like I am.

"I'm sorry," I whisper. "I didn't hear you."

David repeats the question.

"No," I reply offhandedly, rising from the dining chair. "I'm going for a swim."

Speedily, I strip off my sarong revealing my one-piece, blue-camouflage swimsuit below. The turquoise water surrounding the island calls loudly today and for some reason I cannot resist. Actually, I do not plan to resist it at all.

Mom and Dad glance at one another before Mom responds.

"You didn't ask if you could go swimming this afternoon," her tone is short and to the point.

Not liking her response, I frown.

"What's the big deal?" I question as I turn toward the patio area.

The entire family stares at me, but I do not care. I feel trapped like a wolf in a cage pretending to be a dog. If I cannot leave the confines of the villa, I do not know what will happen.

"We are all going into town," Dad tells.

"What for?" I ask, expertly braiding my hair to keep it out of my face.

"It's a gorgeous day to visit another museum in Anacapri," Mom smiles as she explains.

"I'd rather go swimming," I respond with my back facing the table, one foot already out the patio door.

"Selena," my stepfather interrupts. "No swimming today, family time."

Slowly, I turn on my heels. My expression blank. My eyes locked on his.

"You are not my father, *David*," I annunciate every word to make my point.

"*Selena!*" my mother shouts as she bolts out of her seat. "Don't speak to your father like that!"

I turn to her next. Her lips are trembling due to her rising anger. Her voice lowers.

"Apologize!" she hisses. "Right now!"

"Don't tell me what to do, *Marina*," I chuckle.

"Go to your room!" David orders, his accent harsh, the vein at his temple throbbing beneath the skin.

"Humans," I say smugly as I turn and run to the railing on the patio.

Without any hesitation, I boost off of the top propelling my body out, away from the jagged shoreline. Just as expected, my form cuts through the churning sea like a knife as the heavy surf quickly hides all evidence that I was ever there. It is heavenly below the waves.

Peaceful... Perfect.

Grabbing a nearby baby lionfish, I pop it into my mouth. The salty tang is delicious. My stomach growls for more, so I set my sights toward the open sea.

There are lots of things to hunt out there.

CHAPTER TWENTY-FIVE

Quietly, I sit upon the uneven stalagmite form jutting out of the *Marina Piccola* harbor. The hour is late. Much too late for good little girls to be awake. Above, the full moon hangs low in the firmaments; its yellow light illuminating the dark canvas.

I wish I could stay here forever, I think, feeling the spray of the sea against my heated cheeks. The waves glistening below encourage me. Their ever-changing beat mimics my gleeful heart.

Out in the distance, a rhythmic sound catches my attention. It starts low and then expands when it meets the wind. Heavy with bass and percussion. Pounding just like the sea. Closing my eyes, I listen carefully. Segregating each precious note from the sound of Gaia, I realize it is something else. My eyes bolt open. It is a human voice, a pleasant, manly voice that joins the music with perfect timing.

He sings:

"Out on the tar plains, the glides are moving,

All looking for a new place to drive.

You sit beside me so newly charming,

Sweating dewdrops glisten freshing your side... "

Ahh! Duran Duran's, *The Chauffeur*. My mom's favorite 80's pop band.

The song makes me smile.

He sounds professional. The young man is a good distance away. The man whose voice is raspy, yet sweet and at this time he does not see me.

In the moonlight, I can see everything.

He sits on the deck of his exquisite silver yacht, dressed in khaki shorts, a red polo, and tan boat-shoes. His blonde hair waves accosting shimmering amethyst irises. His teeth are straight and bright white which is enhanced by his tanned skin. The ship has been christened *Anna-Sofia* probably after his mother. Although, he does not seem old enough to own such an expensive trinket, he sails it well. Maybe, it belongs to his parents.

In his hand, he holds a sandwich, peanut butter and jelly. Not quite what I was expecting, but charming all-the-same. I know that Ando would not mind sharing.

Suddenly, his cellphone rings. It is loud and shrill against the peacefulness of the evening. The sound hurts my ears even though I am so far away. I feel my pulse quicken.

"*Ciao!*" he greets in Italian.

Even though he is on the phone, I can still hear the female voice that greets back.

"No, mama," he blushes sweetly. "I'm on my way back."

A few moments of silence pass as he stands with the device pressed to his ear. He smiles then frowns then finally laughs. He is adorable.

"I'll be there in fifteen minutes," he blushes once more.

"No... ok... *Dio mio!*... tell papa his boat is being well taken care of—"

He laughs even louder.

"*Ciao!*" he finishes then hangs up the phone.

Quickly, he puts the mobile device back in his pocket and heads to the wheel. He gazes up at the moon and I can see his reluctance to leave. Just like me.

Wanting him to stay a bit longer, I open my mouth.

"Don't be afraid," I sing along with the accompanying orchestra of pounding waves and churning currents. Windy fingers strum a soft bass against the jagged cliffs of towering gray, their percussion low and melancholy. Captivated, he stops and listens then begins to pace, forward, then aft, as he searches for the source of the song.

His forehead furrows and his thick, sun-kissed eyebrows hitch to his hairline.

"Is someone there?" he calls into the night.

For now, I choose to remain silent.

Slowly and with much confusion, he shakes his head and returns to steering the vessel. Not wanting to miss my chance at meeting him, I clear my throat and concentrate, hoping to breach the distance between the rock formation and his cruiser.

"Come with me," I repeat with more effort, more passion.

This time, he turns off the engine and stands on deck... waiting. At last, he sees me as I stand on the edge of the stalagmite form looking at him, my onyx braid blowing like a hefty rope in the breeze.

"I see you," he beams, eyes shining like a lighthouse beacon.

I sing more sweetly.

"Come to me... come to me... .into the sea..."

"Shall I come to you?" his voice sings back, steady and confident.

I smile, unbraiding my hair as I greet the trade winds. The fragrance of broom flowers and night-blooming Jasmine fills my head with anticipation. Even the gulls are watching from overhead, uncaring that the sun has long since gone to sleep.

A passing cloud blocks what little light the moon gives off and we briefly lose sight of each other.

"Are you still there?" he shouts, his voice ever true, ever sure.

Without a doubt, I smile, telling him that I am waiting; telling him that I need him as much as he needs me. I see from my perch when he smiles back.

I know that he is mine.

"Sing for me," he begs, leaning over the bough of the sixty-four-foot luxury yacht. *"Sei una bella donna!"*

I giggle and blush at the same time understanding that he thinks I am a beautiful woman.

"Sing for me, amore mia," the handsome stranger urges me in Italian with sweet words of devotion.

I must oblige.

Closing my eyes, I find the tune again. The tune made just for him. Just for us.

Again, I sing to him.

"Follow me… into the sea… in the ocean's waves we'll play," I sing each word like it is my last, adding more and more vibrato as I fashion my song… only for him.

Thoughtlessly, he dives into the water shattering its surface. Overhead, a glimmering moonbeam wakes him from his trance causing bravery to transmute into dread. His mind tells him to swim back to the protection of the yacht, but his heart takes control urging his body onward. Fear consumes him… washing over him like waves wash over the rocky shoreline of Capri. Looking around, he realizes that he is merely one man, a rich European playboy swimming out toward the purple horizon in some sort of hazardous haze.

But before he can change his mind, the undertow grabs hold of his legs and begins to pull him out towards the indigo depths. Powerless against its desires, he closes his eyes allowing his body to descend, a watery embrace consumes him as he feels his lungs fill with seawater, but he is not afraid. He is at peace for the first time in his short twenty-something year life.

Steadily, seductively, the liquid world starts to fade as he drifts into the emptiness, but in the distance, swimming toward him, are three shapes. As the shapes get closer, he realizes that it is three women: the first with long, curly, crimson tresses resembling the sun's first light. The second, topped with a golden cascade that surrounds her perfect features. The third, adorned with jet black curls spilling downward like inky tentacles. Almost to Death's door, he sees their beautiful aquamarine eyes…

'What are you doing?' Mom grabs the young man around the torso and pulls him up to the surface, allowing him to drink in several deep lungsful of oxygen from the warm summer night.

Ligeia and Leukosia snap inside of my head.

'Have you lost your mind?!'

Confused, I watch them, watching me. Their expressions are of pure shock.

"I'm a Siren," I remind aloud as they glower angrily at me from several yards away.

"You could have killed him!" Ligeia clicks in annoyance.

"That's what I'm supposed to do," I say with a wave of my hand.

"I'll get him back to his boat," my mother informs as she quickly swims away with the water-laden man tucked securely against her body.

"Wipe his memory," Leukosia whistles.

Mom nods her understanding.

"What were you thinking?" the aunts say in stereo.

Rolling my eyes, I reply with annoyance.

"For once, I wasn't thinking," I admit without shame. "I was acting on instinct. That's what you've been teaching me all of these months... *right?*"

"This is not our way," they say together, sadness intermingles with disappointment as they look at me directly.

"We are not mindless killers," they add. "The men who died from our songs, did so by accident. We only kill when absolutely necessary, only for survival."

"Do you understand?" Mom's voice echoes in my ears as I turn to see her returning.

"Marina," Aunt Ligeia says with her no-nonsense tone.

"Yes?" my mother answers softly in Siren.

"It's time."

As I stare at the three most important women in my life, my mother propels her body out of the water like a leaping dolphin, grabs me around my waist and pulls me off of the stalagmite rock and into the sea. It happens so fast that I have no time to get out of the way. Shocked, I switch back to gills as my form slams into the rolling waves.

'Be careful,' both Sirens remind, eyes sad, yet concerned and full of love. Love for me.

My mother nods as she takes my hand firmly in hers. The feeling of déjà vu slams into me as I remember Mom doing the exact same thing, but then I was a screaming toddler throwing a tantrum over a balloon that had popped in a grocery store near our apartment in Ohio. This of course was pre-David when Mom and I were a duo. Right now, I feel like that toddler.

"Where are we going?" I question as we leave the sisters. "Back to the villa?

Mom shakes her head without looking in my direction.

"It can't be prolonged anymore," she clacks in exasperation.

"What can't be prolonged?" I ask, trying to pull my hand away from her tight grip.

"The Calling."

Fear takes hold and I feel more like my human self.

"Bu-but wa-why?" I stammer, unable to curb my terror. "I promise not to do anything bad ever again. I promise!"

Mom ignores me.

"No more trying to kill people! I promise!" I plead, guilt rising as quickly as my blood pressure.

I feel the tears welling in my eyes.

"Suppose something goes wrong... suppose the waters in the Siren Grotto are too strong for me... suppose... "

"No more supposing, Selena!" Mom chastises, still not looking at me. "You have had enough *'hunting'* for a lifetime!"

CHAPTER TWENTY-SIX

My mother has not said anything since we left the young man that I almost murdered.

Murdered! I never thought that word would ever be associated with anything to do with me. That word is reserved for individuals in prison, not with a sixteen-year-old from a tiny island in the Caribbean where the iguanas outnumber the residents. Every time I think about what I tried to do to that man, I feel like *I* am drowning.

"Are we there yet?" I ask for the third time in five minutes.

Mom frowns and gives me an agitated glare.

"No, we are not there yet," she clicks rather loudly making me shrink.

"How far do you think it is?" I question as we swim out of the harbor toward the vast Mediterranean.

"You'll know when we get there," she states matter-of-factly.

"But how?" I realize that I am sounding like my brother.

"You just will," she assures without elaboration.

"But—"

"Selena," Mom clacks then switches to telepathy. *'You'll feel when we're there. Believe me, there is no mistaking the pull it has on us.'*

"Where are Tia Ligeia and Tia Leukosia?" I interrogate flippantly in Siren.

"Away," she responds flatly.

"I thought we are supposed to be taking a family vacation," I whine.

"We are," she sighs, not making eye contact.

"We've only seen them a few times," I remind. "We saw them mostly when we were in Venice and then in Ischia."

Mom finally smiles at me.

"Didn't you like Venice?" she questions with a smirk.

Recalling our time spent there, I smile too.

"I didn't think that the canals would smell funny," I recall, pinching my nostrils together as I pretend to smell it right now.

"The canals have always been like that," she says on a laugh.

"You've been there before?"

Mom blushes then informs.

"That's where I met Leonardo... a long, long time ago."

"I still can't believe you did that," I respond, making a disgusted face. "Posed nude."

"Yup!" she smirks, attempting to hide her embarrassment, but doing a poor job of it.

"Did the aunts know?" I ask, my curiosity taking over.

"Nope!" she confesses with a twinkle in her eyes.

"That is so scandalous," I tease, glad that the tension between us has finally been broken.

"He had the most amazing and interesting inventions and paintings," Mom sighs ignoring my comment. "Don't tell your dad, but I sort of had a crush on him."

"Really?" I squeal, mortified at the idea of my mother having feelings for the famous *Renaissance Man*.

"I was young," she blushes again. "It was during my rebellious stage."

She stops in midsentence making me nervous.

"What's wrong?" I question, feeling abruptly apprehensive.

'*Shh,*' is her only response.

But that sound, said in that tone, spoken inside of my head causes my scales to instantly appear; the itchy sensation almost mocking my fear. Without thought, I begin to scratch. The feel of their smooth, armor-like exterior makes me scratch at them even harder.

'Put your scales away and the itching will stop!' Mom snaps telepathically, making me jump.

"I can't," I admit in Siren, continuing to agitate my arms, then my legs, then finally... .*Oh great... my face!* "I have them on my face? They're on my face!"

Mom rolls her eyes.

"Calm down, please," she demands firmly.

"What the hell!" I scream creating a curtain of multi-shaped bubbles.

Swiftly, my mother swims over to me and takes my hands in hers.

"Listen to me," she soothes. "Hear my words."

I watch her, watching me. Her gaze is full of empathy and love. She might be upset with me, but she will always accept and protect me.

"I don't know why I can't control anything," I grumble feeling my eyes well with tears just as salty as the sea.

'Baby girl,' she whispers in my mind. 'Listen to your mother.'

I nod my understanding.

'Close your eyes,' Mom requests in a calming voice.

I do as I am told.

'Open your mouth,' she unexpectedly adds.

Shocked at her comment, my eyes fly open and stay wide.

"Huh?" is my only response.

'Please open your mouth,' she states in a composed, rational voice.

"Why?" I ask with narrowed eyes.

"I can give you some of my venom," Mom informs. "It will ease the itchiness."

Reluctantly, I obey. Then before my wide-opened eyes my mother's scales appear, blues, greens, and emerald with a few streaks of coral and gold. She is gorgeous. Shimmering scales similarly colored as mine cover her entire body including her face. Under the sea they almost blend in completely like camouflage. I cannot help but smile.

"Is that what I look like?" I ask with a proud grin.

"Yes," she replies grinning just as large.

Mom calls her talons and readies to cut into a small gold one, but I stop her before she makes the incision.

Attacked by another wave of itchiness, I start to scratch again.

"How do I get rid of them?" I beg in complete dismay. "Without you butchering yourself."

"Remember what I told you before," Mom reminds. "They are a survival mechanism. They will appear during times of stress until you learn to control them."

"But they are so freaking itchy," I whine, scratching them again which makes her laugh.

"The only way to get rid of them immediately is... " her words trail off then she cocks her head to the side and listens.

Her brows and forehead instantly furrow as she informs of danger.

'Keep your scales up for the moment,' she says inside of my head instead of out loud. *'We're almost there.'*

We swim for another thirty minutes or so, all the while my chest is tight and my mouth dry. My adrenal gland kicks-in and I begin to sweat underwater... again. Unfortunately, my scales are still bothering me, but my mother insists that I leave them alone and try to focus on something else.

Well... let's see. Swimming toward something that may eat us or kill us in a most unflattering way just for fun... That strategy does not help. At all!

"Selena, stop it!" Mom barks in our Siren language.

"Stop what?" I ask innocently.

"Thinking so loudly," she sighs. "You are giving me a migraine."

Before I can make more fun of our impending doom, I feel *'it'*. In actuality, I see *it*.

'What is this?' I whisper to my mother through thoughts as one hand reaches out to touch the strange substance, study it.

"I'll explain later," she whispers.

"Is this what we saw from the villa?" I ask, running my fingers through the oily substance.

"Yes, kind of," she blurts impatiently.

With a mind of their own, my scales harden even more making me feel like I am wearing an actual combat tank over my limbs. Then the darkness appears. A better description would be mist; a mist so dark and thick that it shifts and morphs into blue, then black, then a dark-bruise-like-purple. It resembles octopus ink.

"Watch out!" Mom yells a warning that vibrates the water around us. "On your left!"

Instinctively, I shift my body to the right almost bumping into my mother. She grabs me by the wrist and takes off like a rocket through the otherwise placid sea, her grip so strong I am thankful that my scales are protecting my bones.

As we fly through the watery expanse, fleeing from something I have yet to see, it hits me. The smell I hate. That all too familiar copper scent that, God forbid, sometimes makes my stomach growl. I look down to where she holds me and gasp as my eyes lock on to the long ebony talons that are breaking through my scales.

"Stop thinking!" she orders, her mind racing through different battle strategies and fighting moves. "You're a Siren! You heal fast!"

"Why are we—"

The thought never fully forms when I see what is chasing us; a school of sharks, all moving and swimming in tight precision like a squadron of fighter jets through the depths. However, not just any type of shark, *Carcharhinus brevipinna,* more commonly known as Spinner Sharks. Tia Ligeia would be pleased to know that her lessons on sharks were not in vain.

Surprisingly, Mom begins to move faster.

'Kick your feet!' she yells in my head.

'Huh?' is my only thought, my only reaction, as I stare at the group of sharks hunting us like... guppies!

"Kick your feet!" Mom clicks and clacks loudly.

Finally, I kick my feet as hard and as fast as I can manage. In fact, I move them so vigorously that the muscles begin to ache then burn. We are moving too fast. My stomach begins to churn, and I will it to behave.

"Mom!" I gasp breathlessly. "I need to stop! I'm… going… to….throw up!"

"Well… don't!"

It is at that moment that my vision clears and locks onto our salvation.

"Dive down!" I clack pointing to a small cleft in the rocky seabed.

"Where?" she says following the direction that I am currently pointing.

"It's to our left, near the red coral!" I clack, click, and whistle my answer.

Just as fast, we aim down not noticing the smallest, fastest female predator is right on our heels. I hear a loud snap and see the water around us turn red. I try to see where it is coming from or rather who it is coming from. To my disbelief, it is not coming from me.

"Just a few more feet, Mom!" I encourage, feeling hope growing inside of me.

"Okay, hold on tight!" she orders, and I oblige; wrapping my arms and legs around her like a baby koala bear attaches to its mother.

Mom gives one last kick of her webbed feet catapulting us forward, so fast that the pressure in my ear's pop, causing them to bleed from the depths we are at now. With a swift paddle of her arms, we reach the entrance and squeeze our bodies through, first me then my mother.

"Are you okay?" she pants out of breath.

"I'm fine," I answer with a smile. "How are you?"

Her smile is faint and her eyes are glazed over.

"Not so good," she softly chuckles.

Slowly... painfully, she moves her hand away from her right side and reveals the softball-size chunk of flesh that is missing.

Dear Father!

"Mom!"

Everything is moving in slow motion, but this time it is just my mind playing tricks on me. With great difficulty, Mom treads water beside me. Her breathing is labored and shallow and every few minutes she coughs. Unfortunately, the last cough is mingled with some of her blood.

"What should I do?" I ask trying to hold back tears.

"Break off one of your scales," she whimpers through clenched teeth.

"What?" I ask, doing a double take.

"Break off one of your scales," Mom requests. "Only a small one is necessary for a wound this size."

My eyes grow larger as I contemplate what I am being asked to do.

"Will it hurt?" I probe, swallowing my remaining saliva.

"Of course not," she answers with a wink and I instantly know that she is lying.

I can't believe this is happening!

Believing that I am cursed, I shake my head and roll my eyes before grabbing one of the small emerald scales near my calve.

"No! Not that one," Mom wheezes. "Take one from the same area where my injury is… that one."

With trembling hands, she touches the two-inch scale on my right hip.

I give it a strong, determined tug, but nothing happens.

"It's not coming off," I inform, filled with a small semblance of relief.

"You need to use something sharp," Mom coughs her reply in Siren. "Use your talons."

"I don't have talons," I remind as my chest does that tightening again.

"You are going to need to call for them," she says coughing up more blood; the sight of it makes me queasy.

"I've never done that before," I remind. "I didn't even know that we had *talons* until you threatened Melody with them."

In agony, my mother grips her side harder, but the bleeding does not stop. Soon we are floating in a metallic-scented maroon cloud. With each passing moment, Mom is becoming weaker and weaker. Without a doubt, soon she will—

"Please," she whimpers. "Stop thinking so negatively."

"Sorry," I reply, feeling more guilt.

"Close your eyes and concentrate," she states very coolly.

Following her instructions, I close my red-rimmed eyes.

"Think about your fingers," she instructs. "In your mind see below your scales, underneath your human skin, picture your fingernails. See them in your mind elongating… sharpening."

"Ouch!" I shout on a muffled whimper as the two-inch, knife-like, nails cut through my skin then my scales like a red-hot poker stabbing through a block of butter.

Mom, even in her delicate condition, gives a wicked snicker.

"I thought you said it wouldn't hurt?" I admonish with a growl.

Playfully, she nudges me with her elbow.

"You knew I wasn't telling the truth," she gives a little laugh.

"I know," I answer with a frown. "I just don't like pain."

"Selena—" she tries to finish the sentence but cannot.

"Mom," I say as my stomach lurches forward like it is trying to leave my abdomen. "Mama?"

"Slice off the scale and place it over my injury... hurry!"

Her eyes close and her breathing slows to barely anything.

Don't panic! I order myself. *Don't you dare panic!*

Mustering my courage, I hold the scale away from the others between my shaking fingers. Next, I position the talon against the flesh nearest to my body, close my eyes, hold my breath and slice.

"Holy crap!"

Although, truth be told, that was not the phrase I wanted to say, but fear of my mother hearing me, even on her dying breath, was enough to suppress that idea. She would probably ground me for the rest of my life from the Great Beyond, and being a Siren, the rest of my life might last for a very long time.

Restlessly, I float within the protection of the underwater cave, enjoying the deafening silence... all but the gentle snores of my sleeping mother. Glancing at my diver's watch, I realize that several hours have passed. My tummy reminds me that it is dinnertime. I close my eyes and concentrate, trying to contact Ando, but it does not work. At last, my mother opens her lovely aquamarine eyes.

"How long have I been out?" she asks with a muffled yawn.

"A few hours," I reveal with a genuine smile.

"I'm famished," she states, stretching her scaly arms above her head.

I laugh out loud making another stream of bubbles.

"Me too."

"Can we go back to Capri now?" I ask, hoping she will stop this ridiculous, not to mention, dangerous quest.

"Soon," she gives me another mischievous wink. "It's not too far now."

"Not too far?" I say, looking around the pitch-black space.

"You'll see," she giggles, reminding me of Ando.

"Mom," I start with my hands on my hips. "You're hurt and—"

She cuts me off by pointing to her side. To my surprise the wound is closed completely, and several new scales have already grown over it. I touch the area gently.

"You're healed," I whisper and giggle at the same time.

"Look down at where you took off your scale," Mom requests.

Nervously, I do and notice that my scale is back too. Running my hand over the spot, I feel the smooth healthy regrown scale that has appeared. If I had not cut it off myself, I never would have known that there was ever an injury there.

"That is so amazing!" I blurt with enthusiasm.

Mom chuckles to herself.

"Yes, it certainly is."

After a few more minutes of just hanging around treading water as Mom finds her feet, my mother makes a request.

"Look down toward the floor of the cave," she says with a smile.

Reluctantly, I look down and only see more darkness.

"I can't see anything," I pout, wondering if I will eventually get better at being a Siren.

"Adjust your eyes," Mom instructs.

I try, but nothing happens.

As usual.

"Will your eyes to see beyond," my recuperating mother states firmly.

"Beyond?" I repeat. "Beyond what?"

"Beyond this world," my mother articulates, like I should already understand the concept of *'beyond'*.

"You must have lost a lot of blood," I tease, poking her already healed scale.

"Just try it," she huffs, folding her arms across her chest.

"Here goes nothing," I state, trying to do something right.

And just as I suspect, I still see only the natural brightness illuminating from Mom's irises.

"Don't worry," she says with compassion. "It will all fall into place one day."

"If you say so," I pout.

"Swim down," she instructs, motioning toward the bottom of the cave floor. "Follow me."

Compliantly, I do. I follow her, our hands clasped tightly. I feel nauseous once again.

Mom searches the rocky wall nearest her looking for something. In the darkness, I hear her pull down on something that sounds heavy and old. Then, without warning, she lets out a wail so loud so blood-curdling that I release her hand to cover my ears.

The water around us begins to glow and become warmer. The cave walls surrounding us illuminate themselves as if thousands of tiny multicolored lightbulbs have suddenly been switched on. Over the rocky surface, are drawings of sea creatures of all shapes and sizes; shiny shimmering rubies, diamonds, pearls and an array of precious jewels and metals light our way further down into the bowels of the sea. My eyes are almost blinded and just as I think I might truly lose my sight; I hear my mother's voice inside of my head.

"Open your eyes, Selena," she whispers in Siren.

I do. The sight that greets me is overwhelming, more incredible than anything… *Ever!*

It is what I imagine Heaven to look like!

"Where are we?" I gawk, swallowing the gigantic lump forming in my throat.

My mother bursts into joyful tears as she hugs me.

"We are home!"

The End?
(Definitely not!)

EPILOGUE

"Open your eyes, Selena," his masculine voice beckons. "Look at your kingdom."

Slowly, purposefully, I open my eyes and drink it all in.

The wonder.

The awe of this place.

It is everything I have ever desired.

"This is mine?" my voice awe-filled at the gift he offers.

"It can be," his words swoon inside of my head. "All you have to do is want it."

I do want it.

I deserve it!

Seductively, Ares takes my hand, his fingers gently glides over my heated skin making my toes curl.

"Do you want it, dear, sweet, lovely, Selena?" he probes as he encircles my waist with sturdy arms.

As I stand watching the world below, it all suddenly becomes clear.

"Yes, I want it," I grin. *"I want it all."*

ABOUT THE AUTHOR

 Alisa K. Michaels, an American author and schoolteacher, lives with her husband in the South-Eastern United States. Michaels is a Rollins College Alumna having degrees both in English and Secondary Education.

She brings to her authorship her experiences growing up on a beautiful, tropical island paradise in the U.S. Virgin Islands before coming to the mainland in her youth. She draws from those experiences to create her fantastical vision.

Alisa K. Michaels is a proud mother of three grown daughters, and a closet monster named, Bucky.

Coming Soon by Alisa K. Michaels!

Acapella

Book Three of The Siren Series

Selena's Song

Book One of The Siren Series

See how it all starts!

Available Everywhere (even on Mars)

www.alisakmichaels.com

www.ingramcontent.com/pod-product-compliance
Lightning Source LLC
LaVergne TN
LVHW010252260326
834688LV00044B/1244